"Freaky Friday gone wr[o]
stories, *Entangled* quic[k]
favourites… I highly re[c]
fans, but if you love wit[c]

MW00938546

— Xpresso Reads

"Entangled mixes Sabrina, the Teenage Witch with Freaky Friday in an intriguing, entertaining story with characters the reader will both love, and love to hate. Fast-paced and filled with page-turning action, Entangled is a must-read for lovers of young adult paranormal."

— Misti Pyles, Examiner.com

"Nikki has nailed the "twin" relationship beautifully. Being a twin myself, I could fully relate to the twin characters' banter and jealousy toward one another."

— Nicole Steinhaus

"I loved this book from the first page. The mix of magic, romance, sibling rivalry, teen angst, friendship and loyalty made this a perfect read."

— Melissa's Eclectic Bookshelf

"I stayed up until 4 am reading, I literally could not put the book down until I knew how it ended… I found myself in a fit of laughter that managed to wake my son across the hall."

—Lover of Paranormal Reviews

"I could not put this story down. I ate it up and loved every moment of it."

— Alluring Reads

SPELLBOUND #1

Entangled

This is a work of fiction. Names, characters, places, and incidents are products of the author's imagination, or the author has used them fictitiously.

Cover design by Najla Qamber Designs
Editing by Sara Meadows

Second Edition, Revised and Updated.
Copyright © 2012, 2016 Nikki Jefford

All rights reserved

ISBN-13: 978-1536827286
ISBN-10: 1536827282

Entangled is dedicated in loving memory to Grandma May

Chapter 1

I f Gray's twin sister wanted to be taken seriously, she should have threatened to step in front of a bus rather than off a building. She was a witch. Heights weren't particularly a problem.

"I'm going to do it, Lee. I mean it."

Gray joined Charlene on the roof of McKinley High and peered over the edge at the damp walkway below. It led into the student parking lot. Everyone was in fifth period . . . everyone except for the identical twins standing over the heads of their oblivious classmates and teachers.

A suicide threat, seriously? This is why Gray was missing English?

They were supposed to be discussing Yeats that afternoon and Gray didn't appreciate having Charlene's minion stop her on the way to class with a message that her sister planned on plunging to her death before the day was out.

That would teach Blake Foster—or so Charlene thought. The jerk had dumped her sister after first period and, worse, had been seen sucking face with Stacey Morehouse at lunch.

Gray started shivering the moment she'd stepped onto the roof. It was friggin' February for crying out loud and she was wearing shorts. Granted, she had thick black tights on underneath, but still—brrr! Couldn't Charlene have scheduled her dramatic death scene in the warmth of their home over a bottle of pills?

"What about me? You expect me to watch?" Gray said. "Sure, that won't haunt me the rest of my days."

Charlene's face contorted. "You're so freaking selfish!"

"Me? What about you? Do you know what this would do to Mom? And what about me? How am I going to get through the rest of the semester when I'm all sad and stuff?"

Charlene snorted. "Like you'd care." She had to be cold in her skinny jeans, but at least she was wearing a sweater.

The cold seeped down to Gray's bones. The tips of her fingers felt as though they'd been dipped in ice water. She tried to conjure up warmth, but her body didn't respond.

"Of course I care. You're my sister." Gray nodded at the building's edge. "It's not like the fall would kill you, anyway."

"It wouldn't?"

"Nah. We're not high enough. It'd just cripple you." Gray bent her neck in, hunched over and held her arms close to her body, and then proceeded to walk around like a gimp. "Hey, Char, here's you walking down the halls of McKinley."

Charlene's lips tightened.

Gray shuffled around. It helped warm her up. Charlene was fighting back a smile. "Don't you dare make me laugh!"

"Hey, Char. Here you are at prom." Gray moved like a T. rex, flopping her hands back and forth against her chest.

Finally Charlene couldn't hold it back any longer. Her body shook. It was a good thing she was laughing because Gray couldn't contain her mirth any longer. Then Charlene's laughter turned to tears.

Gray rushed over, reached out, then stopped herself. Charlene wasn't the hugging type, not even when her heartthrob dumped her out of the blue.

"I'm not going to prom," Charlene sobbed. "Not anymore."

Gray patted Charlene's back. "There's always next year. Anyway, there's plenty of time to find another date. Heck, it's only February second."

Charlene ceased crying abruptly. "I don't want another date! I want Blake!"

"What's so special about that dumbass, anyway?"

"Lee, he's the love of my life." Charlene's voice broke.

"I think we ought to turn him into a toad."

Charlene pulled back. "Oh, no, don't do anything to Blake."

No, good ol' Blake was beyond reproach in Charlene's book. They'd gone to homecoming together and been inseparable ever since . . . well, until today. Not that Gray would do anything bad to him either way. Both she and Charlene had taken the Vow of Honor at age twelve, and that meant absolutely no black magic.

Gray lifted her hands in surrender. "Fine, I won't make a Blake Foster voodoo doll when I get home."

Charlene's eyes widened.

"But don't blame me if his car gets keyed."

"Lee, don't touch Blake's truck, either."

"Why not?"

"When we get back together I don't want to see a scratch on Blake or his truck."

"Oh, so now you're getting back together?"

"Blake just needs to realize the error of his ways." Charlene flipped a long strands of blond hair over her shoulder and smiled right before turning away.

"Char . . ." Gray said in a warning voice.

Wonder of all wonders, Charlene ignored her. She took one gigantic step off the building.

Gray hurried to the edge in time to see her sister float gently to the walkway below.

"Brat," Gray muttered under her breath. Charlene knew she was buoyantly challenged. Not to mention they were at school, for freak's sake. What if someone was watching them from a parked car?

And way to leave her high and dry—or rather, high and chilled to the bone.

Gray stormed to the door leading back inside McKinley.

Ryan was on the other side. His pear-shaped head craned around her, the corners of his mouth curving down like a weepy clown's when he didn't see Charlene. "Oh my god, she jumped."

Gray rolled her eyes. "No, she floated."

Ryan took in a gasping breath. "Thank god."

Gray pushed ahead of Ryan and hurried down the stairwell. She paused in front of the door leading into the second floor hallway. Ryan caught up to her and looked at her with big round eyes.

"Now what?" Gray asked herself. "If I walk into English late Mrs. Pritchett is going to skin me alive. If I'm absent without an excuse . . ." Gray tapped her toe then looked down at Ryan. "Well? What are you waiting for?"

Ryan looked at the door and cleared his throat. "I don't know. What are you going to do?"

Gray stopped tapping her foot and smiled suddenly. "I know what I'm going to do."

She squeezed her eyes closed and disappeared before Ryan's eyes. The last thing Gray heard before she pushed the door open into the school was Ryan sucking air.

He would be surprised. Invisibility was advanced magic. Gray doubted that even the peer leaders at Gathering could disappear from sight.

Gray's clogs clomped across the deserted hallway. Lucky for her Mrs. Pritchett hadn't closed the door to her classroom yet.

Gray slipped in and skirted the row of desks nearest the wall. She sidestepped backpacks and heavy textbooks.

"Casey!" Mrs. Pritchett snapped. "If I hear your mouth again I'm sending you straight to Principal Coleman."

Gray winced and counted her lucky stars Mrs. Pritchett wasn't a witch . . . at least in the magical sense.

Gray's classmates weren't the only ones who couldn't see her; Gray couldn't see herself or her foot when it rolled over a pencil. She sucked in a breath and picked her way to the back of the room.

The use of magic in the presence of normal humans was forbidden by their coven—except in case of emergencies. She highly doubted that getting out of a tardy counted, but Charlene started it, and Gray had obeyed till now. If anything, she eschewed magic in public. She simply wanted to be a normal high school student. And forget about ever dating a magically inclined member of the male species. She wasn't passing on her wonky witch genes to her children. Not that dating a warlock automatically led to children, but one could never be too careful.

Gray surveyed the back row. This would be her best bet. Sneaking into English as Invisi-girl was easy. Reappearing without anyone noticing—not so much.

Gray set her pack onto the floor and slid sideways into the desk. She looked side to side.

"Turn to page fifty-two. Brian, read the first verse of 'Leda and the Swan,'" Mrs. Pritchett commanded.

Good, everyone was looking down. Gray pinched her eyes closed and filled herself in like a line drawing in a coloring book, except at warp speed. It wouldn't do to appear with half a body, or decapitated. She always started from the toes up—backpack last. When she reopened her eyes she saw her arms resting on her desktop. A wry smile formed over her lips. She couldn't help it. She didn't know anyone else capable of invisibility.

Gray reached into her now visible pack and quickly withdrew her poetry book and flipped to page fifty-two.

When the bell rang she stuffed her book back inside. Everyone leapt from their desks to make for sixth period. Sadie Howard glanced back then did a double take when she saw Gray. They usually sat together. How was Gray going to explain that one?

Just as she headed toward Sadie, Gray was bumped from behind. The force of the body against hers sent her pack flying out of her hands onto the ground. Okay, now she was pissed. "What's your . . ."

Gray whipped around to find herself face-to-face with Raj McKenna.

" . . . problem," Gray finished, the word fading like bleached denim.

Raj flicked his Zippo open and closed in his left hand while studying Gray.

Raj had the kind of bronze-toned skin the socialites of McKinley tried obsessively to replicate in tanning booths. The only thing they managed to enhance was their orange-ish glow. Raj's was a hundred percent authentic. His mother was Indian—as in India Indian. He'd inherited her lush dark hair and exotic eyes, the color of which he got from his American father; green like a panther's, which fit him well, 'cause he looked ready to pounce if you made the mistake of turning your back to him. Case in point: ramming Gray as he'd just done now.

The Zippo clicked shut again. Raj really shouldn't be playing with a lighter considering he'd burnt down his last house.

"Sorry, didn't *see* you."

Gray's jaw dropped.

This time, Raj's eyes met hers. There was a glint there, or maybe that was just the flash from Raj's lighter as he flicked it open and closed again.

As Yeats might've said back in the day, *bloody hell.*

The last person Gray wanted knowing about her newfound disappearing act was Raj McKenna.

Raj was the kind of warlock who didn't take vows of honor. An invisibility spell had no place inside Raj's bag of tricks. He probably hadn't considered it before and now Gray had gone and put the idea into his delinquent head. Friggin' great.

Raj didn't belong at McKinley High. He ought to be sent off to one of the coven's rehabilitation campsites far from civilization. But no order had been handed down, not even when Raj's own mother had taken his younger sister and gotten the hell away from him.

Mr. McKenna no longer showed up for meets. They said Raj had driven his dad to drink and the boy was left unsupervised in the ramshackle home where he and his father had relocated in a seedy part of town.

Raj's smile widened. "See you around, Gray."

Not if she could help it. Gray bent down and picked her pack off the floor. If only she knew how to do a memory spell on Raj and make him forget what he'd seen . . . or rather not seen. But Gray had no talent for messing with memories or emotions. She was content to let the world go on without her interference. She simply wanted to be left alone. Maybe that's why she was so good at disappearing.

Chapter 2

"Mom, Charlene's gone off the deep end!" Gray yelled when she arrived home.

She entered the kitchen in time to see her mom attempting to wrench a six-inch knife out of Charlene's hand. "Charlene, give me the knife."

"I'm going to kill her!"

At least Charlene wasn't trying to take her own life. She gripped the knife so hard her knuckles were turning white. "Stacey Morehouse moved in on my man. She so picked the wrong girl to double-cross."

"Charlene, I know you're upset, but you can't go using magic on someone you're unhappy with," Mom said.

"Who said anything about magic?" Charlene snapped. She lifted the knife and grinned. "I don't need a spell to take care of Stacey *Whorehouse*."

"Right, because stabbing her without the use of magic doesn't make it evil." Probably not the best time for sarcasm.

Charlene gave Gray a look that curled her toes. Charlene gasped a moment later when the knife turned into a spatula.

"Charlene Perez," their mother said. "You are not leaving this house until you calm down."

Charlene threw the spatula to the ground. "Fine!" she snapped. "Then I'll stay here forever!" She turned on her heel and stomped up the stairs to her room. Her door slammed shut with a force that shook the house.

"Wow. You don't think she'd really . . ." Gray cleared her throat. "Hurt someone?"

"I don't know," Mom admitted.

They avoided each other's eyes. Gray looked around the kitchen. Her mom sighed. "I better work on a protection spell for Stacey—just in case."

Gray nodded. "Good idea."

* * *

"I heard about your sister and Blake Foster." Gray's best friend, Thea, plopped into the seat next to hers in first period the next morning. "She must be suicidal."

Thea had no idea. "She didn't get out of bed this morning," Gray said.

"That bad?"

Gray nodded as Mr. Houser began roll call.

After class, Charlene's best friends, Brittany and Kiki, practically shoved Thea aside to get to Gray. Both girls were wearing long leather boots over skinny jeans.

"Where's Charlene?" Brittany demanded at the same time Kiki asked, "How is she?"

"She's at home and she's fine."

"Obviously she's not fine. She just had her heart ripped out," Brittany said.

"And yet it still beats," Gray said. "Excuse me, ladies; I've got to get to class." She felt bad ditching Thea that way, but she wasn't about to stick around for a lecture on broken hearts from Thing One and Thing Two.

And speaking of heartbreakers, Stacey turned the corner with Blake's arm draped over her shoulder.

Glaring at Stacey Morehouse came naturally. Her beauty was as blinding as the sun. She was all legs, perky Victoria's Secret–sized breasts, and as blond as a Barbie. Charlene didn't stand a chance.

Gray dodged a group of freshmen and pounded her way up the stairs to the second floor. As she rounded the corner, Raj McKenna stepped in her way.

Just great. If she'd known the Annoying People Parade was scheduled that day, Gray might've elected to stay home, too.

Raj leaned into her. "Pretty neat trick yesterday."

Gray frowned. "I have no idea what you're talking about."

Raj put his hand out, blocking Gray as she tried to walk past him. He grinned. "Of course you do. What about the whole Vow of Honor thing? No magic in public?"

"That's not part of the Vow of Honor, and anyway, it was just that one time."

Raj's grin widened. "That's how it starts."

"Starts? I'm not starting anything." Gray decided it was worth touching Raj to push past him.

Raj quickly caught up. "How about you teach me your invisibility spell?"

"You're the last person I'd teach."

"I'd make it worth your while." Raj's lids closed halfway and his voice turned husky.

Gray focused on the disgust his tone elicited in her and laughed. "Not on your life."

Suddenly, Gray was no longer walking. She was frozen in place, paralyzed. Not only was Gray rooted to the ground, her mouth wouldn't work. She could only follow Raj with her eyes as he circled her like a jungle cat.

Her head finally moved, but only when Raj pulled it back by her ponytail. His breath was moist on her neck. "Hair like gold," he said. "What a contradiction, *Gray*."

Gray tried to move, to strike out at him. She felt herself break through the spell. Perhaps Raj had released her. Her eyes stung from having her hair pulled, or maybe it was from the unshed tears of anger at having been so grotesquely violated.

Raj waited as though expecting Gray's outcry. Instead, she turned and ran. Her clogs pounded down the hallway. Even after she turned the first corner she kept running.

When Mrs. Ryerson called on her in third period, Gray sounded like an idiot, sputtering, "Huh? What?"

Several students chuckled.

"What's wrong with you?" Thea asked at lunch.

"Huh?" There it was again. That creep Raj had ruined her entire day. Gray could still feel his breath on her skin as she stood powerless under his spell. It was the worst feeling in the world. Guys like Raj McKenna should be stripped of their abilities. There had to be some kind of magical binding spell out there.

"Hey, earth to Gray," Thea said, waving her peanut butter and jelly sandwich in front of Gray's face.

She blinked several times. "Sorry, I'm on drama overload."

Thea's expression turned sympathetic, eyes crinkling at the corners. She lowered her chin and voice. "It's times like these I'm glad I'm an only child."

"Try having an identical twin—it's two times worse." When the lunch bell rang, Gray groaned. "Fifth period . . . with Mrs. Pritchett."

"Say no more," Thea said.

But again, Gray was kidding herself. The real reason she had to pry herself away from the cafeteria was because of a certain lighter-snapping warlock. This compelled Gray to hustle to class and select a seat in the front row. She didn't look up from her book. For all she knew, Raj never came to class. When class ended, she shot out of her desk and made her way to last period.

This time, she sat in the back row, and before class was out Gray made herself invisible, promising herself this would be the last time she'd erase herself at school. But hadn't her mother said magic should be used in a case of emergency?

As far as Gray was concerned, getting even with Raj McKenna was an emergency of extreme importance.

* * *

It didn't take a locator spell to find Raj's junk heap. The idiot hadn't even locked the doors, not that that would have hindered Gray. Unbolting spells were practically Magic 101. Even after her powers had turned unreliable, Gray could manage unlocking a door. Still, it was nice not relying on mystical aid to climb into the backseat of McKenna's car.

Gray didn't need magic to protect herself. She wasn't above getting her hands dirty the good old-fashioned way.

Well, okay. At the moment she was invisible—as was the shoelace wound tightly in each fist.

She sat poised and ready on the edge of the backseat. She didn't have to wait long. Raj was out moments after the final bell rang. For once, his lighter was tucked away as he swung his ring of keys around his left finger.

Gray's heart rate quickened.

Raj opened the car door and landed with a thud in the driver's seat. "Another day in paradise," he mumbled under his breath.

He reached forward with his key, but before he could stick it in the ignition he dropped the ring with a clink. Gray had the string around his neck.

"Don't move. Don't speak," Gray hissed.

Raj glanced into his rearview mirror. Gray had already made herself visible. She wanted Raj to see her plain as day, the one in control this round. If she hadn't been so angry it might have surprised her to see the unease in his expression.

Yeah, not the best feeling being at someone else's mercy.

"Now listen carefully, McKenna." Gray's lips brushed his ear.

So maybe she was getting off on the whole revenge thing just a tad. She'd tasted something sweet, but after she set the creep straight no more—she was back to Graylee Perez, model citizen, hardworking student, and honorable witch of the 42nd Coven, Kent Chapter.

But first things first.

She tightened the string. Raj inhaled sharply.

"If you ever use a spell on me again I'll bury you alive."

Gray tightened the shoelace one last time for emphasis before releasing it and grabbing the handle of the car. Before she could get out the locks clicked shut with a sound reminiscent of the snap of Raj's lighter.

So much for a dramatic exit. "What did I just say?" Gray said through gritted teeth.

Raj lifted his arms in the air. "I'm not performing a spell on *you*."

The locks reopened with barely a thought from Gray. Like she said, Magic 101.

They bolted shut just as suddenly.

Gray caught Raj's eye in the rearview mirror. He was neither smiling nor frowning. Something was brewing between them. Something that could only lead to a world of regret and self-loathing. Gray had to get out of there.

The locks sprang open and closed. Open and closed.

The pounding at her window nearly made Gray shriek. She was instantly relieved to see Thea standing beside her door peering inside. Even without magical abilities, her friend was a guardian angel.

"Gray? What in the heck are you doing in there?"

God, this didn't look good. Getting out of Raj McKenna's car like they'd snuck off to . . .

Gray threw open the door, swiftly followed by her legs and everything that went with them. She high-kicked the door shut and glared at Raj. In response he snatched up his keys, shoved them into the ignition, and floored the gas pedal. The vehicle roared.

Gray linked arms with Thea and dragged her away.

Chapter 3

Raj revved the engine one last time then eased up when Gray was a good thirty feet away. It was a damn waste of gas, but it helped ease the pounding in his chest. Gray had spooked him good. He'd never dreamed he'd need a protection spell on his car. Its rundown exterior—not to mention the fact that it belonged to him—had always been protection enough.

Till now.

Not that Gray would ever hide in Raj's backseat again. No, that thought now landed somewhere in the realm of fantasy and fantasies had a way of never coming true.

Raj pulled his Zippo out of his jeans pocket and flipped it open and closed, watching Gray get inside a vehicle with Thea Johnston. He glanced at the shoelace she'd dropped and wound it slowly around his knuckle.

Raj wanted Graylee Perez. Hell, he wanted her more than her invisibility spell. Chances of getting either were somewhere in the ballpark of nil.

Raj loosened his fist and shook the shoestring off his hand onto the empty seat beside him. He drove straight home without thinking. If he'd been thinking he would have hit the arcades or gone to a matinee at the cinema and snuck into two more flicks before the night was out.

If he knew Gray's invisibility spell he wouldn't have to pay for the matinee to begin with.

But no, not thinking had brought him directly home.

Home, bitter home.

His father had found them a rundown shack in Shitsville. A former tenant had ripped out all the carpeting and never replaced it. Plywood stairs met Raj just inside the door, ascending into the gloom overhead. A narrow hallway to the right led into their scrap of kitchen—a room that never smelled of anything nice. No more of Mom's curries or homemade naan.

"Raj, that you?"

Raj lifted a finger and the front door shut behind him. With hollow steps he entered the kitchen. Inside, his dad sat at a fold-out table for two sipping from his bottomless cocktail. It was hard to breathe through all the smoke. The ashtray on the table was already full, a book of matches tossed beside it.

His dad coughed before asking, "How was school?"

Raj shrugged. "Same old."

"You stay out of trouble?"

"Yep."

His dad finished the last of his whiskey or brandy or whatever the hell he was drinking and scooted back. He traveled three steps to the kitchen sink and poured himself a glass of water. When his finger touched the glass the liquid turned amber.

"I'm going over to Shay's to do homework," Raj said.

His dad gave him a hard stare. "Be back by ten."

Raj didn't answer as he headed for the front door. The man had no business telling him what to do.

* * *

Shay was playing the flute when Raj tapped at her door and walked into her room. Her fingers kept moving, her breath a continual stream producing a tune that haunted and hypnotized Raj at the same time. He lowered himself to the carpet, leaned against the wall, and watched Shay's head sway with the instrument.

Once she finished the song Raj clapped. "Bravo."

Shay tossed the flute onto her bed. "I'm bored with that thing."

Raj fought back a laugh. "It took you what, three days to master the flute?"

Shay mastered instruments the way linguists mastered languages.

"I'm not sure what's next. Maybe the sax?" Shay glanced toward the ceiling thoughtfully as she spoke. "Unless I got some snakes to accompany me."

"I think you'll need some new sheet music for that. You don't see serpents swaying to the classical beat. And I'm sure your mom would just love having a cobra take up residence in your room."

Shay gave Raj a blank stare. "Mom's not afraid of snakes."

Shay Baxter had been Raj's best friend since the third grade. She'd stuck by him after everything that had gone down, when his own mother had left him. Shay acted as though everything was the way it'd always been, which had its ups and down.

Mrs. Baxter was the adult version of Shay, a friendly, accepting woman who had no interest in gossip, which meant neither lady asked for Raj's version of events.

Fine, like he needed a couple of meddlesome women in his life.

A girlfriend, on the other hand, was sounding more and more appealing.

Raj glanced from his place on the floor to Shay, who'd taken a seat at her desk and began moving her mouse around and clicking at her computer. Shay had full-bodied, dark-blond hair and freckled skin. She was pretty and rational, but she'd never gotten Raj's blood pumping. Not like Graylee Perez.

Right, and even if he had harbored any secret feelings for Shay, she was practically engaged to Max Curry. They already acted like a married couple. Worse. A perfectly harmonious married couple. Juniors in high school. Sad.

If Raj wanted to go out with a witch, his options at McKinley were limited. There were only three in the whole junior class: Shay, Charlene, and Gray.

Raj cleared his throat. "Hey, do you still make those good luck amulets?"

"Hold that thought," Shay said without turning. "Max is writing a paper on acid rain and I found an article I want to send him."

Raj scratched behind his ear. "Max actually reads and does homework?"

"Max and I believe it's important to exercise our brains," Shay answered.

"Performing spells takes a lot of thought."

"Intellectually speaking." Shay clicked a few more times, then swiveled her seat to face Raj. "So you need a luck charm. What happened to the one I made you in seventh grade?"

"It's not for me."

"Oh, I see."

And like that she did. It could have been for Raj's sister, but Shay knew better. Shay seemed to know everything.

"Basic or fancy?"

"Fancy," Raj answered immediately.

"Moonstone will cost you extra."

"Do it." Raj picked at the stiff burlap carpeting beside his knee. "Think you can have it done soon?" He didn't have to look to see the smile spreading over Shay's face.

"Got a special date in mind?"

"By the weekend of the twelfth."

Raj could hear the smile in her words. "You mean the weekend before St. Valentine's Day?"

"Can you finish in time?"

"Of course I can. Let me jot down the particulars." Shay snatched a pen and notepad off her desk and sat on top of her bed with a bounce.

"Color preference?"

"Blue."

"Symbols?"

"Your call."

"Initials?"

"Not necessary."

Shay tapped her pen against her notepad. "I need initials, Raj."

He hesitated.

Shay sighed. "You know the charm works better if it's personalized."

"Fine. It's GP."

"G what?"

"G-P," Raj said louder.

"GP, GP," Shay repeated. "I assume this is a girl from our class."

"Does it matter?"

"Of course it matters. I want to know what girl at McKinley has managed to capture your heart."

"It has nothing to do with the heart."

She studied him a moment then got up and went to her bookshelf.

"What are you doing?"

Shay pulled her yearbook out and sat cross-legged on top of her bed. "Now I have to know. I'm looking up every GP."

"Please don't."

She spread the yearbook open. "Look at that," she said innocently. "I opened to the Ps."

"Total coincidence, I'm sure," Raj grumbled.

Shay tapped her head. "Think it and it is so."

Which reminded Raj . . . "Don't go reading my mind."

"Please," Shay said, affronted. "I'd never do such a thing. Anyway, the process of elimination is so much more interesting." She bent her head back down. "Now let's see. Grace Peterson."

Raj snorted and relaxed a fraction. "What a smart couple we'd make."

"Gabby Peck."

"Fat chance. Emphasis on *fat*."

"Don't be a jerk," Shay said and threw her pen at him. She flipped several pages and leaned in closer. "Graylee Perez . . ." A long pause followed. Shay's forehead wrinkled.

"What?" he asked defensively.

"Oh, Raj," Shay chided. "I thought you wanted to go out with a normal girl."

Raj straightened his spine. "So you've decided it's Graylee Perez—just like that."

She pierced him with a look. "Raj, cut the bull." She glanced back down at the picture.

Raj wanted to look at it, too. It wasn't like he had his own yearbook at home, but the sudden awkwardness prevented him from joining Shay's side for a look at Gray in still life.

Shay looked up again. "At least she's not as bad as her sister."

"They're nothing alike."

Shay snorted. "They're everything alike. They're identical twins."

"You know what I mean." Raj got up.

"Fine, I'll make a charm for Graylee Perez."

Before Raj could thank her, Shay added, "You know the rules—payment up front."

"I need this in time for Valentine's Day."

"Rules are rules."

"Just make the amulet. I'll get you your money."

"No stealing from your father's wallet," Shay said. "Or anyone else's."

Raj paused in her doorframe. His lips opened and closed. Shay was back at her desk instant messaging with someone, probably Max. Raj pressed his lips together tightly and walked out.

* * *

Raj arrived at fifth period early. A first. He took his seat in the back row and kept an eye on the door.

It was funny how you could not notice a person then notice them all of a sudden. Back when he attended Gatherings, the Perez twins hadn't been part of his clique. At some point, Gray had morphed into the magically inhibited girl parents felt sorry for and students ridiculed. When Raj remembered past reactions, he wanted to travel back in time and punch the faces of the kids who'd laughed when Gray fell on her ass after their peer leader suggested she might have better luck floating if she started by stepping off a desk.

Raj still remembered the expression in Gray's eyes after she landed on the ground. It was about the only thing he remembered of her. He'd been startled by the utter disbelief in that look. She could have landed on her feet, but she'd fully expected to float. Raj wasn't sure why when she'd failed so many attempts before.

He hadn't thought of it till now.

Now look at the girl. She was a spook. Raj knew of no one else powerful enough to disappear. If he were Graylee Perez, he'd show up at the next Gathering and go all poltergeist on every kid who'd ever laughed at her.

Maybe her magical ineptitude had been an act.

No.

Raj recalled her sprawled over the floor again. Definitely not an act. Humiliation was as good a motivation as any. She'd finally caught up and surpassed them all.

Raj sucked in a breath when Sadie Howard walked in. Gray was right behind her, wearing a pair of tweed shorts. Her black tights gave the illusion of cover, but they didn't hide her slim legs.

Gray's eyes found his and she quickly looked away. Raj followed her movements to a seat near the front. His eyes lingered on her before she sat.

The bell rang and Mrs. Pritchett's voice filled the room.

Raj stared at the back of Gray's head. She'd braided her hair. He had to fight the urge to loosen the strands from their weave. No magic, she'd said.

"Mr. McKenna."

Raj kept concentrating on Gray's hair and what he'd like to do with it.

"Mr. McKenna." Mrs. Pritchett's voice went several octaves higher.

Gray's shoulders tensed and Raj moved his eyes from her to the angry glare of Mrs. Pritchett. "Mr. McKenna, if you don't plan on being mentally present in my class, I suggest you leave."

The light feeling left Raj's stomach, to be replaced by the acidic burn of humiliation and rage. He leveled a cold stare at Mrs. Pritchett—one that made her take two steps back. She opened her lips to speak, but no words came out, like a guppy floundering inside a tank.

Gray turned and looked at him with widening eyes. Was this what it took to get her attention for more than two seconds?

Anger bubbled up in Raj's chest, then burst. Mrs. Pritchett's blouse popped open. Her gasp filled the air as she slapped her arms across her supersized white silk bra and ran out of the room. The moment she left, laughter erupted.

"Oh my god!" a girl in the front row cried.

There was movement and chatter. Students got out of their desks to sit on top or join friends in the aisles. Someone knocked a book off their desk with a loud thud. Through the activity, Raj saw Gray stand up and hurry out of the room.

Raj was right behind her. He followed her down the empty hall until she turned around. "Just stop it, Raj! You can't do things like that." Her voice was pure anger, but in her eyes he saw fear. Just like everyone else. Why would Graylee Perez be any different? She hugged her backpack to her chest.

Raj stepped closer, certain he'd caught Gray flinch. "Why do you look so worried, Gray? I haven't forgotten our *arrangement*." Raj smirked at his use of the word as though referring to something untoward. He circled Gray and she stood rooted in place of her own accord. Raj glanced at her lips. He remembered them on his ear. What would it take to get them on his mouth, her tongue against his tongue? Raj took a step back. "Anyway, I won't be needing magic to get your shirt off."

The fear left Gray's face as she put a free hand on her hip. "And what does that mean?"

Raj pulled out his Zippo and flicked it open. "We'd make a powerful couple, you and me. We've got a lot in common. Think about it." Raj snapped the lighter shut. He moved his thumb to flick it open again then stopped when he saw the way Gray stared at him. The expression was hard to make out. Then it changed.

"You really want the invisibility spell that bad? Well, forget it. I'm not giving it to you and I wouldn't go out with you if you were the last person on Earth."

Raj grinned. This wasn't rejection—just a bit of foreplay between a witch and a warlock. "That would be nice. You, me, and the world to ourselves."

Gray loosened her grip on her pack and let it dangle from her fingers next to her knees. "Sounds like my idea of hell."

"At least in hell we could be wicked."

"You're wicked enough already."

Their eyes locked. Raj felt himself drawn to Gray by an invisible force. He'd never wanted to kiss a girl so badly. Maybe if he imagined her resolve melting away, it'd happen. But he didn't have any magical abilities at the moment. Foolishly, Raj had let down his guard and allowed himself to fall under the spell of a girl—the kind of spell any normal was in danger of tripping headfirst into.

It was as though one of his own spells had backfired and frozen him on the spot, gawking at Gray like some kind of pathetic fool.

She shook her head and huffed before walking away, leaving Raj staring after her long after she'd disappeared.

Chapter 4

"Hello? Anybody home?" Gray called into the kitchen after finding the living room deserted. She leaned into the stairs. "Char? Mom?"

Just as her heart started an uneasy drumming inside her chest, Gray heard her mom call out, "Up here, hon."

Gray heard laughter and followed it straight into her mother's bedroom. Charlene was wearing a dress and had done her hair and makeup. She looked downright perky.

"What's going on?" Gray asked.

Charlene's face dropped for a fraction of a second. It was so quick Gray couldn't be sure that she hadn't imagined it. Her mom, on the other hand, grinned from ear to ear. "Your sister and I have just been planning Operation Get Blake Back."

Gray's mouth dropped. "Operation what?"

"Get Blake Back," Charlene enunciated, as though Gray were hearing impaired.

"Yeah, I caught that and again, *what?*"

"All that boy needs is to see your sister's pretty face and it won't take him long to realize what he's missing," Mom said. "So how about the three of us have a girls' night out at the mall and do a bit of shopping, followed by dinner and a movie?"

Gray started to protest then stopped herself. Was she really going to argue against the mall and a movie?

She grinned. "Let's do it."

"That's the spirit! When should we go?"

Charlene gave Gray a once-over. "I'm ready now, but maybe Lee wants to change."

Gray looked down at her shorts and tights. Cute, but not Barbie-cute; urban hip, in her estimation. Charlene must have read her hesitation as something else.

"Here, let me help you." Charlene snapped her fingers and like that Gray was wearing the pastel dress she'd worn to their cousin Myra's graduation.

Speaking of violations . . .

"Charlene, you know I hate it when you do that!"

Charlene blew on her fingernails. They'd been painted pink—if Charlene had indeed taken the time to paint them herself.

"I can dress myself. Besides, I'd never choose this."

Charlene looked up. "But you look so cute in that dress. You really ought to rethink your wardrobe."

"Mom!"

Their mother moved to the door. "I don't know about you girls, but I'm ready to go shopping."

"I'm not leaving in this dress," Gray said, heading toward her bedroom.

"Fine, if you're going to be pouty." Charlene snapped her fingers again and Gray's original outfit appeared.

Charlene was lucky she'd just gotten her heart broken; otherwise, Gray might've paid her sister a midnight visit, shoestring in hand. If only Charlene's magical advances were as easy to put the kibosh on as Raj McKenna's. *Raj.* The thought of him made Gray shudder. She put a hand on her hip. "Guess I'm ready to go then. We should hustle since Char's so bored she has nothing better to do than play dress-up."

Charlene's eyes narrowed and she raised her fingers like she might snap again, but was interrupted by their mother's loud clap. "All right, let's get this show on the road."

"I call front seat," Charlene said.

It was then Gray wished she could snap her own fingers or nod her head like Barbara Eden in *I Dream of Jeannie* and teleport herself into the front seat of the Volkswagen Bug. She'd been working on the spell for months. Few witches could transport, but then again, few could make themselves invisible and that's what had given Gray the gumption to try.

Invisibility had come unexpectedly, but thank god it did. Gray was driving home alone after a late-night movie fest with Thea and had gotten a flat. The first thing she'd done was call her mom using her cell phone; second, she swore to herself she'd ask Ryan's dad to show her how to change a tire; and third, she noted the hooligans lurking about while her mother was still a good fifteen minutes away. Gray had imagined herself invisible to calm her mind, working out all the details of the transformation process and then, somehow, it had happened. She'd known because she saw her arms disappear. Immediately she'd looked in the rearview mirror. No reflection.

It'd been an amazing moment. But then her mom had pulled up and started to panic when she didn't see Gray so she'd filled herself in quickly as her mom hurried back to her own car.

Once they were safely home, Gray tried to demonstrate the spell, but nothing happened. Her mom had given her an encouraging look.

"I was invisible, Mom. I swear."

Her mom had smiled. "I believe you, sweetie. Our abilities are like that sometimes. They respond to our commands when we most need them—like in the case of tonight. You put yourself under magical protection."

Maybe it had been stress that allowed her to hide in plain sight. But Gray hadn't been stressed when she turned invisible to sneak into Mrs. Pritchett's class.

Either way, it didn't look good for Gray that her twin could keep up with their peers at Gathering on Sundays while Gray floundered, literally, to so much as float—a spell even the preteens had mastered.

Gray suppressed a sigh. She took the seat behind her mother. Think of all the time it'd save her if she could be dressed with the snap of a finger. In her dreams. It wasn't like Charlene ever tried to help her develop her powers. At least her sister couldn't create new clothes. Then Gray really would have to hate her. Charlene might be able to make outfits appear on her body, but only articles she already owned. Thus, the trip to the mall.

In the parking lot, Charlene vacated the passenger's seat before Gray or her mom had a chance to open their car door. Her sister led the way into the mall and began pawing through clothes in the shop by the entrance.

"How was your day?" Mom asked as they followed Charlene in.

"Fine." Gray touched a green sweater hanging in front of her. Soft.

"Anything interesting happen today?"

Immediately Raj McKenna popped into Gray's head. "Nope," she said, turning away from the sweater. "What about you?"

"Not really. Marc and I went out for lunch."

Their mother was kinda sorta dating Ryan's dad, Mr. Phillips. Her mom had the opposite rule as Gray; she only dated warlocks. She said she'd dated a normal once before and she couldn't be herself with him.

Thankfully, their mother hadn't dated much in the five years since their father's death. Gray had a feeling she was waiting till she and Char graduated from high school.

"What about boys?"

"Boys?" Gray repeated. Why was her mom suddenly asking her about boys?

"Got any new crushes this semester? I haven't heard you mention a boy's name since Hart Hensley."

Yeah, since he started going out with Trish Roberts.

"Boys are overrated."

Her mother chuckled and held out a multicolored scarf. "This looks like something you'd wear."

As Gray reached out to take it, Charlene squealed and held up a dusty-rose miniskirt with several tiers of ruffles. "This is so cute!" she called across the store.

Their mom smiled, set the scarf down, and started toward Charlene. "Try it on."

"I will, but first I need to find a top." Charlene scurried around the shop, holding the skirt against various blouses and sweaters.

"How about this?" Mom asked, holding up a gray turtleneck.

Charlene made a face. She yanked a sleeveless beige top that sagged at the neckline from a hanging rack. "I like this one." Gray and her mom followed her to the dressing room.

It should have taken Charlene a second to snap into the skirt, not several minutes. It felt as though she was making them wait on purpose.

Then finally, the dressing room door flew open and Charlene stepped out, showing more skin than cloth. Gray had to admit she looked good.

"Oh, Char," Mom said, a grin brightening her entire face. "You'll have Blake eating out of your hand before the week is out."

Charlene's smile nearly reached her ears. The hem of her skirt twirled as she spun around and returned to the dressing room.

Gray turned to her mom and whispered, "Don't tell me you're encouraging this?"

"I have to keep her distracted somehow."

They followed Charlene into a shoe shop, followed by intimates. Gray started looking through the panty tables for fun designs before gravitating toward the wall of hanging bras. A ruby-red push-up bra with black lace edging caught her eye. She found one in a B-cup and held it out in front of her.

"Whatcha got there, Gray?"

Gray attempted to obscure the bra from her sister by turning her body, but Charlene was already grabbing herself a matching bra off the wall. "Good pick, sis."

"You know I don't like wearing the same things."

"Oh, please, like anyone would ever know." Charlene nudged Gray with her elbow. "Hey, Lee. Wanna flash the guys at their next game?"

Gray rolled her eyes. "Is that part of Operation Get Blake Back?"

Charlene chewed on her lip. "Perhaps."

Gray studied her sister's face. For a brief moment she imagined them as a team: dressing alike, teasing the boys, laughing so hard they cried. Why couldn't they be those kind of twins?

"Fine," Gray said. "Get the same bra—just don't mix it up with mine."

Charlene bounced in place. "Great! Now let's grab ourselves the matching panties. Size extra small," she added in a jokey voice.

Gray laughed. As they left the shop with their latest purchase, Charlene linked arms with Gray. Bonding over bras. Sometimes it was the most unexpected things.

After dumping their bags in the trunk of the car and nabbing a bite, they headed for the cinema.

"We should watch a romantic comedy—make sure we're putting the right kind of energy into the air," Mom said.

"Or we could see the latest slasher," Gray suggested. "Nothing says Valentine's like a gore-fest."

Mom laughed.

Charlene's nose wrinkled. "I don't like scary movies."

No, of course not. What Charlene did like was stupid comedies. At least it was good to hear her laughing again. By the time they were turning in for bed, Gray could almost swear the whole "Blake affair" had never happened. Charlene seemed like her usual self, which was better than an unhappy Charlene.

Before bed, Gray tried on the new bra in front of her mirror. Sexy was never a word she'd associated with herself, but when she saw the way the bra lifted her bust she did a double take and stared at her reflection way too long, like a boy gaping at a photo in *Maxim* magazine.

Gray tossed the bra into her hamper and pulled a T-shirt over her head before turning in for the night.

Weird dreams were Gray's specialty, but tonight the word she'd have chosen for them was "disturbing." Raj was in one, standing in her room. And Gray—god—was wearing the new bra and a pair of tight blue jeans.

"I like it," Raj said, looking her over.

The worst part was Gray liked that he liked it.

Did a person's sleeping lips form a grin when they smiled in their dreams? Gray should have been glowering, not grinning like an idiot. Raj took her smile as an invitation to approach the bed.

Gray had gone from standing to lying under the covers. Raj leaned over her. His breath on her face felt way too close and way too real.

Gray woke up with a jerk. Charlene was sitting on her bed looking into the dark chamber thoughtfully. "Lee, I've figured it out."

It took a moment for Gray to calm her racing heart and manage words. She sat up. "Figured what out?"

"How to get Blake back."

This was the reason Charlene had nearly given her a heart attack? Well, of course, 'cause what was more important than Blake Foster?

"Put on a new dress and extra makeup?" Gray asked hopefully.

Charlene continued as though Gray had never spoken. "I've been holding out on Blake, thinking he'd enjoy the challenge. But everyone needs gratification, Lee. Everyone. I mean, think of the most popular celebrities. They put out."

Now Gray was fully awake. "So, you're a celebrity in this scenario?"

"Exactly," Charlene said, missing her sarcasm. "I'm one of the most popular girls at school. In terms of McKinley High, I'm on the A-list. And what do A-list celebrities do?"

"Sing? Act?"

"They party, Lee. They sleep around. It's all about notoriety. That's what puts them in the spotlight. It's what makes them get noticed and talked about."

"So you want everyone talking about how much you get around?"

Charlene grinned and eased herself off the bed. "Sleep tight, Lee."

Gray watched Charlene leave before muttering, "You, too, Britney."

She punched her pillow and lay on her side, then on her stomach, then on her back, and finally back on her side.

Go to sleep. Go to sleep. Go to sleep, she chanted in her head at the same time Raj's voice repeated, *I like it. I like it. I like it.*

* * *

At one time, Gray had been the most gifted student in the Kent Chapter Coven. Until the day she'd messed up a spell.

Her cheeks heated at the memory. Like a bad dream—the one where you stood naked in front of everyone—but Gray's ultimate humiliation hadn't been a dream.

She was in sixth grade, the coven's star pupil. After group lecture she'd followed the kids down to the basement as she'd done every Sunday afternoon since she could remember.

Their peer leader had them lay out a second outfit on the long table and work on changing their clothes without touching the garments.

Sure, Gray had become somewhat cocky as only a rising star can be. Magic fascinated her, and she allotted all her free hours to perfecting her spells and trying new ones. Like any other talent or ability, magic took practice. Just because one was a witch didn't mean she could perform the same level of magic as her peers. She had to work for it.

Gray could already change in an instant. She'd practiced that one for weeks in her bedroom, never tiring of the elation when the new outfit materialized over her body. So she'd lifted her chin and snapped her fingers. And that's when it happened.

The clothes she'd worn were successfully removed, but her second outfit hadn't moved from the table. Except for her cotton underpants and bra, she stood stark naked.

Gray could still hear the laughter as it erupted. Like the hyenas in Mrs. Pritchett's class Friday afternoon. She almost felt sorry for the woman, no matter how mean she was. Raj McKenna was trouble and acted out of spite and self-indulgence. Just like Charlene.

Thank goodness he'd been absent from Gathering the day Gray exposed herself. He probably would have liked that. Raj was a relatively quiet boy back then. Dare she say it? Well-behaved. He always partnered with Shay Baxter and glared at anyone who giggled and whispered about the two of them being secretly in love. Nothing had come of it. They'd been thick as thieves until Raj quit attending and Max Curry made an advance on Shay. Shay Baxter, consequently, had taken Gray's place as the most gifted student of the 42nd Coven, Kent Chapter.

Gray couldn't help hating her just a little and Charlene had been happy to join in. Worse than losing her spot at the top, Gray hadn't been able to perform magic without freezing up after streaking in front of her peers.

Raj McKenna clearly respected power. That's what he really wanted from Gray—to strip her of her most prized spell and make it his own. Let's how fast he'd ditch her once he'd gotten what he wanted.

Gray pushed her bowl of oatmeal aside and stared across the dining table at her mother. It'd been just the two of them for breakfast the past few days.

"Can I stay home, too?" Gray asked.

If Charlene didn't have to attend Gathering, Gray didn't see why she had to go. It wasn't like she was able to participate or anything, but that excuse always led to Mom's rejoinder: "I don't want you to miss lecture."

"Can't you give me a summary tonight?"

"You know how important Gatherings are," Mom said. "We need to stick with our own kind, those who understand us, who keep us in check as we ensure they don't lose their way in return."

Gray tilted her head back. "I'm not the one you need to worry about."

Mom looked side to side then leaned in, barely speaking above a whisper. "Don't worry about Blake Foster or that Stacey girl. Your sister's magic is useless against them."

Yeah, 'cause Blake and Stacey were such big concerns of hers.

"Still," Gray said, "I should probably stay home and make sure Char doesn't hurt herself."

"Your sister will be fine. She just needs some time alone."

Chapter 5

Gatherings were held in a light bluish-gray brick building surrounded by a large parking lot. The outside looked conspicuously like a church or rec center. Take your pick.

That morning's lecture, predictably, had to do with St. Valentine's and the dangers of love spells. Gray's mom listened attentively on the bench beside her as their chapter president, Mr. Holloway, spoke.

"Love is a more powerful force than magic. You can trick the mind and even the heart, but never the soul. When a person is not free to love with their soul, that is not love and that is why a love spell can never truly work."

Blah, blah, blah. Gray picked at her cuticles. Mind control and love spells had never interested her. Now moving objects with the mind—that was fun.

"It can get lonely, being gifted," Mr. Holloway droned on. "But that is why we're here. We're here for each other."

Oh, brother. Gray pictured Charlene curled up on the couch at home watching back-to-back episodes of *Glee*, and had to bite back a frustrated sigh. It was at times like these that Gray missed her sister. Neither of them were fond of Gathering. They paired up when partnering was required, which today—naturally—it was.

After the lecture, their peer leader asked that they team up with a partner. Gray felt her palms begin to sweat. She was fairly certain that Ryan had glanced in her direction. There was no way she was enduring an hour of one-on-one time with Ryan Phillips. He'd probably spend the hour peppering her with questions about Charlene. If she didn't act fast, she'd be stuck. Ryan was already moving her way.

Gray took three large steps over to Nolan Knapp. "Hey, want to be partners?"

His initial surprise was immediately followed by a smile. "Yeah."

Nolan was cute in a boy band sorta way. Although they were in the same grade at McKinley High, Gray never saw him around school. He'd moved to Kent sophomore year. She might have crushed on him if he weren't a warlock—another preference Gray and her sister shared: no dating warlocks!

Nolan brushed his bangs out of his eyes and smiled as if to say, *Why not? Think about it.*

There was nothing to think about. Gray didn't date warlocks, period. Anyway, he didn't make her heart patter.

Shay Baxter stared in their direction before joining a group of children in the adjoining room. Shay had been recruited as a peer leader to coach the coven's youngest members. Gray would have loved working with kids, sharing her joy of magic and discovery. But she had nothing to teach.

"Today we'll work on basics then discuss how they can be used for advanced purposes," their peer leader announced. "You and your partner should start by practicing what you consider elementary magic."

Elementary magic. Was this for Gray's benefit?

She turned to Nolan and pasted a smile over her face. As far as he knew, Gray was merely related to witches.

"Elementary," Nolan mused. His brows lifted. "Moving small objects. Opening and closing doors. Floating."

He was probably being nice by listing these abilities rather than performing them. Beside them, Ryan was already floating two feet off the floor. Not all witches and warlocks were capable of performing the same spells, but certain basics, like the aforementioned, should have come naturally to any offspring of a witch and warlock.

Gray looked from Ryan to Nolan. "I wish I could float."

Nolan's forehead wrinkled. "Why can't you?"

"I was able to. Once."

"If you could do it once, you can do it again."

Gray frowned. "It's not that easy."

"You need to have faith in yourself. I have faith in you."

Gray rolled her eyes. "That's corny." Not to mention Nolan barely knew her.

"Give it a try."

Gray sighed. "Okay. I have faith in myself."

Nolan nodded. "Now try floating."

"You're serious, aren't you?"

Nolan stared back at her with his liquid blue eyes.

Finally Gray closed her eyes. "All right. I'm going to float. All I have to do is imagine my body getting lighter. Lighter and lighter. Lighter than air. I don't weigh a thing." Gray chuckled at the last bit. She kept her eyes squeezed tightly because it was easier than watching herself fail yet again.

Lighter and lighter. Lighter than air.

Gray wasn't big on words. She was more of a visualizer. She stopped chanting in her head, breathed in and out, and imagined herself hovering above the floorboards. In her mind she was suspended in air. She stopped trying. She let go. The ground gave way beneath her.

"Open your eyes," Nolan said softly.

Gray didn't need to. She smiled, eyes still closed. "And ruin the moment?" She had no sight, no hearing, only feeling and the sensation of soaring beyond reach.

The room became quiet and then Gray heard the applause. She opened her eyes and saw their peer leader clapping, along with her peers. Their hands smacked together in metered tempo. Nolan simply grinned at her.

Gray smiled and bowed, still hovering in the air.

Everyone laughed in the good sense of the word, making her feel more buoyant. It was like no other feeling. Gray had forgotten it. It was sensational.

"So, um, are you able to come down?" Nolan asked when Gray remained floating.

His cheeks dimpled when he smiled.

"I like it up here."

She could see Nolan wasn't sure if that meant she was stuck like a helium balloon at the top of a ceiling—one he might have to jump up and catch and drag down. She imagined her feet as weights and hit the ground harder than she'd intended.

It didn't matter.

Gray could float. After a five-year hiatus, her full abilities had returned. She straightened out and studied Nolan's face.

"What?" he asked.

"You should help with the kids. You'd make a fantastic peer leader."

Nolan looked at his sneakers and grinned. "Thanks." He made a semicircle on the floor with his toe.

The gesture reminded Gray of a girl. But Nolan was no girl. He was tall and fit. His smile was endearing. And he smelled good. Gray felt herself leaning into him, almost as though not of her own free will.

Love spell, she warned herself. Many involved scent.

Couldn't be a love spell. Not if Gray was able to stand there considering it might be a love spell. The Power of Reason: a sure sign that one still had their wits about them.

Not to mention Nolan was the one who looked uncomfortable. Certainly not the stance Raj McKenna would take.

Gray leaned back.

Raj's wicked words came back in a rush. *You, me, and the world to ourselves.*

No one had ever spoken to her that way. And the tone he'd used—it had sounded older, husky, accented. Full of temptation. *We'd make a powerful couple, you and me.*

Gray resisted the urge to shudder. If she hadn't turned invisible, Raj McKenna wouldn't have looked at her twice. And he was wrong. They had nothing in common . . . well, besides the whole children of witches and warlocks and magical inheritance thing. He was big-time bad news. As opposed to Nolan Knapp. Smart. Cute. Wholesome . . . Scratch that, wholesome didn't get a girl's heart racing. Thoughtful. Thoughtful was sexy.

No one had ever tried to help her regain her abilities. Unless you counted the peer leaders over the years, and they'd all used the same tactic—trying to push her into it while the class watched.

"I'm glad I could help."

Gray blinked several times when Nolan spoke. Somewhere in her ponderings she'd lost the thread of their conversation. "Totally," she replied lamely.

Nolan broke out into a wide grin.

Sometimes that was all it took. A smile could be more powerful than the most potent love spell.

"Want to take a break?" Nolan asked.

"Heck, no." Gray grinned mischievously. She'd always known that if her full powers returned she'd never doubt them again. She'd stretch them to the limits—well, within bounds, and make up for all the time she missed. Gray looked at the west wall with its dry erase board. "I'm going to move something."

"Like the eraser?" Nolan said just before the heavy oak desk lurched forward and screeched along the floorboards. Nolan's eyes widened.

Their peer leader looked over.

Gray dragged the desk to her, chuckling to herself when Ryan Phillips had to jump out of the way. When the desk stopped a foot away, Gray leapt forward and levitated the final three feet above the desk. She landed on top as Shay Baxter walked in.

Gray crossed her arms over her chest triumphantly. Everyone stared. Shay was unable to hide a tight frown. Gray saw the disbelief on Miss Perfect's face, as though she believed Gray wasn't capable of excelling at anything.

Gray couldn't help thinking it: once more she was queen of the classroom.

* * *

Monday morning, Gray hopped from foot to foot on the sidewalk in front of her house. In Kent, it was either raining or trying to rain. At the moment, it was drizzling. Her breath leaked out in white puffs. The light rain didn't touch her. She'd erected a shield around her body.

Thea flashed her lights when she saw Gray by the side of the road. Gray waved and walked around to the passenger's side. "Good morning," Gray said cheerfully.

Thea nodded at the Beetle parked in the drive. "Is your sister staying home today?"

Gray looked over her shoulder. "She hasn't left her room yet."

"I take it you've been on suicide watch all weekend?"

"More like criminal watch. Charlene wants Stacey's heart on a plate."

"So she's still not over the whole Blake dumping her thing?"

"Ha."

Brittany and Kiki were standing in the middle of D Hall when Gray and Thea entered the building. "Mind if we go the other way?" Gray asked. "I don't feel like dealing with the brat pack this morning."

"I hear you," Thea answered.

She accompanied Gray to her locker. Thea was in the middle of telling Gray about her trip to the assisted living center to visit her grandmother when Gray felt a light kick against her foot.

Her stomach fluttered when she saw Nolan. The tap against her foot was gentle and deliberate. It sent a current shooting up to her chest. He had the widest grin on his face. "Hey."

Gray's hand stilled inside her locker. She couldn't remember which book she'd been reaching for. She smiled like an idiot. "Hi."

"I saw you standing here so I thought I'd come over and say hi."

"Yeah, cool." Gray noticed Thea staring from her to Nolan. "This is my friend, Thea. Thea, this is Nolan."

Nolan's cheeks dimpled. "How's it going?"

Thea smiled back. "Good."

"Great, so you ladies have a nice day." Nolan tossed Gray one last endearing smile. "See you around, Gray."

She and Thea watched Nolan walk away. They kept staring until he'd disappeared around the corner. Thea's eyes glittered.

"Well, isn't he cute. How come you've never mentioned him before?"

"We never really spoke till this weekend . . . at church."

"Uh-oh," Thea said. Her grin widened.

"What?"

"I see a sin coming on."

Gray swatted her friend. "He just said hi."

"That's how it starts."

Gray's smile faded. Thea's words reminded her of Raj. "Let's go to class."

Maybe Nolan would ask her out. It wasn't beyond the realm of possibility. The sooner he did, the sooner she could put an end to any delusions Raj was entertaining in his head about the two of them and the world to themselves.

It might even be worth breaking her own dating rule.

* * *

"You're in a good mood this evening," Mom said as Gray sat down to dinner.

"Eh," Gray replied with a grin and shrug.

Across from her, Charlene blew on her fingernails, which were now ruby red. Char had been acting eerily nonchalant ever since Gray returned home from school. She'd even applied eyeliner and lipstick, which seemed like a waste considering she hadn't gone anywhere.

"It must be from regaining your powers yesterday. See, I told you Gatherings weren't a complete waste of time."

Sure, let Mom think that was the reason behind her dopey grin.

Charlene stiffened. "What's that?" she asked. "Lee got her abilities back?"

Mom smiled. "Your sister floated yesterday."

"That's great." Charlene practically sneered, dropping her elbows to the table and rocking forward. "About time you caught up to the rest of us."

Gray slammed her fork down. "Way to show your sisterly support."

Mom cleared her throat. "Girls, let's enjoy dinner."

Enjoy dinner? Right, with the bad seed sitting directly across from her?

The clank of Mom's serving spoon against the casserole dish was a distant echo in Gray's ear.

"The squash came out nice," Mom said. "Just needs a little more seasoning." She stretched her hand toward the salt shaker. It stood directly between Gray and Charlene. The salt moved across the oak surface into Mom's hand. Any doubt about who'd moved it was clarified when Charlene said, "Here, let me help you, Mom."

Gray straightened her back and lifted her chin. "Would you like some pepper, as well?" She glared at Charlene and then pushed the pepper grinder toward her mom with her mind. Only it didn't move.

Gray's lower lip dropped. She stared in disbelief at the pepper. Then she caught it: a slight smirk on her sister's lips.

"You!" Gray screamed.

Their mom startled in her seat. "What's going on?"

Gray pointed a finger across the table. "You've been blocking my spells all along!"

Charlene shrugged and stuck her nose up, looking proud rather than ashamed.

"No." Mom looked wide-eyed at Charlene. "She wouldn't do that. She couldn't."

"Five years," Gray all but choked out. Tears were threatening, but she refused to let a single one spill in front of Charlene.

"Charlene, is this true?" Mom asked.

"No."

Gray flexed her fist and practically leapt across the table. "How dare you lie? I know it was you. How come I've never been able to perform spells in your presence? Until yesterday I could never do magic at Gatherings, then low and behold—the one day you're gone suddenly I can."

Charlene's glare was fierce. The best defense was an offense and Charlene rocked the whole "I'm not the one in the wrong, you are" thing.

"Charlene, how could you?"

At least Gray's mother believed her.

Charlene's lip folded over. "Oh, right. So I'm the bad guy. The evil twin."

"Charlene, I didn't say that," their mom said.

Why not? Gray grumbled in her head. It was the truth. Five freaking years she'd been stripped of her abilities and confidence.

"You don't have to," Charlene cried out. Oh sure, now she was the one sobbing. "You love her more. You always have." Charlene sobbed harder, great big gasping breaths as though she was choking. "You'd be happier if it'd just been her—if I'd never been born." Charlene leapt from her chair and ran for the stairs.

"Charlene!" Mom called in alarm. She pushed back her chair and hurried after her.

Gray was left sitting at the table alone. She stared across the table so long everything went out of focus. The dining chairs, the plates, the framed pictures; everything turned to blurred fuzz as though she were altering reality and might cause everything around her to disappear until there was only herself, seated inside an empty room.

Gray squeezed her eyes so tightly her upper lip pressed into her gums. Her desire to transport was so intense that she cried out in frustration when she opened her eyes. The dining room came rushing back into focus.

Gray stood up so abruptly her chair skidded back.

Fine, if she couldn't teleport, she still had her own two feet.

She ran outside into the rain and took off down the street. The rain beat down and she did nothing to stop it from pelting her, absorbing through the layers of her clothes to the skin beneath.

Her own sister had taken everything Gray was and locked it tightly away. She'd let the other kids laugh at her in sixth grade. She'd made Gray doubt herself and feel like a screw-up. What kind of sister would do that?

She hadn't taken her powers from her completely, but enough to make her out for the fool in front of her peers and her own mother. Gray had been hesitant to practice on her own. Just when she thought she was getting into the swing again she'd try something at the dinner table or at Gathering and hit a brick wall once more. Just think what new spells she could have mastered if her sister hadn't blocked her for five years!

Chapter 6

The dim room was making Raj sleepy. Adrian's voice in the main chamber brought it all back into focus.

"Just relax, Mrs. Court, and give me your hands."

Adrian, or Hedrick, as he went by these days, was barely visible through the narrow gap between the velvet curtain and the doorway leading into the back room where Raj was crouched on a low stool. On the other side of the curtain, the dark chamber was lit with dripping candles. Adrian sat in front of his client at a round table covered in a midnight-blue tablecloth. The setting looked better suited to a psychic reading than a healing session.

Luckily Raj could see in the dark. If only he could absorb an entire book with the touch of his palm instead of flipping through a tome on the art and magic of healing terminal diseases.

Adrian had told Raj he'd be fixing a migraine, not a brain tumor.

He shouldn't have been surprised when the shady warlock pulled a fast one on him. There was a reason the coven had stripped Adrian of his powers. The man couldn't be trusted. Adrian did, however, pay cash under the table to those who accepted employment working for the famed Hedrick the Healer. Basically, Raj was doing Adrian's work for him.

Before losing his powers, he'd called himself Adrian the Avenger, and it was his business of avenging that had cost him his powers.

Adrian Hedrick Montez.

Rumor had it he started out in his early youth as Montez the Magician before going on the whole avenger kick. Rumor also had it that Adrian's body wasn't his own. The body one chose for themselves said a lot about a person. Adrian's was about twenty-two years old, tall and muscular with thick brown hair and a snap-your-panties-off smile practically guaranteed to get the bastard laid whenever he wanted. The smooth, smug voice that went with the face grated on Raj's nerves when Adrian next spoke.

"Now I'm going to blindfold you, my dear. Do not be alarmed. The eyes have a tendency to want to open and I need to ensure they stay closed while I take a look inside your brain."

As Adrian tied the blindfold over Mrs. Court's eyes, Raj silently slipped into the chamber and took the seat Adrian had vacated. Mrs. Court's aura crackled. That's what had tipped Raj off about a serious illness to begin with. Without the curtain blocking his view of her, he saw that Mrs. Court transmitted a distinct white.

"Now I'm going to put my hands on your head." Adrian's voice would be coming from behind Mrs. Court, but Raj supposed that added to the illusion of his powers.

Raj reached forward. Mrs. Court's tight curls felt crusty under his palms. The woman must have used half a canister of aerosol. Raj leaned forward and lined his eyes with Mrs. Court's covered eyes. He closed his.

There were bright horizontal lines running across his mind. They were faint and brilliant all at once. Raj worked his fingers through Mrs. Court's curls. He applied his finger pads to her scalp like suctions. The lines moved up like a ripple in the wake of a disturbance.

Raj searched the lines, scrolling through them like text on a machine. But he'd reached the end and seen nothing. He started backwards, slower. Everything looked the same. For all he knew, he was looking at the same static and fuzz he'd see if he were sitting alone with his eyes closed.

This was crazy.

Raj had once tried to make his sister well and she'd only had a common cold. Plus it'd been his sister—he'd had every motivation to heal her. If he'd had the ability to, he would have transferred the cold to himself instead.

Raj spread his fingers wider, as though they were little antennas and all he needed was to pick up the tumor's signal. But now he couldn't move the image up or down. He was stuck inside a static void.

At least Adrian was keeping quiet. Raj swore if he heard the man say, "I think I see something" or "Interesting," he'd take his speech from him.

Perhaps not the best idea. Powers or not, Adrian was not a forgiving man. Raj would just have to shoot him a look. But he couldn't even make out Adrian's breath.

Raj leaned back, relaxed his hold. His mind wandered as though in meditation and then he saw it: a dark mass near Mrs. Court's parietal lobe.

Raj nodded.

"I've located the tumor, Mrs. Court," Adrian said. "I need you to stay relaxed while I do more probing."

Raj began squeezing his eyes again at the sound of Adrian's voice and lost sight of the tumor for a moment. *Relax.* He breathed in and out until his inhalations matched the length of his exhalations. *Concentrate.*

Raj's mother had taught him everything he knew about healing spells. It had been her dream for him to train as one of India's mythic pranic healers. Raj didn't want to live in India. He liked America. And he had no desire to become some spiritual woo-woo witch doctor who most likely meditated eight hours a day.

But at the moment he needed money.

Raj cleared his mind. The dark mass loomed like a mountain at dusk. He tried to make it disappear and when that didn't work, he picked at it. He chiseled. He hammered.

Maybe if he indicated to Adrian that he'd been successful and Adrian told Mrs. Court the mass had been extracted, she'd heal herself with her own belief that everything was going to be fine. The placebo effect.

Or she might return, demanding her money back, or worse, put out bad PR about Hedrick the Phony.

Raj dropped his hands to the table and opened his eyes. What had his mother told him about the most gifted healers? They didn't need to put on a show of physical contact and they worked with their eyes open.

Raj bore into Mrs. Court's forehead.

He felt Adrian slip around the table and stiffen beyond his right shoulder.

Suddenly, Mrs. Court's forehead peeled open before Raj's eyes. He could see blood and tissue and brain.

Adrian must have seen it, too. He inhaled sharply and barely managed a whispered, "Hold very still, Mrs. Court."

In Raj's mind the tumor had been black. Now it glowed cream and white. There was a bright, blinding edge around everything inside Mrs. Court's head. Raj tugged at the tumor gently with his eyes. It began detaching from her brain. Wispy, silk-like threads broke away, freeing the lump. The tumor floated forward as he pulled it out. Once it left the open layer of her head it disappeared in an eruption of tiny sparks that drifted down like shiny particles after an exploding firework, and then disappeared altogether.

Raj sealed her forehead.

The room was silent and then Mrs. Court gasped. "It's gone." Then she whispered, "It's gone, isn't it?"

Raj looked at Adrian and nodded.

Adrian sounded all blustering showman once more. "That's right, Mrs. Court. I have successfully removed the tumor from your brain."

She reached for the blindfold and as she did, Raj ducked behind the velvet curtain, thinking once again that an invisibility spell would have come in handy.

"You are a saint, Mr. Montez." Mrs. Court's voice was muffled through the velvet curtain. "Bless you, young man."

Adrian studied Raj carefully after Mrs. Court had paid and gone.

"What was that back there?"

"A miracle," Raj replied sarcastically.

"I've never witnessed a healing spell work that way."

"I like to give it my own touch." Raj's smooth voice covered the shaking of his hands. His mother had once described a healing session like the one he'd performed on Mrs. Court. She'd told him the mystical tale of a pranic healer in India who'd opened a man's chest up with the power of his mind to extract the patient's cancer.

While there were a few hundred pranic healers in India, she said only three were able to do so with what she called "the extra bells and whistles."

Raj shrugged.

Luckily, Adrian was back to business. "I've got a good one for you tomorrow. Woman wants twenty-twenty vision."

"Let me guess," Raj said. "She's blind."

Adrian grinned. "Think you can make a blind woman see again?"

"Easy."

Adrian laughed and slapped Raj on the shoulder. "Confidence. I love it. You know what they say about magic—it's ten percent ability, ninety percent determination."

And another hundred percent study. Raj was going to have his nose in the books all night now. Granting sight to the blind? There were any number of claims that spiritual healing could cure a person's terminal illness, but cases of the blind regaining full sight were as rare as a phoenix.

Well, no one could say Raj backed away from a challenge. "What time?" he asked.

"Mrs. Ling's coming in at ten."

"In the morning?"

"Is that a problem?"

"I already missed school today."

Clearly that hadn't been the correct answer. Adrian stiffened and looked sideways at Raj. For a man without power, he still knew how to hold an intimidating stance. "Make Mrs. Ling see and I'll pay you double."

Double. Now Adrian was speaking Raj's language. He was still twenty dollars shy of paying off the amulet. "I'll be here," Raj said.

Adrian grinned. "Good."

* * *

When Raj stepped outside he had to blink to adjust his eyes. Compared to Adrian's sealed-off lair, it was downright bright outside even for an overcast afternoon.

"Raj!"

Raj felt his heart soar. "Aahana!" He whipped around. His ears hadn't been playing tricks on him. His little sister stood on the sidewalk not six feet from him. She looked older than he remembered—a mini adult in her khaki pants, black pea coat, scarf, and beret.

Her grin widened. Raj felt his own lips moving up as though Aahana were a ventriloquist controlling the strings on his face.

He lifted his arms and she ran toward him, but before she made it a voice broke in like cracked glass and stopped his sister cold.

"Aahana! Keep away from him!"

Aahana no longer advanced, nor did she retreat. She kept her ground—her expression a mixture of pleasure and pain.

His mother's words might have been hasty, but her advance was not. She was still a beauty—tall, slim, dark-skinned with straight, silky hair that flowed past her shoulders. Men and women were forever staring at Raj's mother. She was no blond-next-door and certainly hadn't adopted the friendly American smile.

Raj straightened and narrowed his eyes at his mother. How dare she look at him with that menacing stare? He was a healer even more gifted than she. She ought to treat him with respect rather than as a child or monster. And she ought to stop treating Aahana like a child while she was at it. Aahana was in junior high now and a beauty in her own right. She was lighter skinned like their father and her smiles came naturally except when their mother was agitated.

"Hello, ladies," Raj said evenly.

"Come on, Aahana, we're going."

"But I want to say hi to Raj."

Their mother's voice went up an octave. "Aahana."

Aahana's face fell. "Yes, Mother."

Raj thought that was the end of it, but then his mother pushed a stray hair from her face and asked, "How's your father?"

"Same old."

His mother pursed her lips. "Some things never change."

"No, they don't," Raj said. He wasn't even sure what that meant, but it felt good to match her cold tone and stare.

"What are you doing in this part of town?"

Raj folded his arms over his chest. This was too much. His mother had abandoned him with a drunkard and wanted to play the parental card. "What's it to you?"

"I know what you're doing," she answered for him. "You're visiting Adrian."

"He goes by Hedrick now."

His mother's eyes narrowed. "Aahana, we're going."

Raj tipped his head before turning. "See you around."

* * *

As usual, it was Mrs. Baxter who answered the front door and greeted Raj when he stopped by. "Hello, Raj. Shay's in her room with Max."

Raj hesitated in the doorway. "Maybe I should come back."

"Nonsense," Mrs. Baxter said, opening the front door wider. "They'll be happy to see you."

Raj wasn't sure if he felt like seeing the happy couple. And for all he knew they were in the middle of a steamy make-out session. He chuckled to himself. Shay and Max—nope, couldn't picture it. Raj stepped inside the foyer. Mrs. Baxter tilted her head toward the staircase.

"Thanks, Mrs. Baxter."

Her smile never wavered—like a Stepford Wife. "You're always welcome."

Raj didn't have to knock at Shay's door. It was open. He could hear Shay's and Max's voices before he even reached it.

"*Le livre d'étudiant*! What's wrong with that?" Shay demanded.

"It's '*le livre de l'étudiant*,' " Max said. "To show possession of a noun you have to use *de* plus the definite article."

"Maybe so, but I don't think my sentence is wrong, either."

"Check with Madame Girard."

"Just because she's a teacher doesn't make her right all the time."

Raj's lips quirked. Imagine if Shay and Max showed half as much interest in their magic as in French grammar. "Knock, knock," Raj called out.

Max smiled instantly. "Raj, how are you, buddy?"

Raj took Max's outstretched hand and shook it. "Keeping out of trouble."

Shay still looked peeved. If a French native were in the room she'd probably insist that she was right and they were wrong. "What's going on?" she asked.

Raj dug inside his pocket. "Here's fifty-five dollars and I'll have another twenty to you tomorrow."

Shay didn't look at the money or take it. In fact, she wasn't looking at him at all. She was turning away. His lips turned down. "What?"

Shay faced him. "I don't think you should give Gray the amulet."

Max took a seat at Shay's desk and bent his head over a textbook.

Raj folded his arms and redirected his attention to Shay. "Why?"

"I don't want to see you get hurt."

"Me? Get hurt?" Raj laughed. The sound reminded him of gagging. "I can't get hurt."

"Of course you can."

Raj frowned. "I need that amulet. Did you make it or not?"

"Of course I did." Shay turned abruptly and went to her desk. "Excuse me," she said and reached over Max to pull open a top drawer. Max leaned to one side as Shay extracted an iridescent-blue sachet bag. She loosened the strings and pulled out the amulet. It dangled from her fingers about three and a half inches.

"It's beautiful," Raj said. He hoped Shay would give it to him tonight. He had a couple more days to pay her the rest of the money before Valentine's, but he'd feel better if he had the amulet now. That, and he wanted a chance to look at it before he gave it away.

Shay grinned and dropped the amulet back inside its pouch. "One of my best," she said. She held it out.

Raj stared at her outstretched hand a moment.

"Go ahead, take it. I know you're good for the remaining payment."

Raj didn't need further encouragement. He snatched the pouch. Shay raised one brow before lowering her arm.

"Thanks." Raj flashed Shay one of his devil-may-care grins. "I'll let you get back to your conjugations."

"Stay awhile," Shay said.

"Nah, I've got my own studying to do."

Shay rolled her eyes. "No kidding. Where were you today?"

"Classified."

Shay gave him a playful punch in the shoulder. It felt good; she rarely joked around like that anymore. "Maybe I'll have to beat it out of you."

Max half laughed, half grunted from Shay's desk. He turned around to face the room. "And she could do it, too."

Raj grinned. "I can withstand a bit of torture."

"Ah, but can you withstand a truth spell?"

Raj squeezed the amulet in a protective fist and tucked it under his folded arm. "You wouldn't dare."

Shay stared him down then laughed, relaxing her shoulders as she did so. "Of course not, that'd be a violation of a witch's rights."

Behind her, Max nodded his agreement.

Chapter 7

Gray entered her house quietly. God knows she should have slammed the door, but she didn't feel like seeing or speaking to her mom or sister and that meant not drawing attention to herself.

Forgiveness was out of the question.

Then again, in order for forgiveness to be denied in the first place it would have to be requested, which Charlene had not done.

"Where were you?" Mom asked.

Gray hadn't noticed her sitting in a dark corner of the living room.

She answered with a flippant, "Out." Gray kicked her shoes off and headed for the stairs.

"Charlene feels terrible about what she did," Mom said. "I know it doesn't excuse her, but it was Ryan Phillips's idea."

Sure, blame pear-faced Ryan Phillips. That's what minions were for—to take the fall.

Gray glanced sideways at her mom through narrowed eyes. There was a tight frown and faraway look on her face.

"Ryan's been a bad influence on Charlene," Mom said.

Gray gripped the banister railing and took the first step up, proceeding forward before her mom could say anything more. She locked herself inside her room and put a pair of headphones over her ears. Jem's "They" began playing. Gray turned up the volume.

At some point, she woke lying atop her bed. Her iPod was beside her on the nightstand. She still had her jean skirt and embroidered blouse on.

Gray tried to sit up, but found she was stuck on her back. A second attempt failed.

What the hell?

Then suddenly Raj McKenna materialized at the foot of the bed.

Gray tried to scream, but no sound emerged. The grin on his face was full of wicked intention. He took a step closer until the bed sheets brushed his thighs. His jeans were tight; even his ribbed cotton tee clung to his torso. He was muscled. More muscled than Nolan, less than Blake, but not as top heavy and bulky as her sister's ex. Gray swallowed and it was no longer to scream. Raj's eyes gleamed in the dark.

Gray was able to lift herself to her elbows. Once she did, her eyes met Raj's gaze. His eyes dropped to her blouse. Gray's heart thundered, but there was nothing she could do to stop him. Her blouse burst open.

Gray shot up in bed, gasping and hugging her hands to her chest. With the flick of her finger, the light flipped on. Gray made a quick scan of her room, but there was no sign of an intruder.

Just a dream, Gray.

Why, then, had she been wearing the exact same clothes she'd had on at school that day? Dreaming in detail—was that normal? Her outfit had been dead on, right down to her new red and black bra.

Gray flung her pillow at the foot of her bed—just in case—but it didn't hit any invisible figures lurking at her bedside. She retrieved the pillow off the floor, punched it into shape, and curled up on her side.

* * *

Snow drifted from a faint blue ceiling overhead in a mass of wet clumps. The particles seemed to hover in the air, in no hurry to touch the pavement, where each speck of white melted upon contact. The flurries blotted out the houses across the street as Gray waited for Thea the next morning.

Her mom suggested she wait inside, but Gray wanted out of the house. Besides, there was something magical about the falling snow—a quietness that enveloped her and sealed out the rest of the world.

"Early dismissal, you think?" Gray asked when she climbed inside Thea's car.

"Nah, it's melting too fast. We're just gonna have to brave another day at McKinley High. Maybe it'll wait and dump down on Valentine's Day. Then everyone will have to keep their chocolate and floral displays to themselves. Boohoo."

"I wish."

"Are you sure about that?"

Gray turned her head. "Yeah, why wouldn't I be?"

Thea shrugged and cranked the wheel at their turn onto the main road. "It seemed like you had a moment with that guy yesterday."

"Nolan?"

"Um-hum."

"We're just friends. Well, not really even friends. We know each other," Gray clarified. Clearly it wasn't working on Thea.

"He seems nice. I do have a few questions for him before he can ask you out."

"Thea!" A moment later Gray laughed. Her cheeks were heating, but it felt good.

"What kind of music does he like?"

"No idea."

"You can tell a lot about a guy by the music he listens to."

Gray leaned forward. "Like what?"

Thea straightened up behind the steering wheel. "Like if he's a lame-o."

"Pray tell, what kind of music do lame-os listen to?"

"Boy bands, Britney, Lady Gaga . . . pop."

"You've just described my sister's favorites."

Thea raised a brow. "Point made. Speaking of, I imagine Charlene will be a no-show on Valentine's Day."

Gray snorted. "Yeah, unless she plans to throw pig's blood on Stacey Morehouse."

Thea chuckled. "Not that she wouldn't deserve it. Stacey Morehouse is pretty heinous."

"So's Charlene." Gray sighed. "Why can't I have a nice twin sister?"

"Yin and yang, baby." Thea shrugged. She flicked her blinker on and took a sharp turn into the student parking lot, coming to an abrupt stop that sent Gray lurching forward in her seat. Thea sighed. "Another day in paradise."

Gray's head snapped toward her. "What did you just say?"

"Another day in paradise," Thea repeated.

"Sorry," Gray said. "It's just I heard Raj McKenna say the exact same thing the other day." *When he didn't realize she was there.*

Thea's eyes lit up. "Oh, now he's delish."

Gray could see Thea's tongue peeking out as though she meant to lick her lips. "Gross," she said.

"Tall, dark, lean, muscled McKenna, gross? You're in denial, babe, face it. And I can guarantee you he doesn't listen to any offending music."

"It's just everything else about him that's offending."

Thea finger combed her bangs over one eye. "He's got depth."

"How do you know?"

"I can just tell." She glanced sideways at Gray out of her visible eye. "And I think you like him."

"Do not!"

Thea grinned mischievously. "Then what were you doing inside his car last week?"

"I told you. He didn't return the pen I lent him in class and I went to retrieve it."

"Right, you must have *loved* that pen to go to such great lengths." Thea chuckled.

"It was my favorite pen, Thea. And let me tell you something about Raj McKenna. He's a delinquent. He burnt down his last house." Gray could have sworn Thea looked even more impressed.

"All right already. No reason to get your panties in a twist."

Gray pushed the car door open and got out. Thea was just as quick. Gray looked over the hood at her. "I hate that expression."

"You hate that I'm right."

* * *

After fourth period, Gray went to her locker to retrieve her lunch bag and found that someone had decorated the outside with pink, shimmery wrapping paper. There was a balloon at the top with a Band-Aid stuck in the middle and some ribbon that curled downwards. When Gray opened her locker she found a white rose and card taped inside.

The card had a picture of two bears seated on a green hill under a blue, sunny sky. The print on the card read, "I'm Sorry I Hurt You."

Inside, Charlene had written:

Dear Sister,

What I did was wrong and I don't blame you if you never want to speak to me again. I don't know what's wrong with me. I have tried so hard to be a good friend and sister to you. I have tried to make you like me. When you started doing so well at Gathering I thought you'd get bored with me and leave me behind. I only wished you wouldn't forget me. I wasn't even aware of what I was doing and by the time I was, I didn't know how to stop. My presence canceled your powers out without me wishing it and I was too ashamed to ask for your help or Mom's.

It is such a relief that the spell is lifted. It is a burden I have carried far too long and the guilt has eaten at me all these years. Be happy knowing that I have been my own worst punishment and that I hate myself for what I did.

I am going to fix this, Lee. I'm going to fix everything.

Your sister,

Charlene

Gray tucked the card between two textbooks and re-taped the rose to the inside of her locker door. She grabbed her sack lunch off the top shelf and smacked the locker door shut. For a moment she looked at the glossy paper covering her locker and thought about tearing it down, then decided there was no point. Anyway, it looked pretty. Maybe Nolan would notice and think she had a secret admirer.

She turned around only to see that Shay Baxter had honed in on her as she was walking by, hand in hand with Max Curry. Of course—it had to be the coven's star couple.

Gray pasted a smile over her face. She didn't know why. Shay wasn't smiling at her. Her gaze flicked from Gray to the papered locker and then back to Gray. Max probably wouldn't have noticed her if Shay hadn't said hi and dragged him to a stop at the last minute.

"Hi," Gray returned.

At least Max smiled.

"That was an impressive comeback at Gathering Sunday," Shay said.

Why was she studying Gray as though she were a specimen under a microscope?

Gray's smile faded. "Not really." What she really wanted to do was inform Her Magic Holiness that it wasn't a comeback at all. Gray hadn't lost her capabilities—they'd merely been blocked . . . by her sister. That was the part she wasn't willing to admit. She might as well tell Shay that her sister had committed murder. She'd judge her just as harshly. As mad as Gray was at Charlene, it was for her to judge, not Shay Baxter.

"Well, it's good to have you back," Max said just before the couple continued down the hall.

Suddenly his smile wasn't as endearing. *Back*. Had Gray been away? Did her presence not count during the years she'd been hindered? Gray recalled the look on Shay's face when the applause for Gray had drawn her attention from the next room. For a fleeting second, Gray had had the suspicion that Shay had done something to block her magic in the past. But that was ludicrous. Not the infallible Shay Baxter.

Gray wished it had been Shay. She wished it'd been anyone but her sister.

* * *

There was no trace of snow by the time school got out. Gray was relieved Charlene's car wasn't parked out front when Thea dropped her home. If Charlene thought she could patch everything up with a bit of shiny paper, she was sorely mistaken.

The kitchen was always Gray's first stop when returning home. Today, parchment paper lined the countertops, with empty molds stacked in a pile. The sink was filled with pots smeared with dark chocolate. There was a stack of clear cellophane bags with little red hearts and a spool of red ribbon beside it. What caught Gray's eye in all the mess were the smoothly molded chocolate hearts set on parchment.

"What's all this?" Gray asked her mom when she walked in.

"Charlene's become something of a chocolatier this week."

"Charlene and chocolate." Gray turned toward her mother with raised brows. "I never thought I'd hear those two words in the same sentence."

"This is the first time I've seen her interested in anything besides Blake. Look how beautifully they turned out."

As if Gray had stopped looking at the chocolates since entering the kitchen. Each heart was smooth, dark, and beckoning to melt on the tip of her tongue.

"They say sugar's the best medicine," Mom said.

"Don't you mean laughter?"

"I think it's a toss-up."

"I could use a bit of chocolate therapy myself." Gray zeroed in on one of the chocolate hearts, only to freeze mid-reach when her mother yelped, "No! Charlene said not to touch anything."

Gray snorted. "What? Does she plan on eating them all herself?"

"No, she's giving them away. I think she wanted it to be a surprise for Valentine's Day."

Gray fought the urge to snort again. It was a bit hard to miss a kitchen filled with chocolate. Well, at the very least, Charlene owed her a bag of handmade chocolates. Gray would take chocolates over flowers any day. And it wasn't like she was expecting anyone else to gift her sweets. No, it would be another Valentine's where she had to buy her own candy. This year she'd take the ones Charlene made. It wasn't like she cared about having it packaged up or presented to her on Valentine's Day.

Once her mom had left the kitchen, Gray snatched a handful of hearts and ran up to her room. She popped a chocolate into her mouth and made a face. Okay, not the best candy she'd ever tasted, but not the worst. Charlene could cross catering off her list of potential careers. Gray sucked on a second piece then bit into it once it'd softened. It was still chocolate, after all.

She spread her geometry book open on her desk. Might as well get her least favorite subject out of the way first. She pulled several sheets of lined paper out of her desk drawer and clicked her mechanical pencil twice. She leaned over the book. Trouble was, geometry problems looked like Chinese and if you didn't speak Chinese how could you translate symbols or, in this case, solve problems?

Maybe she should ease back into homework with something that came more naturally, like English. Now there was a language Gray understood.

She pushed the math book aside and extracted an ink pen from her pen cup. She tapped it on top of the desk then stopped, stared into space, and traced a finger over her lips.

Gray stood and grabbed the Magic 8 Ball off her bookshelf. There wasn't anything magic about it—just a standard-issue toy from Mattel. Still, she liked to think the energy she put into the ball brought forth the truth and tonight she had a very important question to ask.

"Does Nolan Knapp like me?" Gray shook the ball vigorously and turned it around.

Ask again later.

Later, like three seconds later?

Gray shook it again.

Ask again later.

She began shaking the ball with more vigor. *Does Raj McKenna like me?* she asked in her head before she could stop herself.

Yes.

The Magic 8 clunked against the wood shelf when Gray set it down.

Gray returned to her desk and polished off the rest of the chocolates as she did her reading assignment. When it came time to start the essay, she found herself unable to concentrate. For one thing, her stomach hurt.

Good going. She'd given herself a tummy ache.

By the time Gray came down for dinner, Charlene's chocolate factory was closed down and packed away. Gray wasn't sure she could sit at the same dinner table as her sister and just looking at the casserole placed in the center was making her feel ill.

Charlene began to yell from upstairs as Mom walked into the dining room. "Go ahead and eat without me. I just applied my face mask."

Mom smiled at Gray. "Well then, I guess it's just you and me." Her expression changed. Now she was looking at Gray, frowning. "What's the matter, sweetie?"

Gray slouched in her chair. "Nothing. Just a slight tummy ache."

"Did you get into the chocolate?"

Gray tried to flash Mom one of her cute "you caught me" looks, but it was hard to pull off when it felt as though her insides were eating her up.

"Here, this will help." She heaped green salad onto Gray's plate.

"Thanks, Mom." Gray forced the lettuce into her mouth. Hopefully it'd counterbalance the sweets soon. She chewed slowly. "How was your day?" she asked halfheartedly.

"They have me working on another Norwegian thriller."

"Good, at least it's something interesting."

"All books are interesting."

Gray swallowed a mouthful of chewed lettuce then pushed her plate forward. "I think I'm gonna go to bed."

"That's probably a good idea."

Gray felt bad leaving her plate on the table, but at the moment she just wanted to crawl under her covers and curl into a ball.

Chapter 8

I t wasn't the beeping of her alarm, but the pounding of her
head that woke Gray up the next morning. The pressure in
her skull was debilitating. It felt like an anvil pressing her
head into the pillow. She lay in bed a moment longer before
slowly lifting up.

"What the heck?" Gray's mouth fell open.

Why the hell was she in Charlene's bedroom?

Gray felt something scratchy against her bosom. She
looked down. And what the freak was she doing sleeping in
Charlene's lace slip?

The headache was momentarily forgotten. Gray swung her
legs out of bed and stomped to her room. "Charlene!" *If this was
her sister's idea of a joke . . .*

But Charlene wasn't in Gray's room. Obviously she hadn't
slept in Gray's bed, either. It was neatly made. Someone had
tidied up the objects on her armoire and dresser and picked up
her discarded clothes.

"Mom!" Gray called next, marching down the hall to her
mother's room.

She pushed the door open. Empty.

Again, what the freak?

The hospital.

Gray jolted to a stop. Oh, god, Charlene! She'd seemed
okay the night before—she'd been giving herself a facial—but
maybe she just wanted to look her best before offing herself.

Was that why Gray had been sleeping in her sister's bed? Had her mom rushed off to the hospital while Gray fell into Char's pillows sobbing herself to sleep then somehow blocked out the whole traumatic event?

And thrown on Charlene's slip while she was at it?

That was just weird.

Gray hurried down the stairs and into the kitchen. There was a note on the countertop.

Charlene:
Got the call.
I'll be back Friday afternoon.
I love you.
Mom

Some Valentine's week this was turning out to be. Even Gray's own mother didn't love her.

Okay, so of course she knew her mom loved her, but not enough to leave her a note or at least include her in the address.

Well, then, whatever.

Gray stormed back up the stairs and pulled off the negligee. She didn't even want to think about how creepy that was. As she stepped into a pair of underwear, Gray remembered she didn't have to dress herself anymore. Good, 'cause Thea was going to be there to pick her up in less than fifteen minutes. Gray snapped into a pair of embroidered jeans and a blouse.

She hurried down the stairs and poured herself a bowl of cereal. She rushed back up the stairs and began tearing her room apart looking for her backpack. Finally she located it in the far corner of her closet.

She couldn't imagine why her mom would tidy up her room all of a sudden. And what was "the call?" Her mom hadn't mentioned anything. Maybe it had something to do with Charlene. Maybe she was getting her help. They had spent all that time talking in secret. Gray hoped that whatever kind of help it was involved a boarding school—preferably in a foreign country.

She wasn't ready to forgive her sister, especially now that she knew Charlene was okay. Kinda. Gray still wasn't clear where her sister was at the moment.

The sky was solid gray. So what else was new? Except that maybe it was much lighter than it should be, even for an overcast day. And warmer, too. The air didn't have the same bite to it, especially considering it'd been cold enough to snow the day before. Their street was ominously quiet. For a moment Gray had a chilling thought. What if she was the last person alive in the world? She shook it aside and let relief wash over her when a car passed.

Gray checked her watch. This was the latest Thea had ever run. Unzipping the front pouch on her pack, she reached in, but her phone was missing. She rifled through the main pouch, but it wasn't there, either.

When twelve minutes had passed, Gray headed back up her driveway. She leaned over and picked up the rolled newspaper and tossed it on the kitchen counter right before checking the answering machine.

No messages.

Gray dialed Thea's house. The Johnstons' answering machine picked up as Gray hung up. She dialed her mom's phone next. It went directly to her answering machine. "Hey, it's me," Gray said. "Just wondering where the heck you are. Give me a call."

Gray set the phone in its cradle and looked around the kitchen. There were a couple of glasses and a bowl and spoon inside the sink. Gray circled the kitchen, pausing in front of the trash bin. She wasn't sure what she was looking for. She stepped on the lever that lifted the bin's lid. Inside were several empty cans of soup and Slim Fast diet shakes.

Great on the recycling effort, Char.

Gray removed her foot from the lever and the lid snapped shut.

She sighed. Loudly. It was comforting to hear sound of any kind in the deserted house.

Gray grabbed the keys to the Beetle from the key peg by the door. Charlene obviously wasn't using them and who knew what the heck had happened to Thea. The world had gone mad.

* * *

The rain was holding back for the moment, but it didn't make the parking lot look any less gloomy. Her windshield faced McKinley. Gray studied the building for any activity going in or out. She chuckled softly. It felt like she was on a stakeout. Gray waited an extra twenty-five minutes. It was too late to go to first period. No more disappearing acts, especially not halfway through the period.

When the bell rang, Gray stepped out of the car. Was it her imagination, or were people staring at her in the hallway? She looked down at her blouse and jeans. Everything looked fine. Gray patted her hair. She'd put it up in a high ponytail then braided it Lara Croft Tomb Raider-style, but blond and, let's face it—not as badass when you considered the embroidered jeans and blouse. Still, everything had looked good before she left the house and she'd checked twice: once before waiting for Thea, the next before nabbing the Beetle.

Gray paused in front of her locker. The pink paper was gone. Had Charlene taken it down? She couldn't see any reason why she would—she was after Gray's forgiveness, after all. Someone else must have. That was just rude.

Gray began turning the combo on her locker. She could feel a pair of eyes on her so she glanced to the left. Curtis Read gaped at her fifteen lockers down. She really needed to check her face in her locker mirror. Gray finished the combination and pulled down on the latch. It didn't budge. She yanked harder.

Curtis had thrown her off. If she had something on her face someone really ought to say something.

She spun the combo again with the same results. A groaning sound worked its way through her lips.

Fine. Magic it was, then. She lifted a finger and the lock unlatched. Gray pulled on the latch and gasped.

Her locker was completely bare.

She blinked several times. No, her eyes weren't playing tricks on her. There was nothing inside her locker. Her pictures and mirror had been removed as well.

Someone had some explaining to do and they better start doing it fast. It took Gray a moment to tear her eyes from the empty shell of her locker. She made a quick scan of the hall, searching for the guilty party, but the crowd had thinned out and begun to make their way to second period.

The warning bell chimed. She smacked the locker shut and headed to second period.

Someone was playing a joke on her. Raj? No, that didn't make any sense. Charlene? No. It couldn't be. Not this time.

Gray took her seat in geometry class. Again she was met with peculiar stares and now, whispering. *"What's she doing here?"* She pulled at her collar. Sweat was beading in the crooks of her armpits, ready to swell and leak down her arms at any minute. She dug inside her backpack and arranged her geometry book on her desktop along with her spiral notebook and mechanical pencil.

Mr. Burke turned to face the class with his attendance sheet. The moment his eyes left the paper, they landed on Gray. "Miss Perez," he said, startled. "What are you doing in my class?"

So even the teachers were in on it.

Gray swallowed. Her heart was hammering inside her chest. Everyone was staring at her. It was like some horrible nightmare. Maybe the coven was punishing her for performing magic at school. Enough to manipulate reality? She couldn't begin to imagine the kind of power that'd take, followed by the repairs and brain washes at the conclusion of her day of humiliation. It didn't make any sense.

"The same thing I do every day, learning math under your tutelage, Mr. Burke," Gray answered. Maybe she could get him to crack a smile and admit he couldn't keep a straight face any longer.

But Mr. Burke didn't smile. His jaw tensed. "Is this a joke?"

She would have liked to ask him the same question, but Mr. Burke didn't look like he was playing around.

Everyone seemed to be holding their breath around her.

"I don't know," Gray said slowly. "Maybe you can tell me what's going on."

Mr. Burke just stared at her.

Gray sat up. "Did I get transferred to another geometry class and someone forgot to mention it to me?" *Or to another school? Why was her locker cleared out?*

"You've never been in my geometry class, Charlene."

Charlene! Gray's heart skipped. "I'm not Charlene!"

There were gasps all around her.

"Who are you then?" Mike Matthews asked from beside her.

"Oh, for Pete's sake, you know very well I'm Gray."

Louder gasps, followed by a rush of whispers coming from all directions. It was like being sucked into the eye of a hurricane with chatter hurled and swirled all around her. Gray looked to Mr. Burke, imploring him with her eyes to make this charade end.

"Enough!" he shouted and the clamor stopped. Mr. Burke looked at Gray and spoke softly. "Miss Perez, please come with me."

Gray stuffed her things inside her pack and vacated her desk. She was more than ready to get out of that room.

She joined Mr. Burke in the hallway, where he shut the classroom door behind him. Gray could practically hear the jabber begin anew the moment the door clicked in place. *Hyenas.* She'd like to see how her classmates handled a day in the Twilight Zone.

Gray turned to Mr. Burke. He looked upset, so she was surprised by the gentleness of his voice. "Miss Perez, I know this has been a difficult time for you." Mr. Burke reached out and applied a soft amount of pressure to Gray's shoulder blade, guiding her forward. "Not only losing a sister, but a twin," he continued. "I know it feels like a part of you has died and it must hurt to let go of that part of yourself."

Gray stopped in her tracks. "What?" No, it couldn't be. Everyone was confused. Gray had missed something important. Blocked it out. It had to be Charlene. This was some kind of horrible mix-up. She gulped. "Did something happen to Charlene?"

Mr. Burke stared at her a moment then stretched the arm he'd previously had on her back into the hall. "Come with me."

"Where are we going?"

"To the office. I think you need to speak with Mrs. Knight."

Sure, 'cause McKinley High's career counselor would be able to straighten this all out. Not knowing what else to do, Gray followed Mr. Burke.

The office secretary lifted her head the moment Mr. Burke and Gray walked into the compact waiting room outside the counselors' offices.

"I need Mrs. Knight right away," Mr. Burke said.

The secretary nodded then stood. Wow, she was fetching Mrs. Knight by foot. Something was definitely amiss. Mrs. Knight walked out moments later. McKinley's career counselor was the office beauty: slim long legs and dark silky hair that bobbed just above her shoulders.

"Good morning, Mr. Burke. Hello, Charlene. What seems to be the problem?"

"I'm not Charlene, I'm Gray."

Mrs. Knight's eyes darted to Mr. Burke. He took a step back. "She's all yours, Mrs. Knight. I left my class unattended." Mr. Burke spun around and left.

Mrs. Knight's eyes latched onto Gray. "Charlene, why don't you step inside my office?"

Gray's cheeks heated. "I'm not Charlene!"

"Follow me, please." Mrs. Knight turned her back and started to her office.

Did she really expect Gray to follow her after that display? Gray grumbled and shuffled behind Mrs. Knight. What else was she supposed to do?

"Close the door, please." Mrs. Knight was already seated behind her desk when Gray walked in.

Gray shut the door and took a seat in front of Mrs. Knight's desk. The office was as tidy and prim as the woman seated in black slacks before her. She stared at the counselor and the counselor stared back. Unlike Mr. Burke, Mrs. Knight didn't look surprised. "You know what's happening, don't you?"

Gray leaned forward in her chair. "No, I really don't."

"You haven't taken time out to grieve. Remember our talk last month?"

Seriously? "No."

"I warned you that if you kept pushing your feelings aside they'd only build and end up bursting out. You can't block the pain forever, Charlene."

Gray snorted. If she really had died, it would be just like Charlene not to grieve.

Mrs. Knight's lips formed a tight pucker. The counselor looked dead serious. This was getting a little frightening. What kind of evil magic had Gray gotten in the middle of? And why had she been targeted?

"I'd like to go home," Gray said.

"I think that's a good idea, Charlene. Go home and take time to grieve your loss."

Gray narrowed her eyes. The woman was purposely saying her sister's name every chance she got. Even if she was under a spell, there was no reason to be so rude.

"I'll call your mother and let her know we spoke and that you're headed straight home."

"My mom's out of town."

The frown on Mrs. Knight's face deepened. "Your mom left you alone?"

Gray didn't like Mrs. Knight's tone when she asked the question—like her mother was negligent or something.

"Yeah," Gray responded, sounding a bit snooty. "Well, I am seventeen."

"I don't think you should be alone right now," Mrs. Knight shot back. "When is your mother returning?"

"Friday."

"Next Friday?"

"No. I don't know. I think she meant this Friday."

"Today's Friday."

Okay, now they were really messing with her. "Today's Wednesday."

"Nooo," Mrs. Knight said slowly. "Today's Friday." Then dawning seemed to appear on her face. "Friday, April first." She looked Gray over carefully.

Gray squinted across the desk. "So this is like a joke?" That made absolutely no sense—an April Fools' joke in February?

"Is it?" Mrs. Knight quipped. Her frown looked as taut as a rubber band and ready to snap if it became any deeper. She snatched a piece of paper and pen.

The movement startled Gray.

"Does your mother have a cell phone?"

"Yes."

"Number?"

Gray recited the numbers reluctantly, not that she cared if Mrs. Knight called her mom; she was just smarting over her general attitude.

"Can I go home now?"

"Not yet."

Great.

Chapter 9

R aj held the amulet three inches in front of his face and stared till it went out of focus. This had become his habit for the past two months. He barely touched his Zippo any more. He was slouched in his seat, one elbow propped on the desk—the moonstones, the charms, the initials "GP" dangling in front of him.

Beyond the amulet he could see students arriving to class. They were silhouettes, mannequins without faces.

"Did you hear about Charlene Perez?"

Raj barely registered the words.

" . . . pretending to be her dead sister."

"That's messed up."

"Maybe she's having a nervous breakdown."

"Or is playing the sickest April Fools' joke in history."

Raj shot out of his desk, closing his fingers around the amulet as he walked swiftly out of the room. His feet carried him over the polished hallway. He didn't even know where he was going. Raj squeezed the amulet in his hand so tightly the crystal felt as though it would cut into his palm.

He rounded a corner and made for the student center. The halls were clearing out as the last seconds before the final bell hovered in the air. It rang as he crossed over the school crest in the middle of the student center. A wall of light caught his eye from the triple sets of double doors beside the main office. Raj headed for them.

As he neared, a figure stepped out of the office lobby into the deserted hallway. Her hair was pulled into a long braid and she was wearing embroidered jeans. Raj's heart lurched inside his chest.

It wasn't possible.

"Gray!" he yelled.

She looked over her shoulder, startled. Her eyes widened and she began walking faster.

Raj picked up his pace. When she saw him gaining ground she began running.

"Gray!"

He wanted to stop her in place, make her stand still. He had to confirm it was her. He had to know. But he'd promised her.

Raj began sprinting.

She pushed through the double doors out into the breaking light. Raj reached the doors right before they clicked shut, shoved them open, and hit the pavement on the walkway leading out.

Gray had shot across the pickup lane into a patch of grass between the teachers' parking lot and the road. Raj sprinted toward the grass. Gray had just about made it to the road. She slowed and looked over her shoulder one last time before vanishing.

"Gray!" Her name burned all the way down Raj's throat.

He'd lost her again. Oh god, he'd lost her again.

Chapter 10

Gray's feet smacked the pavement. She didn't stop running until she'd reached home. She couldn't even think straight enough to remember she was invisible until she reached for the light switch in the kitchen. Gray filled herself in as though she were an Etch A Sketch. The spell was a quick scribble in her head.

Gray pulled the newspaper out of its plastic cover and spread it over the countertop.

Mrs. Knight had been telling the truth. The date said it was Friday, April 1st.

Gray flipped through, looking for any headlines that might stand out. Nothing out of the ordinary. Her stomach growled. She felt like she hadn't eaten in ages.

Time warp! she thought suddenly, then dismissed it as quickly. That didn't explain any of the anomalies going on at school.

Gray went to her room and began opening drawers. Aside from the tidiness, everything was still there—unlike her locker. Gray paced the room. She walked through Charlene's room next. She'd only caught a fleeting glance of her sister's domain that morning. Everything was exactly as she remembered it. Charlene hadn't even bothered taking down the pictures of herself and Blake framing the edges of her wall mirror.

Going through her mother's room caused a moment's hesitation, but Gray needed answers. She skipped the dresser and went straight to her mom's desk. For all her exterior organization, Mom's interior spaces were a mess. The top drawer was filled with recipes she'd ripped out of magazines; receipts; greeting cards; pens; paperclips; and, rubber bands. Gray opened the next drawer. This one looked neat at first. Mom had lined up her stapler, tape, and calculator, but in the space behind those items were more scraps. The third drawer was deeper. Mom's dream journals and spell books were tossed inside along with her French, German, and Norwegian dictionaries.

Gray pushed the drawers shut and began grabbing things off the desk. She held Mom's glass cubed paperweight. She'd seen her holding it often enough while working on translations, but the only reading Gray picked up was a faraway, foreign chattering. The weight clunked on the desk as Gray abandoned it for Mom's nightstand. When she yanked open the top drawer she inhaled sharply. The drawer was just as disorganized as the ones in the desk, but instead of recipes and receipts, this one was filled with photographs of Gray.

Gray reached in and wrapped her fingers around a pile of photos. She began flipping through, letting the images drop one by one on top of her mom's bed. It was a mix of toddler and grade school pictures. Charlene was in a couple of them. From the looks of it, Mom had cherry-picked the ones where she and Charlene were holding hands or smiling at the same time.

There were more photos in the nightstand and a piece of newspaper folded in half. Gray unfolded it. There she was in black and white. They'd printed her sophomore yearbook picture. It appeared just below the article's headline:

Teenager, 17, found dead at family home

Thursday, February 10

Graylee Perez, 17, was found dead at her family home, in Kent, Wash., on February 9.

Her body was discovered in her bed by her identical twin sister when she failed to wake on Wednesday morning. It is not yet known how she died.

Paramedics were called to the scene at 6:45 a.m., but they could not save her.

The article fluttered to the ground.

Gray grabbed the remaining photos and scraps from the drawer and dumped them onto her mom's bed. She sifted through the pile, but there weren't any more news articles.

Gray clicked her laptop open inside her room and jabbed the power key with her thumb. Before she began a search of her mysterious death, Gray went to her Facebook page out of habit. Her eyes scanned her wall.

RIP Gray.

You'll be missed.

I can't believe we won't be sitting together in English anymore. Graylee Perez was one of the nicest girls I ever knew.

Gone too soon.

A beautiful girl and a tremendous loss for all of Kent and McKinley High.

Gray flexed her fingers. She had to resist the urge to type, I'M BACK!!!!!!!!!!!
Enough of that. She opened a new window and began a search. "Graylee Perez found dead" should do the trick. Typing the words was uncanny. She stopped and stared at each letter on the screen then hit enter.

There was a follow-up article dated Saturday, February 12.

McKinley High student Gray Perez dies suddenly

A TEENAGE STUDENT from McKinley High died mysteriously in her sleep Wednesday morning.

The body of Graylee Perez, 17, was discovered by her family early Wednesday morning, February 9.

Time and cause of death have not yet been determined.

Gray opened more articles, all of which were regurgitated versions of the first stating "unexpectedly," "unknown," and "mysterious," but these with a sprinkling of quotes from teachers and students praising Gray as a "wonderful person we were privileged to know."

The closest Gray could get to an explanation, which wasn't an explanation at all, was a line from their local daily saying, "An inquest has not yet been opened into Perez's death."

What kind of reporting was that? People didn't just die in their sleep. At least not healthy teenagers. Maybe if Gray had ODed or drank two gallons of tequila.

Gray's tummy rumbled.

The last thing Gray should be thinking about right now was her stomach, so sue her, but she had to eat. It wasn't like she was a corpse anymore.

She snatched up the nearest phone and dialed the number of her favorite pizza parlor. Forty-three minutes later a large Bella Luna was delivered to the front door. Gray set it on the table and began eating directly out of the box.

Half the pie had been gobbled up when Gray heard a car pull up in the driveway. She lowered the piece she'd picked up and walked into the living room. Her eyes focused on the front door. Her heart did a drumroll inside her chest.

A key was shoved inside the lock and jiggled before the deadbolt began to turn, which meant it wasn't her mom or sister. They used magic, not keys, to open doors.

Gray looked around for the nearest heavy object. She lifted their family portrait off the wall. She could always smash it over the person's head. The pane of glass over the front should do at least a little damage.

Gray lifted it as the door opened.

There was a question on Mom's face when she stepped inside the house. Her eyes met Gray's as though she'd expected to see her standing there all along.

Gray set the picture against the wall with a clunk and gaped at her mom. She meant to demand answers—and while she was at it, why was her mother using a key to get inside the house?

But without warning, Gray looked into her mother's eyes and burst into tears.

In her mind she'd seen her mom just yesterday, but she could sense their separation in her soul. Her life had been taken from her.

Gray's mom pulled her into a hug. Gray buried her face into her mother's shoulder. Her mom's body began to shake as she sobbed. Gray cried harder.

When the tears finally subsided, Gray pulled her face away and took a step back. "Mom, did I die?"

Tears were still streaming down her mother's face as she nodded.

"And you brought me back?"

Mom nodded again slowly. She stroked her hair. "I've missed you so much, baby girl."

"How did you do it? How did you bring me back to life?" It was extraordinary, really. Only a handful of witches were capable of reanimation, and that was only in theory. Gray couldn't recall a single story of a person being successfully brought back to life.

"It wasn't me exactly. I hired someone."

"Someone? Who?"

"I swore I wouldn't tell anyone."

"Yeah, I get that, but it's me—reanimated girl—your daughter!"

Mom swallowed. "I swore on your life. That was the deal."

"Oh." Gray's face dropped. "Can you tell me where you were?"

"I went to the mountains."

"What? Like the Cascades?"

"Yeah," Mom said slowly. "What about you? I can't believe I missed your reentry. Did you 'poof' appear?"

"No, actually, I woke up in Charlene's bed this morning."

That's when Mom asked the million-dollar question. "Where is Charlene?"

Gray and her mother stared at one another. "I don't know," Gray said.

"You didn't see her today?"

"She wasn't here when I woke up and I never saw her at school. Then again, I didn't stick around McKinley very long once it became apparent that everyone thought I was CRAZY!"

Mom bowed her head. "I should have been here for your reentry, sweetie. I came home as fast as I could."

They walked into the kitchen together. Gray glanced at the note her mom had written Charlene. "When did you leave?"

"Early Monday after Charlene left for school." Mom glanced around the kitchen. Her face lit up suddenly. "She must be with Blake."

Gray's jaw dropped. "Charlene and Blake are back together?"

Mom nodded.

"When did that happen?"

"I don't know when exactly. Last month?"

"Well, it's good to know everyone moved on without me." So she grumbled a little. Who wouldn't? Gray felt guilty an instant later when she saw her mom's face.

"My life could never go on without you." Mom's lower lip quivered.

Gray felt tears gathering in her eyes.

Mom beat a fist to her chest. "A part of me died when you did."

"I'm sorry, Mom," Gray said softly. She cleared her throat a moment later. "How about trying her phone?"

Mom shook her head a moment later. "It just goes to voicemail. I'll try Blake's house," she said as she dialed the number. "Hi, Mr. Foster. This is Charlene's mom. Is Charlene there by any chance? All right, thanks. If you see her could you have her call? Thanks." Her mom placed the phone very gently on the counter, then looked at Gray. "Oh, god, what have I done?"

* * *

"You don't know that she's gone," Gray said for the tenth time in the past hour.

They'd retreated to Charlene's room, where Mom was inspecting what she called The Point of Reentry. Gray had already gone over every minute detail from the time she'd woken that morning. Sharing the detail about waking in the silk slip had only increased her mother's distress.

"I killed her. In exchange for one daughter's life I obliterated the other. How could I be so foolish? Our coven has warned us time and again that to engage in the black arts is to invite grave consequences."

Gray flopped back onto Charlene's bed. None of this felt real. "Now what? Do you have to take it back? Am I doomed to return to the hereafter once more? By the way, there's no heaven. There's nothing. Do I have to go back to the nothing?"

"No!" her mother all but screamed. "I can't lose you again!" Mom took a deep breath. "I was very specific about keeping both my daughters." She straightened up. "Excuse me a moment."

Once Gray realized Mom was headed to her own room she called out, "Sorry about the mess."

No reason for her to stick around Charlene's room any longer, either.

Gray finished reading her Facebook wall page, polished off the rest of her pizza, and began watching *Glee* in the living room. During one of the musical numbers, Gray felt a presence behind her. She turned suddenly and caught her mom watching her.

"Learn anything?" Gray asked.

"I left my contact a message."

"What now?"

"There's not much we can do at this point. I think it'd be best if you got a good night's rest and were refreshed for tomorrow. At least it's the weekend."

Gray turned off the TV. "Mom? How did I die?"

Her mom pressed her lips together and took a seat in the chair across from Gray. She folded her hands in her lap, breathed in and out. Her lashes fluttered and for a moment Gray thought she might cry, but her mom's voice was steady. "The doctors think it was sudden unexpected death syndrome."

"Which is what exactly? I mean besides sudden and unexpected."

"Not much is known about SUDS."

"SUDS, huh?" Gray forced a chuckle. "Sounds like a warm bubble bath—not unexpected DEATH!"

"I had Mr. Holloway look into it personally. He ruled out any kind of magical foul play."

"I can't imagine anyone wanting me dead."

"Neither could I," Mom said. "But I had to be sure."

Gray pushed herself off the couch. "So that's it? I died suddenly and unexpectedly in my sleep. That's the grand finale for Graylee Perez?"

Mom took a step forward. "No, it's not." She reached out and put a hand on each of Gray's shoulders. She pulled her into a hug and squeezed her tightly. "You came back and I'm never letting you go."

Gray extended her arms around her mom. She breathed in her scent. She'd never considered that she might not see her mom again. Maybe she was back, but for how long? Who was to say she wouldn't die all over again? If there was one thing Gray remembered from lectures it was this: you can't cheat death.

Chapter 11

Gray woke up with a start. She lifted her head a couple inches off the pillow and saw the two bedposts on either side of her—Charlene's bed. Gray threw back the covers. She was wearing a red and black silk, lace babydoll.

Not again.

Oh, god. What if her life was turning into the Bill Murray movie *Groundhog Day*? At least in Bill Murray's version he got to be himself every day.

Gray snapped into her cotton pajama pants and a tank top. She peeked inside her mother's room. It was empty. When noises below and the scent of raisin bread reached her, her heart surged with happiness. Gray flew down the stairs.

Mom turned from where she stood in front of the stove and smiled. "Morning, hon. Would you like some oatmeal and raisin bread?"

"Yes, please."

"Did you sleep well?" Mom asked as she dished Gray up.

"Um, yeah." Gray buttered her toast while Mom sprinkled berries, walnuts, and brown sugar on top of her oatmeal. Gray glanced at her mom. "I woke up in Charlene's bed again."

Mom didn't meet her eyes when she handed her the bowl of oatmeal. "I can explain that."

"Thank goodness." Gray took a seat on a barstool at the counter and scooped a bite of oatmeal with all the goodies onto her spoon.

"The good news is I didn't accidentally purge Charlene from existence."

"And the bad news?" 'Cause of course there was bad news—probably horrible news. This was a resurrection spell, for freak's sake, and Charlene wasn't present.

Mom released the breath she'd been holding. "There's just no easy way to say this. At the moment you and Charlene are sharing the same body."

Gray dropped her spoon. "What?!"

Mom extended an arm toward Gray. "At the moment there's only this one body—Charlene's—and both of you are using it."

"Like multiple personality disorder?"

"No, like fifty-fifty split. After you went to sleep Friday night, Charlene woke up Saturday morning in your bed."

Gray got off the stool. She couldn't sit any longer. "What's today?"

"Sunday."

"So you're saying tomorrow I'll be Charlene?"

Mom nodded.

"And on Tuesday I'll be me again?"

A pot clanked inside the kitchen sink as Mom started putting in the dirty dishes.

"How did this happen?"

"Apparently I didn't specify wanting you in separate bodies."

Oh, those pesky little details. Gray didn't share this thought. She was beyond sarcasm. She wanted back inside her body pronto. Black magic had a way of coming back around and biting one in the ass. "Your contact needs to fix this!"

"It's not that easy."

"What do you mean?"

"In removing you from Charlene's body you could be removed altogether."

"What am I supposed to do—live half a life in someone else's body?"

"We're working on it."

"And in the meantime?"

"In the meantime you need to pretend to be your sister. No one at school can know."

"And the coven?"

"You know what would happen if they found out."

"Banishment?" Gray whispered.

Mom nodded.

Gray studied her mom. "You'll fix this, right?"

"I'll do everything I can."

"And for now I'm supposed to pretend to be Charlene?"

Mom brought a notebook over. "Yes, and your sister left some notes to help you out."

Gray stared at the notebook a moment before taking it. She flipped it open.

NO MORE PIZZA, YOU PIG!!! I GAINED 2 POUNDS BECAUSE OF YOU!

No wearing your clothes in public. I will choose an outfit for you to wear to school on the days you're me.

Hair must be worn down. No pigtails, ponytails, hair clips or goofy Princess Leia-style buns on the side of your head.

No leaving the house without makeup. I have taped examples and tips in the following pages on how to create a smoky eye.

Gray flipped back to several pages of magazine print and step-by-step illustrated guides for creating a smoldering look. She flipped back to the front page.

No speaking to anyone at McKinley who isn't on the approved list (see the following pages). Don't even think about trying to visit with your old friends unless you want to get us committed to an insane asylum.

Absolutely no—UNDER ANY CIRCUMSTANCES— having sex with Blake.

Gray's nose wrinkled. *Ewwww!*

She looked up, her face still contorted. "Did you read this?"

Mom was putting away the brown sugar. "No, Charlene told me not to."

"And you listened to her?"

Mom looked directly at Gray. "She said it was private."

More like psychotic.

No more sleeping in your room. I want to wake up in my own bed in the morning.

Yeah? Well, join the club.

Gray closed the notebook. "You'd think I'd feel happy to have a second shot at life."

"Hang in there. I'll get this sorted out."

Gray glanced at the wall clock. "If it's Sunday shouldn't we be going to Gathering?"

"Charlene and I stopped attending after you died. How about you and I spend the day together instead? We can do whatever you want."

"Except eat pizza."

Mom raised a brow. Gray smiled suddenly. "Then again, Char didn't say anything about a burger and fries."

"You know what?" Mom said. "I haven't had French fries in a really long time." She grabbed her purse off the counter. "Where do you want to go? Driftwood Café has those homemade zucchini-nut burgers."

"Just so long as I don't run into anyone from McKinley High," Gray said. "Good luck to Charlene explaining the scene I made in Mr. Burke's class when she returns to school tomorrow."

Mom chewed on her lower lip a moment. "We should think of something."

Gray raised a brow. "Temporary insanity?"

Her mom laughed. It was a beautiful sound. Gray followed her out of the house and passed her on the walkway. She stopped and turned slowly when she saw her mom with the key in the lock of the door. "What's with the key?"

Mom looked pleased with herself when she got the bolt turned and clicked into place. "Call me paranoid, but I haven't wanted to perform spells after partaking in something this big."

She glanced at Gray. "I was lucky. There was one kink, but I got you back. I'm afraid to chance anything else."

Gray watched Mom's fingers close around the keys.

It made sense that she didn't want to tempt fate, but what could go wrong with a simple locking spell? And that was one big kink of a resurrection spell. Still, Gray was alive and she was with her mom. What more could she ask for . . . other than her own body back? They'd fix this. They had to. She wasn't ready to think about the alternative.

The impossible part was accomplished: Gray was back from the dead. A body transfer should be a piece of cake in comparison.

Speaking of cake, for now Gray had every intention of doing the pigging out and letting Charlene work it off on her days. There was one advantage.

Chapter 12

Raj was waiting in the student parking lot early Monday morning. He flipped his Zippo open and closed. Friday night he'd driven by McKinley and spotted Charlene Perez's lone car in the lot. By Saturday afternoon it was gone.

There was one space left in the front row of the parking lot. Several cars passed it as though it were taken. Five minutes later Charlene pulled into the spot.

Clever witch.

Raj grinned, snapped the Zippo shut, and stuffed it inside his pocket. He stalked over to Charlene and pivoted to walk into the building beside her. "Hey," Raj said casually.

Charlene's eyes screwed up. She had on her standard miniskirt and tight sweater. "What do you want?"

"I never got a chance to express my condolences for your loss."

Charlene's eyes narrowed. "What's it to you?"

"Losing your twin must feel two times worse," Raj said without missing a beat. "Might tempt you to try a resurrection spell."

Charlene snorted. "Yeah, right, there are only like three witches in the world who might have even the remotest chance of pulling that off." She batted her long, dark lashes. "Not that I'm without talent."

"So you've got connections?"

"I've got all kinds of connections—doesn't mean I'd use them."

"Still, must get lonely."

Charlene stopped walking and turned. "Do I seem lonely to you?" she demanded. Before Raj could answer Charlene's frown morphed into a wicked grin. "Why are you asking me about my sister, anyway? Do you have some kind of weird obsession with her? 'Cause she never mentioned you before."

If Charlene was searching Raj's face for signs of hurt she could go on and look all day long. Insults rolled off Raj like water off a duck.

He raised a brow. "And I'm sure the two of you were super close."

Charlene opened her mouth to speak, but no sound came out.

"Now, now, Charlene. If you can't say anything nice . . ." Raj grinned. He wasn't breaking any promises by performing a muting spell on Charlene. After all, Gray hadn't asked him not to use magic on her sister.

Charlene's eyes widened. If he weren't so aggravated, it might have been funny to watch her try to scream at him. Suddenly she stopped. A look came over her face and she began to lift a finger toward him.

Raj quickly froze it. He didn't want to find out what kind of whammy she'd been planning.

Rage flashed in Charlene's eyes.

Raj clucked his tongue. "Careful, Charlene, you're still in the coven's good graces. As much as I'd enjoy being the cause of your expulsion, I think your mom's had enough to deal with this year. Now I'm going to release you, but before I do I want to know why you pretended to be your sister on Friday. The truth, Charlene."

Raj pulled out his Zippo and pushed the lid open with his thumb. When he snapped it shut again Charlene was free. She nearly stumbled forward. "You bastard!"

"Curse me all you want, but I'll freeze you again if you don't answer my question. Why were you pretending to be Gray?"

"I was under a spell!" Charlene screamed.

"Who did the spell?"

"No freaking idea! You are so going to pay for using magic on me, McKenna. The coven should strip you of your powers like they did to Adrian Montez. You shouldn't even be allowed to pull a bunny from a top hat. No wonder your mom took off and left you."

Raj fluttered his lashes and yawned. He turned and headed back inside. "Nice chatting."

"Asshole!" Charlene called after him.

Her words barely registered in his mind. Why would someone want to make Charlene think she was her sister? It had to be an April Fools' joke. That was the most likely explanation. Witches and warlocks could be brutal on the first of April. They had it in their powers to pull some pretty elaborate pranks.

Then there was the other explanation—the one Raj didn't dare dream of. Maybe someone had managed to bring Gray to life temporarily. It was a far easier feat to accomplish than a resurrection. Both were virtually unheard of. The girl he'd seen had certainly dressed like Graylee Perez. He had no clue if she'd behaved like Gray. All he'd caught was a fleeting glimpse of her running. She'd looked frightened.

Like she'd been awakened from the dead.

Raj had to face the facts—Gray was gone. Death was final. Even the death of a witch.

There was only one thing left to do: find the sick freak who'd performed the spell on Charlene and make them pay.

Chapter 13

The worst thing about being Charlene wasn't the hair or even the miniskirt—it was hanging out with her twin's diabolical friends.

Don't think of it as being Charlene, her mom had instructed. *Imagine yourself as an actress on Glee . . . without the singing and dancing.*

Gray reached around to her backside for the tenth time that morning. It felt like her pleated skirt was tucked inside her underwear, but alas, it was just really short. That was why she kept feeling a cool draft on her bare bronzed legs. Leave it to Charlene to come up with a tanning spell. Charlene hadn't figured out how to make it permanent, though, and it had to be "applied" every morning—like putting on clothes.

"Oh my god, Char, you look great," Kiki said.

Time for her lines and they didn't include "Thanks."

"How else would I look?"

Kiki giggled.

Apparently being rude wasn't just clever, but witty as well.

Brittany smirked. Her skirt was equally micro, but her legs were shorter, which made it less obvious.

"Hi, beautiful." Blake approached from behind and wrapped his arms around Gray. Spiced clove filled her nostrils. She wasn't sure if it was supposed to be deodorant or cologne. Blake's arms tightened and he squeezed her against his torso and thighs.

Gray resisted the urge to swat him away or stomp on his foot. This became increasingly difficult when one hand slid down to her backside.

Thank god for Charlene's "No Sex with Blake" rule or Gray might just throw herself at him. Gag!

Gray took a step forward. "God, Blake, can't you keep your hands to yourself for one second?"

He grinned. "Not when you're around."

Kiki giggled.

Gray heard the snap of a lighter and turned her head. Raj McKenna was walking by. Gray's heart pounded inside her ribcage, but Raj barely glanced at her. She watched him pass and then stared at his back. It was almost as if she'd imagined him calling out her name and running after her the week before.

Her real name.

How had Raj known?

Obviously he didn't think that was the case now, unless his nonchalance was an act. Her heart dropped into the pit of her stomach as he rounded the corner.

Gray was dead to the rest of the world. Literally.

Brittany looped her arm around Gray's and took off with her down the hall. "Does Blake know you hooked up with Todd Hanson?" She didn't even bother whispering.

"What?" Gray glanced quickly over her shoulder, but Blake and Kiki were no longer standing by their lockers.

She tried to think fast. Charlene hadn't made any notations about Todd Hanson. Why would she hook up with the senior basketball captain when she was in love with Blake?

"I don't think so," Gray said. She turned to Brittany. "Do you?"

Brittany considered this for several seconds before scrunching up her pert nose. "Nah."

"Todd is really hot," Gray said, fishing for information.

"I'd do him."

Not the kind of information she was looking for.

"Do you think Blake would dump me if he found out?"

"Whatever. It's not like you two are exclusive. If he can screw Jenna Hocking you have every right to go get some hot senior ass."

Gray nearly choked. "Jenna Hocking! But she's ugly." Okay, so that was rude, but at least she sounded like Charlene. And Jenna Hocking? The girl was bucktoothed and frizzy-haired. Sure, she had jugs the size of melons, but it was a bit hard to believe that Blake Foster would sleep with her—not when he'd snagged the school's beauty queen, Stacey Morehouse. So this was the soap opera that was her sister's life? Gray wanted to ask how Charlene had won Blake back from Stacey's clutches, but couldn't think of a way to ask without sounding like she had just stepped out of Looneyville.

Brittany laughed. "I know, right. You showed Blake by hooking up with Todd."

Gray stopped suddenly. "I need to go to first period biology."

"See you in fourth," Brittany said.

Gray unfolded her cheat sheet.

First period biology with Mr. Darling. B Hall, room 104. Sit next to Ryan.

Gray turned down B Hall. Ryan was already seated five rows back, boring holes into her with his big, round eyes. A student's pen rolled off a desk as Gray made her way back. She knelt down, bending at the knees so she wouldn't flash her panties at everyone behind her.

The girl's eyes widened from behind her glasses when Gray handed the pen back. "Thanks," she squeaked.

Ryan was frowning at Gray. "What?" she demanded as she took her seat.

"That's not something your sister would do."

So Ryan was aware of their entanglement. Gray should have been relieved that someone knew—if only that someone had been anyone other than Ryan Phillips.

"Yeah, well, my sister's a bitch," Gray said.

Ryan winced. "That's not nice and it's not true, either. You just don't know her like I do."

"Sure, I don't know my twin sister as well as the boy she barely hangs out with." Gray dumped Charlene's messenger bag on the floor beside her desk. "So Charlene told you about our little dilemma?"

Ryan looked like he was inspecting Gray as she spoke. "Yes, and she's given me the task of helping you out on the days you're . . . you."

"You mean she wants you to keep tabs on me?"

Ryan shrugged. "We have three classes together."

"Lucky me."

"You didn't say anything suspicious to Blake or Brittany this morning, did you?"

"I don't think so." Gray smoothed her cheat sheet over her desk. She'd already looked it over a dozen times, but she kept forgetting what order her classes were in. It was like the first day of school. After biology, she noticed, Gray had Advanced French with Madame Girard. Just great. Gray knew two words of French: bonjour and oui.

Gray glanced back over at Ryan. He was still staring at her.

"You look like you've seen a ghost." Gray chuckled to herself. "Hey, what's the deal with Charlene and Blake?"

"They're going out."

"Uh, yeah, but they weren't before I died." Ryan managed to break eye contact when she said the last word. The eyes in his pear-shaped face darted around the room before returning to her. "Rooftop—Charlene threatening to jump. Ring any bells?"

"Blake Foster realized the error of his ways."

"Ah, a spell, was it?"

"No, it wasn't a spell!" Ryan spit out. He squirmed once more when the girl in the seat in front of him glanced back. "Look," Ryan said in a whisper, "Blake felt really bad for your sister after she lost you. He's been a great comfort to her during this time of tragedy."

Tragedy, indeed, if the only outcome of Gray's death was to bring her sister and Blake Foster back together.

"What about Todd Hanson?"

"What about him?"

"Brittany says he and Charlene hooked up."

Gray could've sworn she saw Ryan wince. He lifted his round chin. "I don't think that's really either of our business."

Gray hid a grin. "So I should deny any accusations?"

Ryan's forehead wrinkled. "Who's accusing you?"

"No one. Well, except Brittany. And it wasn't so much of an accusation as a statement."

"Good morning, class," Mr. Darling called out.

Gray faced forward and ignored Ryan for the rest of the period. She meant to stride out of the room without him after the bell rang, but he caught her elbow. His words hissed inside her ear. "Look, it's a well-known fact that Charlene and Blake aren't exclusive. For whatever reason, he makes her happy, but that doesn't mean she has to remain chaste while he screws around. That's all you need to know."

"And Charlene's okay with him sleeping around?"

Ryan shifted in place and looked around. Gray sighed and was about to start walking again when Ryan leaned forward to whisper, "Charlene says leniency is the key to a successful relationship."

Gray rolled her eyes. "Oh, yeah? Dr. Perez ought to write a book on the subject."

Ryan started blinking again.

"Okay, whatever." Gray was getting tired of his ineptitude. She would have been better off with him not knowing who she was. The lame-oid hadn't even asked how she, Graylee Perez, was doing, or welcomed her back to the world of the living. Gray was a magical marvel. The least Ryan could do was act impressed rather than waste her time with this ridiculous high school melodrama.

Gray climbed the stairs to second period French class with Madame Girard. Charlene had made a notation to sit beside Trish Roberts—the girl who'd stolen Hart Hensley from Gray.

This day was just getting better and better.

But when Gray walked into class, there was no sign of Trish.

Now what?

Shay Baxter and Max Curry were seated side by side in the front row. Gray walked past them. Her eyes raced around the room and came to a skidding halt when they landed on Nolan Knapp.

Charlene had French with Nolan?

Two witches and two warlocks—quite the little gathering in French class. Shay Baxter was no surprise, but Gray would have seen Nolan as more of a fun, fiesta Spanish sort. French tended to attract stuck-ups like Shay and Charlene.

Gray walked back to where Nolan was seated and slipped into the desk beside him. He glanced at her and then back at a piece of paper on his desk. It looked like he was drawing cartoons with captions—or so it appeared from the corner of Gray's eye.

She crossed her legs, hitting her knee against the underbelly of her desk as she did so. Gray cursed softly. Nolan kept doodling.

She managed to get the leg over the other one and began shaking her foot.

The final bell rang and Madame Girard walked to the front of the class. "*Bonjour*," she called out in a booming voice.

"*Bonjour, Madame*," the class chorused.

Bonjour. That was a word Gray recognized. So far, so good, though she would have been better off in Señora Gomez's Spanish class in room 156 on the first floor.

The French teacher looked around the room. Gray slouched in her seat. "*Monsieur* Curry, *qu'avez-vous fait cette fin de semaine?*"

"*J'ai fait mes devoirs. J'ai nettoyé ma chambre et j'ai cuisiné le diner—J'ai aussi étudier pour le français.*"

Everyone chuckled.

Great, so not only was everyone semi-fluent, but they were making jokes.

"*Bon!*" Madame Girard said.

So maybe Gray knew three French words. She knew *bon* was "good."

"Now, I want you to find a partner and take turns telling each other what you did over the weekend."

Okay, the fact that the instructions were said in English was appreciated, but partner? Speak French? There was no way Gray was going to pull this off.

Without thinking, she turned to Nolan. "Be my partner."

The pen stilled in his hand. His face flushed. "Yeah," he said. "Sure."

Gray couldn't tell if he was just really bashful or what. "I didn't know you liked to draw," she said.

Nolan took the drawing he'd been working on and slipped it inside a folder. "Um, yeah."

"That's cool."

He looked up and really stared at her this time. Gray smiled big—a smile that said, I'm keeping a mega secret.

"*J'écoute les etudiants parler en anglais,*" Madame Girard cried. "*En français, s'il vous plait. Raconter votre fin de semaine à votre camarade.*"

Gray met Nolan's eye. "You first."

"*J'ai regardé la télévision. J'ai nourri mon poisson . . . Je me suis lavé les cheveux. J'ai dessiné. J'ai rencontré des amis.*" Nolan glanced upwards as he thought. "*J'ai mangé,*" Nolan finished after he'd thought for a while. "*Et toi?*"

Gray had no idea what Nolan was mumbling on about.

"*Yo estaba vivo.*"

Nolan's forehead wrinkled in confusion.

"It's Spanish," Gray whispered. She leaned closer. Her eyes locked with Nolan's. "It means I was alive."

Nolan stared back. It was nice to look into his eyes again, even if she could see that the information she wanted to convey wasn't registering.

"Alive is good," Gray continued, sounding like a foreign student on the other side of the globe attempting basic English.

"*Mademoiselle* Perez," their teacher called from the front of the room.

Gray hit her knee a second time, sitting up in attention.

"Why don't you share what you did over the weekend with the class?"

Gray could feel her eyes widening like saucers over her face. "Uh, oui," she began. Her eyes darted around the room—all those faces staring at her. If only she could channel her mother, who spoke French better than most natives. Gray sent out a silent plea, but no one answered her SOS.

Madame Girard tapped her foot.

Gray cleared her throat. "I went to *zee* restaurant with my *mozther.*" Maybe if she spoke with an accent the class wouldn't notice her words were in English.

There was a giggle. No, apparently everyone was on to her. Shay and Max had turned fully in their chairs to look at her.

Gray looked at the French teacher and shrugged helplessly.

She raised one very domineering brow. "*Amusant, Mademoiselle* Perez. *En français cette fois.*"

"*Oui.*"

Someone snorted.

Gray cleared her throat. "May I please be excused?"

"*Pourquoi?*"

Gray glanced at Nolan. *Why*, he mouthed. She looked back at Madame Girard. "Because I'm going to throw up!" she cried suddenly. It was impromptu, not really something out of *Glee*, unless she was playing the impregnated Quinn. It did succeed in getting her out of French class, though. Blowing chunks was disgusting in any language.

Chapter 14

In her haste to leave behind the humiliation that was French class—let Charlene smooth that one out tomorrow—Gray forgot her, or rather Charlene's, messenger bag. In hindsight, it was a bit like one of those cheesy maneuvers from a romantic comedy. Though when Nolan walked up with her bag after class she had to admit it worked like a charm.

Gray waited across the hall for the dismissal bell to ring.

She folded her arms over her chest and stared down any classmate who dared glance her way, including Shay Baxter. Once Nolan walked out with her bag she dropped her arms. He smiled as he crossed the hall and handed the bag over.

"Thanks, I couldn't go back in there," Gray said.

"Are you all right?"

"Yeah, why?"

"Um." Nolan looked at his feet.

"Just kidding," Gray said. "God, that was humiliating."

Nolan swept his bangs back. "What happened?"

"I don't know what I'm going to do," Gray said, staring down the hall. "I don't know French. Well, besides *bonjour, oui,* and now *pourquoi.*" She looked at Nolan. "Do you think there's a spell for instant language fluency?"

Nolan's brows jumped. He looked around quickly and stepped closer to Gray. "Maybe we shouldn't be talking about that around here."

Gray stared him in the eyes. What she really wanted was to tell him she was back. If Charlene could tell Ryan, Gray ought to be allowed to tell Nolan. The hallway probably wasn't the right place to do it. Nolan already looked startled that she'd addressed him at all. Was Charlene that intimidating? And he'd all but had an epileptic fit when she mentioned the word *magic* in public. Imagine his reaction if she did something really crazy, like go invisible?

Gray instantly thought of Raj. He delighted in magical misbehavior. But McKenna was still an unsolved mystery. Why had he run after her one day and ignored her the next?

Some questions were better left unanswered.

Nolan Knapp suddenly seemed feeble-minded compared to Raj. Live a little. That was Gray's philosophy since dying, anyway. She lifted her chin. "Have I said something to make you uncomfortable? My, what a good little warlock you are."

She saw his frown deepen, whether at being called a warlock in public or the obvious set down she couldn't be sure. "*Merci* for the assistance with my bag."

Hey, she knew a fifth French word.

Gray turned on her heel and walked away before Nolan could answer. She wanted to believe that her snooty words were all part of the act she was putting on, but the truth was Nolan had frustrated her.

As promised, Ryan appeared in two more of her classes. Before the day was out Gray had been groped no less than ten times by Blake, gotten slapped on the ass by Pete Sutherland (just how many guys was her sister sleeping with at school?), endured Brittany and Kiki's mean-spirited blather, and worst yet, had nothing but a chocolate Slim Fast for lunch. At least Blake spent lunch with his homeboys. If he'd tried to feel her up in the cafeteria, Gray would've been way too tempted to throw the shake in his face.

Speaking of the boyfriend, he was waiting for her after the last bell rang. Gray had to turn away from him to get inside Charlene's locker and Blake took that opportunity to run his hand down her back.

His hand didn't linger long before he began scratching at his head. The smile on Gray's face was hidden with her head inside the locker. So maybe she'd given Blake a slight case of the itchies across that thick skull of his. She couldn't exactly slap him across the face. Not unless she wanted Charlene to murder her in her sleep.

Her smile expanded. Charlene couldn't touch her.

Gray shut her locker and pushed past Blake. "Hey," he said, falling into step beside her and sliding an arm around her waist. "Wanna come over . . . maybe fool around?" He pulled her against his side.

"Sorry, Blake, I have plans."

He stopped abruptly. "With who?"

"Myself."

Blake grinned slowly. "Oh, yourself, huh?" He began poking her in different places. "And what do you have planned for yourself? A little rub and poke?"

"Blake, stop it!" Gray stomped her foot on the ground as she spoke.

Without warning, Blake stopped and sighed. "All right, what did I do now?"

"What do you mean?"

"Why don't you just tell me so I can stop guessing?"

Gray followed the movements of students in their rain coats exiting the building. If only she could be so lucky. She turned to Blake and tried to speak in her most convincing voice. "You didn't do anything. I just have plans, okay?"

"Right," he said, straightening up. "Fine. See you tomorrow."

Yeah, and why don't you go screw Jenna Hocking?

Okay, where did that come from? It wasn't like Blake was Gray's boyfriend. But he was cheating on her sister. Her cheating sister. Ugh, Gray was stuck inside Charlene's own sleazy high school soap opera. Maybe this was hell.

She needed her body back.

* * *

What did one bring to her own gravesite? Flowers? Trinkets . . . shovel?

Gray parked on the road outside St. Ann's Cemetery and trudged through the iron gates. Cemeteries had always seemed like such a waste of good parkland, but today Gray was relieved her body was encased in a box below the earth rather than incinerated.

Her steps slowed along the paved path. She hadn't been to see her father's grave in a couple of years. She used to visit on his birthday and Father's Day. No one could accuse her of neglecting to pay her respects anymore. Now her body was a few feet from his. A corpse for company.

Dad's gravesite was on the other side of a big oak.

To Gray's annoyance, there was a figure lingering in the area of her gravesite. This was a private matter. As she neared, she saw the figure wasn't just in the vicinity of her resting place—he stood right in front of it. At least someone hadn't forgotten about her—even if that someone was Raj McKenna.

For a moment she considered making herself invisible. Given her surroundings, it felt too creepy and oddly disrespectful toward the dead. But god, it was tempting, especially when Gray saw Raj take an object out of his pocket, set it on her tombstone, then snatch it away when he caught her movement from the corner of his eye.

Gray walked up beside him. "Boo."

Gray may have been smiling, but Raj certainly wasn't. His anger gave her the chills. It wasn't as though she'd caught him doing anything embarrassing like crying. No, McKenna looked every bit as badass as Gray remembered him. He wore a black jacket over a pair of tight dark jeans. Like the ones in her dream.

Gray shook the thought away and nodded toward her grave. "Didn't figure you as the sentimental sort, McKenna."

"Funny, I was just thinking the same thing about you." Raj gave her a look of pure loathing. "What do you want, Charlene?"

Gray's smile widened. "I'm not Charlene."

Raj folded his arms over his chest. "Oh, you're not, are you? Someone put you under a spell again?"

Gray nodded. "I am under a spell—a resurrection spell gone wrong."

Raj's mouth was tight. His expression made Gray want to laugh. He wanted to believe it so bad. She could see the begging in his eyes. Raj probably never dreamed he'd meet a resurrected soul. It'd blow his mind. Forget the invisibility spell. That was a card trick in comparison.

"Don't believe me?" Gray asked cheerfully.

"No," Raj said. The word came out as a faint whisper.

Gray circled her grave, coming to a stop in front of the headstone.

Graylee Perez
Forever In Our Hearts

She lowered herself to the ground and lay down, her head barely touching the tombstone.

Raj watched her warily. "What are you doing?"

Cold seeped from the earth into Gray. Goosebumps scattered over her bare legs. She closed her eyes. "Maybe if I concentrate hard enough I can transfer myself back inside my body."

Raj folded his arms. "And then what? Claw your way up to the surface?"

Her eyes popped open. "So you believe me?"

"I don't know."

"What if I made myself invisible?"

"You and your sister could both know that spell."

Gray sat up. "You think Charlene's as powerful a witch as me?"

"No." Raj reached his hand down and Gray took it, relishing the firm warmth of Raj's grip as he helped her to her feet, then quickly released her hand.

"Better not," she said, dusting potential bits of grass off her backside.

"How come you look like Charlene?"

Gray laughed. "How come I look like my identical twin sister?"

"You know what I mean," Raj said, waving his hand over Gray. "Makeup. Hair. Skirt."

Gray glanced down at the pleated miniskirt. "I know, right? What a hussy." Raj didn't return her grin. "What's the matter,

McKenna? Aren't you happy to see me?" Gray would've thought Raj would show a little more pizzazz.

"It's really you?" he asked in the same somber tone.

"It's really me. Well, sorta. This is Charlene's body. I guess mine's still buried six feet deep." Gray glanced down and kicked at the damp grass. She chuckled. "Caught in the ol' casket. Nothing but a bag of bones." She noticed the tight frown over Raj's face. "What?"

"It's not funny."

"Just trying to lighten the mood with a bit of comic relief. How do you think I feel knowing my corpse is rotting in the earth?"

"Is that what went wrong with the resurrection spell—you were put inside Charlene's body?"

Jeez, he was all business.

"Worse. We're stuck sharing this body, fifty-fifty. I get it every other day."

"When does the switch happen?"

"At three every morning. My mom thinks that's when I died."

"Have you tried staying up for the switch?"

"Of course. I stayed awake Sunday night into Monday morning. I watched the time change."

"And what happened?"

"Nothing happened. I thought I'd found a loophole, but then I woke my mom up and she said it was Tuesday morning—THIS morning."

"So it's really you?" Raj asked again.

"Yeah, it's me."

"Good." Raj put his hands in both pockets.

Gray followed the movement with her eyes. "What was that you put on my grave?"

"Nothing."

"I saw you start to put something on my tombstone. I want to know what it was." Gray took a step closer and reached for Raj's pocket. He grabbed her wrist before she could dig inside his pants for the mystery object, then secured her second wrist. She writhed under his grasp and Raj tightened his hold.

"Keep your hands to yourself, Perez."

Gray nearly laughed. After being groped all day by Blake, Raj was telling *her* to keep her hands to herself? "What's the deal, McKenna? You were about to give me some trinket, anyway. Do I only get it if I'm dead?"

Raj released her and took a step back. The pained look on his face made Gray instantly regret the taunt. "I meant to give it to you earlier." His gaze was mysterious and somber. Eyes like those could hypnotize a person. "A couple days after you . . . died."

"Valentine's Day?" Gray wasn't sure she'd heard correctly.

Raj began studying the lawn of the cemetery.

Gray suddenly understood Raj's fascination with the ground. The grass was obnoxiously green. Probably from all the human fertilizer below.

"Want to get out of here?" Raj asked.

Gray glanced sideways at her grave then nodded. "I don't think lying in the damp grass above my grave is going to solve my problem."

Chapter 15

"So what are you going to do?" Raj asked as they headed to the parking lot.

"I don't know. My mom's waiting for her mysterious contact to get back to her. Whoever brought me back better be able to fix this. I can't spend the rest of my life trapped inside Charlene's body. I don't even get full access to it. I'm a part-timer. Half a human. And I don't even get a cool identity. I get to be the sister skank."

"I take it she's aware of what's happening."

Gray snorted. "She made me a manual on 'How to Be Charlene.' Oh yeah, there're instructions on everything from hair and makeup to acceptable behavior. I've got a dress code and everything." Gray glanced down once more. "Thus the miniskirt. Even when I'm myself I don't get to be me."

Gray had only been half paying attention as she walked alongside Raj to the parking lot. His car was the sole vehicle around. "Did you drive?" he asked.

"I'm parked on the street."

"Wanna grab a mocha at The Daily Grind?"

A hot mocha sounded good and it wasn't like this was a date. Gray had bumped into Raj. They just happened to be two people in the same place at the same time with a simultaneous craving for caffeinated chocolate.

Gray walked around Raj's car and opened the door of the passenger's side. The handle lifted without interference. "Still not locking your doors, McKenna?" She caught his eye across the hood of the car. Raj flashed her the first smile she'd seen since . . . well, since she'd died. She hadn't realized how much she'd missed that mischievous, self-assured grin.

"At least this time I can see you getting in." They both settled into their seats. Raj rested his arms on the steering wheel and stole a look at Gray. "You still haven't explained your invisibility spell to me."

"You really want to know that spell?" Gray asked.

"Yes, I do."

She grinned and motioned him closer with her finger. Raj pressed his lips together and shook his head so Gray leaned across the armrest. "I'll take it to my grave."

* * *

Raj chose the table in the back corner of The Daily Grind. The Grind wasn't your typical dark-paneled, cozy coffee house. The outer walls were glass and the place had a high ceiling. It looked modern, light, and clean. There was the additional benefit of drawing an older crowd rather than McKinley students.

Gray had already sucked down half her mocha. She was trying to take time to enjoy it, but it was way too tasty.

"What happened with the spell?" Raj asked. He didn't lower his voice or shift uneasily the way Nolan did when discussing magic in public.

Gray drank another sip of her mocha. "No idea. My mom asked to have both her daughters. She didn't specify having us in separate bodies."

Raj, who had been tapping the table before, now tapped his white enamel mug. It was probably better to have him tapping tables and cups than flicking his Zippo on and off inside a café. "How did it happen exactly? Were you pulled out of a magical realm?"

"Nope." Gray took another sip. "There was nothing. No consciousness. Nada."

"There can't just be nothing."

"I'm telling you there was nothing."

Raj stopped tapping his cup. "You must not remember."

"Maybe 'cause there's nothing to remember."

Raj leaned forward. "Or maybe you weren't really dead. Maybe you were in an alternate dimension. That must be why your mom was able to get you back."

Gray crossed her arms over her chest and leaned back in her chair. A smile quirked over her lips. "This really bothers you, doesn't it?"

Raj straightened up. "What?"

"My account of the hereafter . . . or lack thereof."

"I hardly think you're an expert."

"Right. I only died and came back to life. So many people know what that's like . . . for a minute. Don't forget I spent seven whole weeks in sweet oblivion before returning—none of this dead for several seconds, saw the light woo woo."

"You're jaded."

"Funny, I thought that description better suited you." Gray finished the rest of her mocha.

Raj raised a brow. "Would you like another?"

"I probably shouldn't."

Raj stood up. Gray was glad he didn't try to talk her out of it. She began digging through her bag. "Gray," he said. "Let me get it."

She just stared at him and he must have taken her momentary lack of protest as permission. Raj strode over to the order counter. When they first arrived, Gray had made sure to order and pay for her own drink. This was not a date.

She studied his muscular form at the counter. The way he leaned against it, casual, but not sloppy. When the barista turned to make the drink, he commenced tapping the counter with his left pointer finger.

The barista turned to say something to him and Raj stopped. His hand moved down to his pocket and he fingered whatever secret trinket he was hiding in there.

Gray's trinket.

She intended to lift it off him before the day was out. What was it he planned to give her on Valentine's Day? God, please don't let it be jewelry or a promise ring. But that was ridiculous. Those things were only for people who'd been going out and they most certainly were not going out. She wasn't even supposed to be alive.

Raj returned with a large mug and set it in front of Gray. "Thanks," she said.

"My pleasure."

She didn't like the way he was staring at her so she lifted her mug and said, "There are no mochas in heaven. But then again . . . there's no heaven, either."

Worked like a charm. Raj frowned.

"What happens if you can't get back inside your body?"

So she wasn't the only one trying to change the subject, though this topic was about as pleasant as the dark void.

"I don't even want to think of that as a possibility. How would my sister and I choose a college? What if Charlene decided she wanted to attend the Sorbonne?" Gray slapped a hand to her forehead. "And I can forget about a semester abroad in Barcelona. Charlene would never go for that. Maybe this is worse than being dead."

"Don't say that."

Gray looked Raj in the eyes. "Why not?"

He glanced down and hesitated a moment before pulling his hand back and letting it slip under the table. Raj dug inside his pocket and then held out his fist to Gray. After a pause that seemed to last an eternity, Gray placed an open palm under Raj's hand, but he didn't release the object. She jerked her hand with impatience. Did he expect her to pry the trinket out of his fingers? Finally Raj dropped it into her palm and pulled his hand back.

Gray felt the object before she saw it. The beads, stone, and silver were warm from being inside Raj's pocket. The moment it landed in her palm she curled her fingers around it and felt a hum reverberate through her entire body. Passion. Longing. Anguish. "What is it?" she whispered. It had power, whatever it was.

"A luck amulet."

Gray spread her hand open. The amulet itself was a silver sun with a square hole in the center. Multicolored threads had been woven through the hole and branched off into three dangles decorated with silver symbols and beads. The beads were pearly white—like metallic clouds trapped inside a stone. In the middle of the center thread was a crystal and two block-lettered square beads below it: GP.

Gray really shouldn't accept the amulet, but it was so beautiful and besides, she could use all the luck she could get.

"It's lovely," she said in a voice void of emotion. Gray couldn't look at Raj. The charm was gorgeous—more precious to her than any piece of jewelry. She was afraid he would sense how much the gift meant to her. "Thanks."

Raj slouched back in his seat, all casual-cool. "A lot of luck it did you."

Gray squeezed the amulet in her hand as Raj had done moments before her. "I should go. My mom will worry."

Raj pushed back in his seat. "I'll drive you to your car."

Gray thought they might arrive back at the cemetery without having spoken, but then Raj suddenly couldn't stop talking as they neared St. Ann's. "Did your mom tell you anything about the process?" he asked. "Did she share the steps? Was any kind of sacrifice required for the resurrection? Were warnings issued and what were they?"

"Wait a minute. Hold up," Gray said. "Sacrifice? Do you think my mom had to offer up a sacrifice?"

Raj glanced sideways. "It's not uncommon for a spell of that magnitude. You're not just messing with the laws of nature. You're screwing with the spiritual world."

"Are we talking animal sacrifice or human?" *Please don't say animal.*

"It might not be that kind of sacrifice at all. It could've been something of personal value or a promise made."

"What kind of promise?"

The car slowed and came to a gentle halt. Gray hadn't even noticed Raj circle the cemetery and pull in behind her car.

He put the car in park now and looked over at Gray. "I don't know. What has your mom told you?"

"Nothing." Gray said. "She's being really secretive about the whole thing. Believe me, I tried to get info. She said she can't tell me who performed the spell. They made her promise on my life." Gray lifted her head. "Hey, could that be the promise you're talking about?"

"Maybe, but it sounds more like insurance. This witch or warlock doesn't want the word getting out that they defied universal coven rules." Raj frowned. "It's not right to mess with the spiritual world."

Gray couldn't believe what she was hearing. Raj McKenna in a huff over black magic?

She didn't even lift her finger to unbuckle her belt. It popped out by the sheer force of her mind. Gray grabbed the loose belt and pushed if off. "Well, sorry if my existence upsets the moral fabric of your conscience. Maybe you shouldn't be talking to me at all since I'm tainted by unnatural forces."

"That's not what I'm saying."

"Whatever. See you Thursday. Maybe." The car door creaked when Gray pushed it open.

"Gray, wait."

Gray turned her nose up and gave Raj a scathing look, but she waited.

"What can I do to help?"

"Are you sure you want to be involved in this?"

"Yes."

Gray stared at him a moment, then shut herself back inside the car with Raj. It wasn't as though there was anyone around to hear them, but still. "Fine. Keep your eyes and ears open. Let me know what Charlene's up to."

Raj grinned. "That'd be a lot easier if I knew your invisibility spell."

"Yeah, right. For all I know you would use the spell to rob convenience stores or play peeping Tom in the girls' locker room. I don't want that on my conscience."

"What conscience? You're dead."

Gray gave him a look. Raj put up his hands. "You know I'd never use the spell on you."

"Fine. I'll think about it," Gray said. "But first do something for me. Introduce me to Adrian Montez."

"Adrian?" Raj asked, eyebrows furrowing. "Why?"

"He was once a powerful warlock, from what I understand."

"Yeah, *was*."

"I imagine he knows the kind of people who could put me back inside my body."

Raj hesitated a moment before saying, "I can ask."

"I want to meet him," Gray repeated.

"I don't think that's a good idea." Raj began tapping the steering wheel then stopped suddenly when his fingers disappeared. When his head snapped in Gray's direction she flashed him the Cheshire grin. "You can make other people invisible, as well?"

"Other people. Other objects." Gray shrugged. She filled Raj's fingers back in as he stared at them. When he looked at her again she said, "Introduce me to Adrian."

* * *

Mom was pacing the living room when she walked into the house. Her face flooded with relief when Gray came through the door. "You were at the cemetery awhile. I almost drove by, but I figured you wanted to be alone."

"Sorry. I didn't mean to worry you." Gray set down Charlene's messenger bag. "Mind if I change real quick?" Gray snapped her fingers and the skirt and top turned into a pair of soft blue jeans and a ribbed tank top. "Much better," Gray said, flopping onto the couch. "Actually I ran into Raj McKenna and we left in favor of mochas at The Daily Grind."

"Raj McKenna knows you're back?"

"Hey, Charlene told Ryan Phillips. If she can tell her minion what's going on I should be able to tell my . . . well, definitely not minion, but, you know, magically inclined friend." Gray chuckled at the thought of Raj as her minion. "Speaking of Ryan Phillips, are you and Mr. Phillips still an item?" Yes, let's change the subject—obviously Mom was mulling over both the fact that Gray had confided in someone and, more likely, that she'd been out having coffee with a boy.

"Marc and I aren't dating any longer."

Gray tilted her head back on the armrest of the couch. "Oh, why not?"

"I couldn't see him after hearing how Ryan helped Charlene with that blocking spell."

"Oh right, the blocking spell." It'd sorta settled to the back of Gray's memory, what with this whole dying-and-body-sharing development. "Well, that's a relief. If I had to have Ryan Phillips as a stepbrother, I really would wish I were dead."

"No need to. Marc and I are over and I would never marry another man anyway."

"Oh, no?"

Mom twisted her lips. "At least not a warlock."

"Hey, that's my rule. What made you change your mind?"

Mom shrugged. "My days of magical enchantment are over. I'm retired."

"Retired? You can't just retire from being a witch. It's what we are." Gray looked at her mother closer. "Is this about me and the resurrection spell?"

"In some ways."

"I don't want to be the reason you decide not to perform magic again."

Mom's eyes filled with tears. "You're the reason my life is filled with joy."

"Okay, I'm going to my room. This is getting too corny." Gray turned before her mom could see that her tears were becoming contagious.

* * *

Gray's desk was covered in textbooks, and not the school variety, but tomes on magic, spells, and potions. She'd pulled her hair into a loose twist and clipped it against her scalp, keeping it out of her face as she bent over the texts. It was becoming clear very quickly that these books couldn't come close to helping Gray. She needed access to the forbidden volumes.

There was a light knock on Gray's door. Her mom cracked the door open. "Honey, there's a boy here to see you."

Gray groaned. "So long as it's not Blake."

Next time he started molesting her she wouldn't be as nice; she'd give him a butt rash.

"It's not Blake."

Gray's head lifted. "Raj?"

Mom shook her head.

Gray got up. "Well, there's no sense playing twenty questions, let's see who my gentleman caller is."

"It's Nolan Knapp," Mom said as Gray passed her in the hall.

Chapter 16

Nolan waited in the entryway with his hands in his pockets studying the wall pictures up close.

"Nolan? What are you doing here?"

Nolan pulled his hands out of his pockets and brushed aside the hair hanging just above his eyes. "I, um, thought you might like a study partner—for French."

Oh, French. That's right. She hadn't solved the problem of French class. Gray voted dropping it in exchange for study hall second period. She'd jot down the suggestion in The Book of Charlene. Unless Charlene wanted to explain why she had a case of French amnesia every other day.

"A French study buddy," Gray repeated for her mother's benefit. Mom was a couple feet from the staircase, forehead pinched. "How thoughtful, Nolan. Why don't we go up to my room where it's quieter?"

Gray shared a quick look with her mom before leading Nolan up the stairs. She hurried him past her room with its open door. He breezed right past as though it didn't exist.

"Right this way," Gray continued. As soon as Nolan stepped inside Charlene's room Gray sidestepped him to go back out the door. "I'll get another chair."

"I feel bad about earlier," Nolan said before Gray had a chance to vacate the room.

"Earlier?" Gray stared at him.

"Getting all weird when you brought up magic at school."

"Oh." Gray's shoulders dropped. "Don't worry about it."

"No, that was really lame of me."

Gray lifted her shoulders up and down. "The rules are in place for a reason. It shows strength of character that you respect them."

Nolan's cheeks flushed and suddenly it was like they'd traveled back in time—back to where he and Gray had partnered up at Gathering and started saying "hey" in the hall. It seemed rather juvenile now and somewhat insulting. Nolan didn't know it was her, which meant he was going all weird and blushy on Charlene's behalf. No matter. Gray was going to need to get her hands dirty if she expected to have her life back. She had no time for boys.

Nolan cleared his throat. "Why are you having trouble with French all of a sudden?"

Gray sighed. "Nolan, I have bigger problems than French."

"Like what?"

"Believe me, you don't want to know." Gray went to the door. It was already open, but she pulled it all the way into the room for emphasis. "You should probably go." Gray looked at Nolan and saw she'd only succeeded in making him more determined to root himself in place.

"I want to know," he said firmly. "Maybe I can help."

"Doubtful."

Nolan walked past Gray. At first she thought he was leaving, but instead he closed the door. By hand. He turned. He was a tall boy and the door framed his features, which didn't appear so scrawny anymore. "Do you know why my family and I moved here?"

"Well, I know it wasn't for the weather."

Nolan didn't smile. He didn't even brush back the bangs that had resettled over his forehead. "We had to move after our coven kicked me out."

Gray practically snorted. "You? Get kicked out of coven? That's a little farfetched."

She could believe it of Raj, but Nolan—no way. He looked dead serious, though. What was it with Gray and bad boys?

Gray stretched across Charlene's bed and propped her head up with her hand. Nolan followed her motions. Mostly he stared at her legs. "So what did you do? Accidentally turn your peer leader's hair blue?"

Nolan looked directly at Gray. "I slept with her."

"You're joking?" Nolan had always struck her as a virgin, not a boy who'd seduced or been seduced by an older woman.

"Nope."

"Were either of you under a spell or was it just old-fashioned love?"

"It was more of an infatuation." Nolan straddled Charlene's desk chair beside the bed.

"On your part or hers?" Gray prodded. She grinned. Guy gossip. This was way too much fun.

Nolan grinned back. "Hers. She had a thing for adolescent boys and believe it or not, males can be quite impressionable."

"I.e., horny?" Gray said, and they both laughed. "So did your parents find out and freak?" Nolan's parents were older, and old in her mind equated with old-fashioned.

"No, she got bored with me and moved on to my friend Justin. I shouldn't have blamed Justin, but I did."

Gray tucked her legs under her and sat up on her knees. "What did you do to him?"

"I did something to his . . . you know." Nolan's smile widened.

"You didn't!"

The back of the chair dipped as he rocked forward. "I did."

"Now you have to share! What exactly did you do?"

"I made it smaller."

Gray burst into a fit of giggles. She lay on her back laughing.

"Much smaller. Pinky-small," Nolan said.

Gray was now clutching her stomach, tears streaming down her cheeks. She sat up and started laughing anew when her eyes met Nolan's. "Oh, you're bad," she said when she'd recovered. "So your friend figured it out?"

"His father figured everything out. He had our peer leader expelled from Gathering for life. She's on the universal coven's blacklist. I, fortunately, was allowed to join another coven, but I had to leave my own—I performed magic on a fellow warlock."

Gray chewed on her lower lip. In that case Ryan Phillips ought to be given the boot out of their coven. Better yet, he belonged on the blacklist right alongside Ms. Likes Young Hot Ass. "What did your parents say?"

"Not much. I think the whole thing embarrassed them."

"So they didn't even ground you?"

"Ground me?" Nolan's lips puckered into a smile. "I was the victim."

Gray rolled her eyes and got off the bed. "Right. Poor, innocent, young pervert."

"Hey, I wasn't perverted. I was in awe of the woman."

"Right," Gray said again. "Come with me."

Nolan got out of the seat on her command and followed her into the hall. Gray led him into her own room. The smile that'd been plastered over Nolan's face faded as he entered her private domain.

Gray shut the door behind them.

"What are we doing in here?"

"Can you keep a secret?"

"Of course."

Gray twisted her hair up as she walked to her desk and fastened it with the clip she'd tossed on top of her books. "I'm not Charlene. I'm Gray."

Confusion warped Nolan's face. "Gray? Really?"

"Yep—the French mystery has been solved. Phew!" Gray swiped her hand over her face.

"You mean it's been you all along? Charlene's the one who died?"

"No, I died, but I was brought back to life."

"I don't understand. I didn't think that was possible." Nolan walked up to Gray and poked her.

"Hey."

"Just checking." Nolan brushed his bangs to one side. "So you pretend to be Charlene sometimes so you can go to school?"

Gray snorted. "Yeah, right, attending McKinley High is my first choice of activities since returning from the great beyond. Actually, there's a slight problem. At the moment Charlene and I are sharing the same body. Well, technically I'm borrowing her body. There was a glitch in the resurrection spell and only one of us is conscious during a twenty-four hour period before the other awakens."

"So tomorrow . . ."

"I'll be Charlene."

"And the day after that?"

"Me again." Gray waved a finger in the air. "Yay."

Nolan hadn't stopped staring.

"So that's my big secret," Gray said.

"Sorry, it's just a little hard to believe."

"I can hardly believe it myself, but, alas, here I am."

"How did your mom pull off a resurrection spell?"

"Classified and if you mention this to anyone I'll be forced to give you a case of Justin-itus."

Nolan laughed.

Gray swept an arm over her desk. "We're in the middle of Operation Body Transfer, but my texts don't even come close to helping."

Nolan glanced from the pile of books to Gray. His lips twisted then relaxed right before he spoke. "But body transfers have been pulled off without too much trouble in the past—at least temporary ones. Isn't there a way to make the spell permanent?"

"You'd think," Gray said.

"Know anyone who has performed a body transfer?"

Gray smiled. "I know of someone."

She could see Nolan raise his brows under his bangs.

"Adrian Hedrick Montez." Gray punctuated each name as she spoke. "Otherwise known as Adrian the Avenger. Word is he performed one on himself and that his current body isn't even his own. I know for a fact he once transferred some hotshot guy into the body of a troll. Not literally a troll, but some short, fat, balding dude covered in pimples." Gray shot Nolan a mischievous smile and stole a look at his groin region. "Go figure. You two have something in common when it comes to vengeance."

"Did the guy cheat on his girlfriend or something?"

"Nope," Gray said, leaning against her bed. "He cut Adrian off in traffic." She laughed, but Nolan looked appalled.

"You're joking?"

Gray shook her head.

"He doesn't sound like the kind of warlock you want to solicit for help."

Gray pushed away from her bed. "Adrian's harmless. The council stripped him of his powers."

"Imagine if he got them back," Nolan said.

Maybe the possibility of Adrian regaining his abilities should have concerned Gray, but it had no effect. Death did that to a person. It was like conquering one's fear of heights by climbing a mountain or leaping from a plane. Gray had jumped headfirst into the abyss and there was nothing to worry about. No pain or sadness. No limitless existence and endless being.

Why were people so stuck on going to heaven, anyway? Existing forever in a bright, white haze sounded like the epitome of boredom.

Never-ending boredom. Right this way!

"Charlene!" Mom called from downstairs. "Dinner will be ready in ten minutes."

Nolan looked at Gray. "Charlene?"

"You're not supposed to know." Gray opened her door. "Be right down," she called. She turned and faced Nolan. "I told Mom she should start calling me *Graylene*." When Nolan joined her in the upstairs hallway she leaned in and said, "Remember, don't tell a soul."

"Promise."

When they reached the top of the stairs, Nolan put out a hand to stop her. His touch was firmer than Gray would have imagined. "I'll see what I can find out. There have to be warlocks and witches other than Adrian with the ability to perform a body transfer."

Gray shrugged.

"Bye, Nolan," Mom said upon joining them in the entryway. "It was nice of you to stop by."

"We miss seeing you at Gatherings," Nolan said.

"Yes, well, it's been a difficult time."

"I'm sorry, Mrs. Perez."

It was hard for Gray to say good-bye with her mom hovering over them. "See you later," she said and smiled.

"Yeah, see you around." Nolan's cheeks dimpled when he smiled. "Sorry we didn't get a chance to study French."

* * *

"Why didn't you get a chance to study French?" Mom asked as soon as Nolan was out the door.

Gray rolled her eyes and headed toward the nice smell coming from the kitchen. "Oh, please, like you have to worry. I'm not Charlene . . . yet." Gray got two plates out of the cupboard. Fluffy white basmati rice was set on warm in the rice cooker and there was a cast iron skillet filled with curried coconut potatoes and beside it, a smaller skillet with sautéed garlicky kale.

Gray loved healthy food as much as junk so long as the sauces and seasoning were good. Her mom happened to be a wizard in the kitchen . . . or sorceress—whatever.

Gray handed her mom a plate. "Smells delicious."

"Thanks, it's nice to have someone to cook for again."

"I don't get how Charlene does it," Gray said, scooping a heaping pile of rice onto her plate. "Slim Fast is not food!"

Mom chuckled. "So, want to tell me about Nolan Knapp?" she asked when they'd sat down at the table.

"He's nice. Well-behaved and cute—obviously."

Mom picked her fork up. "You know what I mean."

"I told him."

That statement didn't require clarification. Mom leaned forward. "You told him?"

"Well, how else was I supposed to explain not knowing any French after studying the language for supposedly five years? We were partnered in class today—complete humiliation, by the way, almost as bad as last Friday's debacle during second period in Mr. Burke's class. I vote homeschool for the rest of the semester."

"Oh, I'd already forgotten about French class. That does pose a problem."

"Un problema momento—however you say that in French."

"Hmmm," her mom said.

"Know any good language spells?"

Mom studied the contents on her plate. "I'm afraid Charlene's going to have to drop the class."

"Yes!" Gray dove into her curry and took a large, triumphant bite.

"So now Raj McKenna and Nolan Knapp know about you," Mom said. "You don't plan on telling anyone else, do you?"

"Negative, and they're both sworn to secrecy, by the way."

Mom moved her potatoes around her plate, but never took her eyes off Gray. "You never mentioned either boy before."

Gray shrugged. "Raj and I had fifth period together." Right, and they'd been so chummy during class. There's one thing Gray didn't miss about her old life—English with Mrs. Pritchett. "And Nolan and I paired up at Gathering that time I got my abilities back—or unblocked, rather." Gray used her fork like a spatula to scoop up the sautéed kale and slide it between her lips.

"They both seem nice. It's about time boys started taking notice of you."

Yeah, and she'd spent time with two in the same day. All-time record. "Apparently dead girls are a real turn-on. I mean, what warlock wouldn't be interested in a witch from the great beyond?"

"What boy wouldn't be interested in you for yourself, Gray?"

Gray straightened up. "This is strictly business. Raj and Nolan have offered their assistance."

"I'm sure I'll hear back from my contact soon."

"When?"

"I don't know."

"And there isn't any kind of expiration on this spell, is there?"

"No."

Mom's tone wasn't too convincing.

If Raj wouldn't introduce her to Adrian, Gray would just have to go introduce herself.

Chapter 17

Charlene Perez and Ryan Phillips walked out of first period together. Their bodies were touching, mouths moving. They slowed to a full stop in the hall, quickly finished their conversation, and then parted ways. Charlene walked past Raj without noticing him.

Raj knew Charlene's entire class schedule. Gray had given him a copy. He doubted he'd learn much during school hours. Charlene was bound to be discreet around her classmates. Raj didn't have a single class with the witch . . . which meant he no longer had any classes with Gray.

He stared at her empty desk beside Sadie Howard in English. The entire class had avoided that seat after Gray's death and every day during fifth period it remained empty.

Raj still remembered the day Gray appeared from thin air. She'd cast a spell over him instantly. Not consciously, of course, but the consequence had been just as powerful. That day felt like a lifetime ago, not two months.

Sure, learning that she'd been dead and was now sharing her sister's body came as a shock to Gray, but she hadn't suffered through the shock of her actual death. That was something Raj had known he'd never get past. Even in his later years—even when he left McKinley and Kent behind—there'd always be that girl. That one special girl who'd left the physical realm way too early.

Shay stopped by Raj's locker at the end of the day. She was wearing her standard heavy sweater over a pair of khaki pants. It was either that or a long plaid skirt and white blouse. You'd think she was attending Catholic school or something. Still, Shay managed to look beautiful at every moment.

"Can you come by this afternoon?" Shay asked.

"What's up?"

"I'll tell you later."

Raj knew there was a lot they couldn't discuss at school, but Shay didn't have to be so damn cryptic all the time. And why did he feel like the only time he saw her lately was in the secrecy of her home, as though Raj's company was an embarrassment?

Raj was just being moody. None of that was true. Shay was the last person who cared what others thought. She was simply on the fast track to college and that meant spending lunches in lab, student council, or the library. Still, she could've been there for him a little more. Like after his mom and sister moved away or after Gray died.

Get a grip, Raj; who was the girl in this scenario?

He straightened his spine and reached inside his pocket for his Zippo. Fine, if Shay wanted to wait to mention what was on her mind, she'd wait.

* * *

Charlene had gone to Ryan's locker to talk to him. Raj didn't bother with any pretenses, like reading a book in the hallway. People like Charlene and Ryan were easy to observe openly; so engrossed in their own lives that they barely noticed other people around them.

Raj flicked his Zippo open and closed. If either one of them were to look over he wouldn't bother looking away. He'd stare them down till they cowered. It would work on Ryan—probably not Charlene.

She began whispering in Ryan's ear.

Okay, Raj, lip-read. You can do it. But lip-reading wasn't one of his abilities. What Raj was good at reading were auras, and Ryan's went haywire when Charlene pressed her body into his shoulder to speak into his ear. It was the static equivalent of a hard-on.

Long after Charlene had left Ryan's side, the boy stared in the direction she'd walked. Raj had nearly followed her then decided on a different course of action.

Keep an eye on Ryan Phillips while you're at it, Gray had said.

Why?

The little bastard helped Charlene perform a blocking spell on me. There isn't anything he wouldn't do for her.

Raj followed Ryan out to the student parking lot and veered off to get to his car in time to follow Ryan onto the road.

Raj gripped his steering wheel. "All right, you twisted little freak. Let's see what you're up to."

* * *

"What took you so long?" Shay demanded when Raj swung by her house later.

She'd been on the phone with Max when he walked into her room. Whatever she wanted to discuss must be serious because the moment their eyes locked she'd ended her conversation almost immediately. "Max, Raj is here. I'll call you back."

Raj leaned against the wall beside her door. "I had errands. Actually, I'm not quite finished with them. You wanted to say something?"

Shay got up from her desk chair and stood directly in front of Raj. She folded her arms. "Raj," she began carefully, "is there something you're not sharing with me?"

Raj raised a brow. "Regarding?"

"Charlene Perez."

His mouth opened before he could stop himself. Shay naturally caught the motion. "Why are you interested in Charlene Perez all of a sudden?" Raj demanded, trying to go on the offensive.

"There's something funny about that girl lately," Shay said. "Last week I heard that she was pretending to be her sister, that she even had to be escorted out of class—her sister's old class. I saw her in French on Monday and all appeared normal. Then she comes into French Tuesday and suddenly can't recall a word of the language. Then today—totally fine. What'll happen tomorrow, I wonder?"

Raj tried to stare Shay down, but she was the one person this never worked on. He broke eye contact then stole another look. Well, why didn't she share her theory already? "So what are you saying?" Raj asked.

Shay dropped her arms. The only time she took her eyes off Raj was to walk over to her desk, but the moment she was leaning against the edge she looked directly at him. "The other odd thing about yesterday was she sat next to Nolan Knapp."

Raj ground his teeth together and tried to appear neutral. His efforts resulted in an achy jaw.

"She selected him as her partner when it was time to pair up," Shay continued, oblivious to Raj's distress. He didn't need to be able to see his own aura to know it'd smoldered from a healthy glowing green to a smoggy haze of brown and mustard.

Shay maintained a steady blue: relaxed, balanced—a born survivor.

"Right before Gray died she chose him as her partner at Gathering," Shay continued.

Raj dug out his Zippo and flicked it open.

"Please don't do that in here," Shay said.

Raj snapped it shut and stuffed it back inside his pocket.

"Since when did we start keeping secrets from one another?" Shay asked.

Secrets? Had Shay ever bothered asking Raj why one day, out of the blue, he'd tried to burn down his house with his sister inside? Raj loved Shay like a sister, but sometimes she was so damn oblivious. Present circumstances excluded.

"I don't know what you're insinuating," Raj said. "But it sounds pretty crazy to me."

"Is Graylee Perez back?" It was rare for Shay to raise her voice.

"I don't know. Why don't you tell me since you have it all figured out?"

"Raj, if Gray's back this is huge. The coven would flip its lid."

Raj took a step toward Shay. "Don't go telling tales to the coven."

Shay placed a hand on her hip. "Then tell me what's going on."

"Fine." Raj sighed. "Mrs. Perez found someone, we don't know who, to perform a resurrection spell, but it came out wrong. Gray is Charlene and Charlene is Gray. The switch happens every twenty-four hours at three a.m."

Shay looked beyond Raj's shoulder. "Wow. I thought Mrs. Perez was more levelheaded than that."

Of all the observations Shay could make.

Nope, Shay's existence was as clear as the blue sky beyond the clouds engulfing the rest of the city. She couldn't understand what it was like to love someone so much you'd do anything to get them back. Mrs. Perez hadn't used her head. She'd used her heart.

"What are they going to do?" Shay asked.

"Gray's mom is trying to get in touch with her contact."

Shay tsked. "Sounds like he's caused enough problems."

"How do you know it's a he?"

"Please—this has to be the work of a warlock; a witch wouldn't dare."

"Kinda sexist, don't you think?"

Shay didn't even bat an eye. "Totally sexist and also totally true."

Raj put up his arms. "If you say so."

"What's with you?"

"Nothing. Nice chatting."

"Wait a minute," Shay said.

Raj only paused for a moment in her doorframe. "Look, I have to go. See you at school."

Chapter 18

When Gray woke up Thursday morning, it was to the standard-issue lace babydoll. Charlene had left her spiral communications notebook open on her desk beside the bed.

She'd dated her entry and made a notation of the time. Her first entry of the day stated, *I woke up in your room!!!*

"Yeah? Well, I woke up in yours."

Gray snapped into her own PJs and stuffed the notebook under her arm as she walked down the hall to her room. At the bottom of her sock drawer, she'd stowed away the luck amulet Raj had given her. It wasn't just hidden under socks—it was also invisible. Gray filled it in and slipped it inside the pocket of her fuzzy hoodie as she descended the staircase. "Hi, Mom," she said, joining her in the kitchen.

"Hi, honey. How are you this morning?"

"It's a Gray kind of day." Gray began scanning the notebook after she took a seat on the barstool at the counter. "Charlene won't drop French!" Gray looked up. "You're kidding me. Now what the heck am I supposed to do?"

Mom opened the drawer under the phone and pulled out a slip of paper. She handed it to Gray. Gray read it and looked back up. "Dr. Finnegan says I have laryngitis?" Gray looked back down. "'It's not contagious. I have decided it is safe for her to attend classes, but advise that she not speak unless absolutely necessary.'" Gray rolled her eyes. "Oh, brother. And what? I'm going to have laryngitis the rest of the semester?"

"Only in French class, but no, it's only a temporary solution. I pulled out my old Rosetta Stone CDs."

My jaw dropped. "You can't be serious."

Mom shrugged. "I'm sure we'll think of something. In the meantime, it wouldn't hurt to brush up on some basics."

"You mean learn French in one week? Forget it! No merci. Not bon!"

"What's wrong with French?" Mom asked in a teasing tone. "It's a beautiful language." She set a bowl of oatmeal in front of Gray. "Your great-great-grandmother was French."

Gray rolled her eyes. "And Grandpa was Spanish." She went back to reading the notebook while she ate her oatmeal. Marcy Kimble had pissed Charlene off and so Gray was not to acknowledge her. No problem. An essay was due in English. It was finished and inside her folder. At least Charlene was organized.

When I told you not to sleep with Blake I didn't mean avoid him altogether. He said you wouldn't come over after school Tuesday. He also said you acted weird. I had to spend the whole afternoon doing damage control.

Better Charlene than Gray.

Stop snacking, Charlene wrote. *My stomach didn't feel good when I woke up this morning and my skirt felt tight. I have a very simple diet. Grapefruit in the morning with a handful of granola. Slim Fast shake for lunch. Slim Fast shake for dinner or green salad with a squirt of lemon— no croutons.*

If Gray had to stick to that kind of diet she'd rather be dead. She'd never tasted a Slim Fast shake before that week and she had to say it reminded her of chocolate-flavored Pepto-Bismol.

If Charlene could figure out a spell to make herself tan, couldn't she come up with one to keep herself thin?

Gray closed the notebook and reached inside her pocket for the amulet. She slouched over the countertop and dangled the charm in front of her face.

"What's that?"

When Gray looked at her mom she saw that she was now frowning.

"A luck amulet."

"Where did you get it?"

"It was a gift from a guy and no, you wouldn't approve of him."

"Nolan?"

Gray snorted. "What's not to approve about Nolan? Nope, it's from Raj McKenna." Gray glanced up, but her mom merely looked pensive.

"Raj McKenna," she repeated.

"Yeah. Why?"

"Hmmm."

"What's with the face?"

"He used moonstones." Gray could feel her mom studying her. "He must like you a lot."

"It doesn't mean anything," Gray said. "Even if Raj McKenna did like me, I doubt he does anymore. Not since learning I'm a heathen."

"You're not a heathen."

"Of course I am. I don't believe in God. Do you?"

Gray's mother twisted her lips. "I believe in a higher power. I'm a witch, after all."

"Well, sorry I couldn't bring back a message from Dad."

Mom walked over and put a hand on Gray's shoulder. "You listen to me, Graylee Perez. There is nothing wrong with you. It wasn't your time. I believe the spiritual world is as magnificent and vast as the universe and that we cannot begin to understand it. But there's a place for you in the great beyond. There's a place for all of us. It just wasn't your time."

The tears came unexpectedly. Gray put her arms around her mom and blinked them away rapidly so that by the time she pulled her head back her cheeks were dry.

"Raj McKenna always struck me as a good kid. Mrs. Baxter once told me he was one of the most gifted healers she'd come across—and youngest. It's a shame his mother left him with the dad, but then I have trouble understanding any woman who would leave her child."

"Well, he did burn their house down."

"Did he?"

Gray opened and closed her mouth. "He never denied it."

"I don't know. Something didn't feel right about that story."

Gray shrugged. "Well, I'm off to school."

"Have a good day, honey." Her mom gave her another hug. She'd been doing that a lot lately.

Before Gray walked out the door she snapped into a skirt and V-neck sweater.

* * *

Rather than go straight to Charlene's locker, Gray chose an alternate route taking her through the hallways on the east side of McKinley. She thought she knew where Raj's locker was, but without him around it couldn't be confirmed.

Gray felt a tap against her shoulder. She should have known it was Nolan. He was grinning from ear to ear.

"Hi, Nolan. Find a cure?"

"No, but I think I know someone who can help."

Gray fell into step beside him. "Really? Who is it?"

"Brock. He's a warlock up north a couple hours. The guy was put on suspension by his coven for transferring his mother into the body of a younger woman."

Gray rubbed her hands together. "Sounds like the kind of warlock I'd like to meet. Where is he exactly?"

"Bellingham." Nolan's cheeks dimpled. "Wanna take a road trip?"

"How does after school sound?"

"My parents might notice that. What about Saturday?"

"Perfect!" Gray swung around and hugged Nolan. His eyes nearly popped out of his head and his cheeks turned five shades brighter. "Thanks, Nolan!"

"Yeah, totally. Anything to help." He paused for a moment. "Um, do you want to have lunch together today?"

"I wish." Gray snorted. "I have to eat with Tweedledee and Tweedledum—don't want to disturb Charlene's superficial friendships, you know."

Nolan cleared his throat. "No, that's cool."

"Trust me; I'd rather eat with you any day. See you in French class?"

"Okay. What are you going to do if Madame Girard calls on you?"

"Laryngitis," Gray said, pointing to her throat.

Nolan chuckled. "Okay, see you in French." He pressed his hand between her shoulder blades before walking away.

Gray's mouth opened slightly then abruptly closed when she noticed Thea glaring in her direction. If only she could go over to her friend and assure her that no, Charlene wasn't moving in on Gray's old crush. She tried to convey this message with her eyes, but it was no use.

Suddenly Gray was bumped from the side. For such a petite girl, Brittany had a lot of force behind her. Gray rubbed her shoulder.

"So what's the deal with Nolan Knapp?" Brittany demanded. "Have you slept with him?"

Gray lifted her nose. "Wouldn't you like to know?" She wasn't snooty by nature, but somehow it came naturally to her when she was around Brittany. Maybe Charlene wouldn't be as intolerable if she kept better company.

Brittany smirked. "I guess he's cute—in a boyish sorta way."

"He got kicked out of his last school for sleeping with a teacher."

Brittany's eyes nearly popped out of her face. "Shut up!"

"Swear."

Brittany grinned wickedly. "Hello, Nolan. You know he has to be all kinds of naughty between the sheets having gotten instruction by an older woman."

"Maybe."

"Oh, totally. If you don't do him, I will."

"Sorry, Brit. Nolan's off-limits."

"What? So you think you can have all the hotties to yourself?"

Gray tried the chin lift again. "That's right."

"Bitch."

"Super bitch."

Brittany's mouth opened wide on a gasp and then she smiled. "Mega bitch!"

"Super, gigantic, mega bitch."

Both girls were laughing at this point. Gray stopped abruptly when she saw Raj watching her across the hall. "I'll see you later. I have business with a certain annoying boy who is so not on my hook-up list."

Brittany followed Gray's gaze. "McKenna?" Gray was surprised when her voice didn't convey disgust. "I'd do him."

Gray gnashed her teeth together and forced a smile that felt more like a grimace. She couldn't very well tell Brittany that Raj McKenna was off-limits, as well. Way off-limits.

Chapter 19

"Making new friends?" Raj asked when Gray crossed the hall to his side.

Gray really did grimace this time. "Hardly. Maintaining Charlene's façade is all."

"Uh-huh."

"What?"

"Looked like you were having a good time playing the role."

"Don't be a jackass. I'm just good at hiding my inner cringe. Anyway, I bet you'd think a lot better of Brittany if you knew she declared you 'doable.'"

Raj laughed. "In her dreams."

"Look at you all puffed up. Imagine what it would do for your ego if I told you that even my own dear friend Thea said as much to me before I kicked the bucket."

Raj craned his head toward Gray. "Thea Johnston thinks I'm doable?"

"You know her or something?"

"We have some classes together. She's always seemed really cool."

"Then why don't you ask her out or something?" Gray snapped. Her frown stretched to her chin. Why shouldn't Raj think Thea was cool? She was really cool.

"Whoa, who said anything about asking anyone out?" Raj lifted his hands. So far his lighter hadn't appeared in either hand.

Gray kept expecting him to retrieve the blasted thing and start snapping it open and closed. Heck, she felt like flicking the dang Zippo a few times herself. "I'm still processing this information."

"That's right, gloat all you want—two girls at McKinley vote Raj McKenna decidedly doable."

"And you don't?"

"You wish."

"Why not?"

Gray pressed her lips together.

Raj chuckled the longer she refused to respond. Gray picked up the pace. "Speaking of doable, I have to go get my morning embrace with Blake over with."

Raj caught Gray's arm. She was about to demand he let her go, but the words died on her tongue when their eyes met.

"I don't like him touching you."

"It's not me he's touching."

Raj stared deep into Gray's eyes. "It is you."

She swallowed. "Don't worry. I can look out for myself." Gray pulled free from his grasp.

"I don't like it," he repeated as she hurried down the hall.

Raj's words followed Gray right up to Blake Foster, who awaited her at her locker. The grin on his face was sickening. "Last night was incredible," he whispered, invading Gray's personal space and running his gropey hands all over her before she had the chance to cast a rash across his body. "You are one naughty schoolgirl."

So that was what Charlene meant by damage control.

Blake reached a hand up Gray's skirt at the same time he bit down on her earlobe. Gray didn't have enough wits about her to cast a spell. She did, however, have the full force of her natural reflexes and smacked Blake across the face with a resounding slap.

The hand that'd been under Gray's skirt was now pressed against Blake's cheek. Anger flashed across his eyes.

Uh-oh.

Gray chuckled nervously. "And you're a naughty schoolboy."

Blake didn't bite. "Not cool, Charlene," he said. "Not cool at all." And then he stormed off.

* * *

Gray spent first period on the edge of her seat biting her fingernails—a habit she'd supposedly kicked before entering high school. Ryan didn't mention Blake so he must not have heard about it yet.

"Here," Ryan said, slipping Gray a typed report.

Gray glanced down. *Gene Mutation* was in bold text at the top followed by *Charlene Perez, 1st Period Biology/Darling.* "What is this?"

"Charlene's biology report."

"You do her homework for her?"

"Biology is Charlene's most difficult subject," Ryan huffed.

Gray huffed back at him. "Yeah, and gym's mine. Doesn't mean I'm gonna have someone run laps for me."

Ryan straightened up in his desk. "Anyway, Charlene helps me with English."

"Well, good for her." God, Gray was actually looking forward to Mr. Darling's lecture that morning—anything to shut Ryan up. And she had two more classes with him before the day was out. It wasn't like she got them over with in one fell swoop, either. They were strung out over the course of her day. School started with Ryan Phillips and ended with Ryan Phillips. She needed her damn body back.

As much as she loathed keeping Ryan's company, French held even less appeal.

Shay Baxter advanced on Gray as she headed for the seat beside Nolan. "Why don't you sit beside me, Mademoiselle Perez." It wasn't a question.

"And why should I do that?" Gray demanded. Ryan had been warm-up and she was on a roll.

Because I'm going to tell you what to say if Madam Girard calls on you.

Just great. On top of everything else, Shay Baxter had telepathic powers.

If only Gray had the same ability to convey a message of apology to Nolan as she slumped into the desk beside Shay in the front row.

"Why are you helping me?" Gray asked.

"I'm doing this for Raj."

Gray's lip curled back. "You must really care about him."

Shay naturally didn't pick up on Gray's bitter tone. Her stoic pose went uncompromised. "He's my friend," she said matter-of-factly.

Well, he could forget about being Gray's friend. She had a bone to pick with Raj. How could he tell Shay Baxter about the resurrection spell? He probably told Shay everything. They were BFFs, bonded through years of friendship.

Gray had to stop this. Shay was probably reading her thoughts right now.

"I'll also translate everything Madame Girard says so you'll know what's going on in class," Shay said.

"And that's it, right?" Gray asked. "You're not going to invade my thoughts or anything?"

Shay showed the first glimmer of emotion. Maybe it was her version of outrage because her words had a crisp undertone as they dropped from her lips. "That would be a violation of your private rights, not to mention an infringement of coven code. I would never eavesdrop on your personal thoughts."

Of course you wouldn't, Miss Perfect.

Gray checked Shay's face for any indication that she'd heard that thought, but the girl still looked incensed by Gray's accusation. Shay's jaw didn't soften until Max Curry walked in. While they greeted one another, Gray glanced back at Nolan. He was frowning. She lifted a hand and nodded her head toward Shay. Nolan looked down at the piece of paper on his desk and began scribbling furiously.

Gray turned back around to face the front of the room. It wasn't that she wanted to sit beside Shay Baxter. Shay was the last person she wanted to sit next to! But it beat laryngitis.

After class, Gray waited for Nolan in the hallway. He certainly took his time coming out. "Hey," she said when he stepped out of class.

"Hey."

"Sorry I didn't get to sit by you." Gray rolled her eyes. "Shay Baxter ambushed me. At least she's helping me with my language problem."

Nolan stiffened. "So Shay knows what's going on?"

"It's not like I told her. Raj did." Gray screwed up her face. "He's so going to get a piece of my mind—or mouth, rather. I guess Shay really is more gifted than me with her fancy pants telepathic abilities. I'll just have to chew him out the old-fashioned way: with my mouth." Gray chuckled then stopped abruptly when she noticed Nolan wasn't exactly paying attention to her diatribe.

"You told Raj McKenna?"

Gray shrugged. "Well, yeah. He knows that warlock I mentioned, Adrian Montez."

Nolan's lip curled over. "But I was going to help you."

"You still are. I'd much rather solicit the help of this Brock guy than Adrian the Avenger. Adrian doesn't even have powers anymore."

Nolan's mouth returned to normal. "Cool, so we'll make a road trip out of it this weekend."

"Saturday," Gray said. "No overnighters unless you want to wake up next to one very pissed-off twin." She chuckled.

Nolan dimpled and looked at the ground then back up. "All right, if I don't see you later, I'll catch you Saturday morning as soon as I can make a getaway."

* * *

Gray physically winced when she lifted the tab of her French vanilla Slim Fast during lunch hour—and it wasn't just because the chalky substance in front of her was "French." Gray took a sip and made a face. "God, this is foul."

Kiki giggled. Even her salad looked more appetizing.

Gray stood up and grabbed the Slim Fast, practically crushing it in her hand.

"What are you doing?" Brittany asked.

"I'm chucking this and getting tater tots."

"I'll come with you," Kiki said.

Brittany stood. "Well, you can't just leave me here sitting alone."

"I think I'll have a slice of pizza," Kiki said on the way up to the service window.

"You know you guys are going to have pimples tomorrow," Brittany cried out behind them. "And forget fitting into your prom dresses. Guys? Wait up!"

Gray got her tater tots and Kiki had her slice of pizza. Gray made a goofy face at Brittany when the girl glared at her. "What? You want one or something?"

"No, thanks," Brittany sniffed.

Gray thought she'd managed to survive another day at McKinley High as Charlene when Brittany came rushing upon her at the end of sixth period.

"Oh my god, promise you won't get mad at me for telling you this, Charlene."

Gray suppressed a sigh. "What now?"

"Kristy Phelps says Blake and Jenna showed up at the sub shop together during lunch hour. Usually Kristy has fifth period chemistry with Jenna, but Jenna never showed up and when I asked Kiki, she said Blake didn't show up to bio."

Obviously, Gray was supposed to have some kind of reaction to this, but she just wasn't in the mood. "Oh my god, that bastard," Gray said halfheartedly. "At least I showed him with Todd Hanson. Maybe it's time I tap that again."

Brittany hugged her arms around her chest. "Todd is the hottest senior at McKinley. You'll so show Blake!"

"What's he doing with bucktoothed Jenna Hocking, anyway?" Gray mused aloud. "When did Stacey Morehouse stop making the cut?"

Brittany's mouth hung open. "You're joking, right?"

"Apparently." Gray lowered her voice and leaned closer. "Why?"

Brittany took a step back. Her face squeezed together and she looked at Gray with the same kind of disgust one might use when catching sight of roadkill or a whiff of fish guts.

"What's wrong with you lately?"

"I bumped my head this morning. Really hard," Gray added when the first part did nothing to soften the features of Brittany's expression.

"Yeah, well, you might want to have that looked at." Brittany walked away as though Gray's supposed head injury were contagious, or maybe the only contagion she was worried about was keeping company with a person clearly losing her mind.

Fat chance Charlene's friends would stick around if her sister stopped being anything other than perfectly stuck-up and popular. Blake's wasn't the only relationship she had to maintain and that was currently on the fritz thanks to Gray's handy dandy reflexes.

Gray could only begin to imagine what she'd find written in the Book of Charlene come Saturday morning. Her sister would probably rip through the pages with the pressure of her pen. Well, it wasn't easy being Charlene.

Gray noticed Ryan at the end of the hall with his jacket and backpack. He walked toward the double doors leading into the student parking lot. Gray hurried after him. "Hey, Ryan!" As soon as Gray was close enough she asked, "What's the deal with Stacey Morehouse? I asked Brittany why Blake lost interest in her and she looked at me like I was nutso. So what did you fail to mention?"

"Um." Ryan looked side to side. "It's complicated."

"Ryan!"

"She's in a coma."

Gray stepped so close to Ryan their noses practically touched. "How did Stacey get in a coma?"

"She was in a car crash." Ryan's eyes darted to one side.

Gray sucked in a breath. Even when she'd distanced herself from Ryan by a full foot she had trouble getting air into her lungs. Finally, she managed to take in a breath. She wanted to slap him across his pear-shaped face or, better yet, sock him in the jaw. "Realized the error of his ways, my ass." Gray turned on her heel and took off down the hallway.

"Don't go assuming something!" Ryan yelled after her.

But it was far too late for that.

Gray had only one theory, and her name was Charlene.

* * *

Green, Gray thought.

Green. Green. Green.

The lights changed on cue all the way to Valley Medical Hospital. Man oh man, she loved being a witch. Gray didn't have any time to waste. Not that Stacey Morehouse was going anywhere. She just had to see how she was doing for herself.

"Hello, I'm here to see Stacey Morehouse," Gray said, approaching the front desk of the critical care unit.

A large African-American woman, who looked even darker in her white uniform, regarded Gray over her horn-rimmed glasses. "Are you a relative?"

"I'm a friend."

"Sorry, sweetie, only family allowed."

"Thanks," Gray said grudgingly.

No matter. Once she'd rounded the corner and checked that the hallway was deserted, Gray went invisible and turned right back around. It would have helped if she'd known which room Stacey was in. Gray had never been very good at locator spells. If the stationed nurse would go away for a second, Gray could try looking Stacey up on the computer, but the woman was firmly planted in her seat.

Okay, feet, take me to Stacey Morehouse.

Gray walked swiftly down the hall and slipped through a partially open door. An elderly woman emerged from her bathroom. The flush of the toilet still sloshed behind her. Gray was about to mutter an apology, then remembered she was invisible.

She'd just have to look in every room until she found Stacey.

Hospital odors always made her nose twitch. If only invisibility could erase her sense of smell. At least Gray hadn't died inside a hospital. Dying peacefully in her sleep was at the top of Gray's list as far as death scenarios went—just not at seventeen!

Gray was surprised by how much it affected her to see Stacey Morehouse lying comatose on top of her hospital bed.

She'd never been fond of Stacey, but they shared a bond now: the bond of death and the brink of death. Two seventeen-year-old girls knocked down in their prime.

The difference was Stacey shouldn't be lying on her back, breathing through a ventilator, shut off to the world. Gray sent out a silent apology for her sister—if it was, indeed, Charlene. That was what she had to find out.

The windows in Stacey's room overlooked the hospital's green patch of lawn below.

It looked like an interior designer had been hired to personalize Stacey's hospital room. Whoever it was had done a noble job of making it feel more homey. Several framed Monet art prints hung from the wall, and there was a fresh floral bouquet on a side table.

A beautiful patchwork quilt had been spread over Stacey's standard-issue hospital bedspread.

Gray walked tentatively to Stacey's bedside. Why did it feel like she was approaching an open casket?

Stacey's hair was fluffed gently around the pillow on either side of her face as though it had recently been combed. Her brows were perfectly plucked and even her cheeks had a healthy glow to them.

She looked like Sleeping Beauty.

"What did Charlene do to you?" Gray whispered.

Chapter 20

Death and accidents were beginning to feel like a morbid obsession with Gray. Her eyes raced down the article she'd pulled up on the computer inside her room.

McKinley Teen in Critical Condition after Collision

Sunday, February 13

Stacey Lee Morehouse, 17, is in critical condition at Valley Medical Hospital after driving headfirst into a street lamp Friday evening.

Morehouse is the only daughter of local attorney Daniel Morehouse.

This tragedy falls two days after McKinley High junior Graylee Perez, 17, was found dead in her family home the morning of the 9th. Coroners have yet to determine the cause of death. Perez was in the same grade as Morehouse at McKinley High School.

Morehouse crashed into a light pole off Stanton and Third shortly after leaving her boyfriend's house at 9:40 p.m. Friday night. Paramedics performed CPR on the young woman after they arrived on the scene. They said she was found unconscious.

Police have yet to make a statement, but say alcohol was not a factor.

The cause of the crash has not yet been determined.

Oh, for freak's sake—were they kidding her? What was it with their paper and follow through?

Maybe teenage deaths and accidents were just too common an occurrence in Kent these days.

Gray headed toward the stairs to find her mom and grill her, then stopped short. She recalled the dark circles she'd seen under her mom's eyes that morning. Even when Gray had returned from the hospital Mom had been holding her head at the dining room table, ancient texts spread open before her. That was why Gray had greeted then quickly bypassed her in favor of online research before she began firing away questions about Stacey Morehouse's accident.

Mom was worried. She'd already complained of a headache that wouldn't go away. Must be a migraine if Mom couldn't cast it off. Gray had put together a calming potion. Just before heading up to her room she'd seen her mom drinking the warm brew in delicate sips. Gray wasn't about to go upset that calm now.

She took a step backwards, returned to her room, and closed the door.

Gray dialed the number Raj had given her. This was no time to text. Raj had barely answered when Gray fired her first question at him. "What do you know about Stacey Morehouse?"

"The coma girl?"

"Yeah."

"That she's in a coma."

Gray released an impatient sigh. "Was there ever an investigation into the cause of the crash?"

"Yeah, a big one. Her dad's some sort of hotshot attorney."

"So? What did they find?"

"Faulty brakes. Mr. Morehouse sued the car manufacturer."

"And what caused the faulty brakes?"

Gray began tapping her foot as the silence dragged on. Finally Raj said, "I wasn't part of the investigation, you know? Why are you interested in Stacey Morehouse anyway?"

"I think Charlene might have had something to do with her accident."

Another pause followed. Gray felt herself holding her breath. She squeezed her phone. It was one thing to have a sister who was manipulative, vain, selfish, and mentally unstable . . . but murderous?

"What makes you think that?"

Gray momentarily forgot her sister. Raj's voice deepened when it turned serious. Each word was like a sweet husk of corn being peeled back. His voice felt seductive so close to her ear. Gray reminded herself that she was mad at Raj for blabbing her secret to Shay Baxter.

"Before I died, Blake dumped Charlene for Stacey. She actually threatened to kill Stacey. My mom put a protection spell on Stacey, but I think it was only protection against magic. Good old-fashioned foul play might have been up for grabs."

Raj cleared his throat. "Have you asked your mother about this?"

Gray glanced at the door. She uttered a feeble, "No," then continued a little louder, "She's so wrapped up in finding a way to fix this resurrection spell. I haven't been able to bring myself to confront her, but I will. I'll ask her the moment we get off the phone."

"No!" Raj's reply startled her. "Don't worry her even more right now. Let her concentrate on getting you back inside your body and even more importantly, conscious every day—not this split shift. Stacey isn't going anywhere."

"Raj?"

"Yeah?"

Gray pressed her toe into the carpet. "Do you think you could come with me to the hospital—see if you might be able to get inside her mind and find out what happened the night of the crash?"

Raj hesitated. "It's an extremely intrusive spell, Gray."

"I need answers. I need to know if Charlene is dangerous."

"Fine, I'll meet you in front of the hospital in twenty minutes."

Chapter 21

Raj snapped his lighter open and closed faster than usual. Afternoon had turned to early evening and though spring had only just begun, the overcast sky was like the last flickers of a dying wick inside a room of shadows. The light on the Zippo sparked. Raj left it open and stared directly into the flame. It began to flicker and dance.

Beyond the pinprick of light he could see Gray approaching. She wore shorts over black tights, her clogs, and a mesh purple sweater over a black tank top. Gray walked up to him. "Should you be messing around with that thing in front of a hospital?"

Raj snapped the Zippo shut.

"What's with the lighter, anyway? You don't smoke."

"It's a keepsake." Raj held the lighter in front of his face between his pointer and thumb. "A reminder that even the people who are supposed to look out for you are capable of letting you down and that the only person you can count on is yourself."

"You got all that from a lighter?"

Raj stuffed it inside his pocket. "Yeah."

Gray was still frowning when Raj looked at her again. At least she looked more like herself in her own clothes.

"Why did you tell Shay Baxter I was alive? I thought you were going to keep your mouth shut."

Raj tried to hide the flinch her tone caused. "Sorry, but she pretty much figured it out herself."

"Of course she did," Gray grumbled. "Shay knows everything."

"What's that supposed to mean? Shay said she was going to help you in French. Didn't she?"

Gray folded her arms over her chest. "Oh, Shay helped, all right. She told me where to sit and what to say. She practically told me what to think, being inside my mind and all. She's heaps of help!"

Raj's mouth fell open. Gray looked really angry. He thought she would have appreciated Shay's help. "I'm sorry. I can tell her to back off if you like."

"Don't you dare! I don't want you discussing me with Shay Baxter any more." Gray kicked at the pavement.

"Should we go inside?"

"Yeah, let's hope you're as good at getting inside people's heads as Shay Baxter." Gray stormed ahead.

Raj's shoulders slumped as he followed Gray past the sliding doors. He walked behind her like a lackey to the elevators. It wasn't until the doors closed that Gray acknowledged him again. "They only allow family inside so I'm going to need to make us both invisible."

"Or you could teach me how to make myself invisible."

"Not right now."

Most likely never. Gray would dangle the damn spell like a carrot over his head, thinking that was the key to getting his help when being around her was reward enough. The elevator doors opened and Gray stepped out. Raj followed her down a hallway. As they approached a corner, Gray disappeared and then Raj disappeared after her.

This time it wasn't just his fingers missing. He couldn't see his arms or legs. He couldn't see any part of himself. Raj nearly tripped. His hand shot out and smacked into Gray's arm. The moment it did, he grasped her as though steadying himself.

"You're invisible, not blind, McKenna!"

Raj let go of her abruptly. He came to a stop in the middle of the hallway, blending into the white sterile surroundings. For a moment he truly felt as though he didn't exist. He had no idea if Gray waited for him or not until he heard her voice further down the hall. "Raj? Raj, where are you?" she whispered.

Raj pressed his lips into a tight frown. Not that she'd see it. If he listened close he could hear her footsteps coming back down the hallway. "Raj? Raj!" she said more insistently.

"Here." His voice sounded rough and deep when he was angry. Gray must have recognized it because he heard her footsteps stop abruptly.

"What's the matter?"

"You sounded like your sister just a moment ago. I came here to help you, remember?"

Silence followed by more silence. Then suddenly she took his hand. Raj didn't know how she'd found it, but somehow she grasped his fingers on the first try. Maybe he'd missed her filling his hand in temporarily. He stopped wondering when she gave his hand a gentle squeeze and pulled gently to lead him down the hall.

"I forgot how uncanny it can be the first time," she said. "It's kinda a wild sensation, isn't it?"

"Yeah." Raj swallowed. Gray still had hold of his hand.

He might have been the one who was invisible, but in those moments Gray held his hand in hers it was as though the walls and people around him disappeared. Before Raj knew it, they'd slipped inside a patient's room. Gray closed the door behind them and let go of Raj's hand. She appeared in front of him then looked back and remembered he was still invisible. "Whoops."

The first thing Raj saw was his shoulders. He began to fill in, the spell working its way down to his toes. Raj held his arms in front of him in wonder and looked at Gray, but she was beside the hospital bed staring down. "Do you think you can reach her?"

Raj approached the girl. He hadn't known Stacey Morehouse well at all. They didn't exactly run in the same circle.

Raj took in a breath. It felt more like it had been stolen from him by an unseen force.

Stacey's aura was white. A white aura was more like a noise than a color. It indicated serious health problems in a person. It was also the color preceding death.

"We shouldn't be here," Raj said.

"Don't chicken out on me now, McKenna."

He shot Gray a look.

"I'll teach you the invisibility spell."

"This doesn't feel right."

Gray walked over to Raj's side. "What if she's trapped in there just waiting for the chance to communicate with someone?"

Raj looked down at Stacey. His fingers twitched at his side. That was exactly what he was afraid of.

"Fine," he said finally. "I'll try. I'm not making any promises, but I'll try."

Gray smiled. "That's all I'm asking."

Raj positioned himself beside Stacey's head. He was so close to the bedside his thighs brushed the blankets. He looked down. Even comatose, Stacey Morehouse was a beautiful girl, but looks weren't everything. In fact, they meant nothing if the person inside wasn't nice. Still, it was a shame to see someone so young and, in all appearances, physically healthy, laid low. And if Gray's sister had caused this . . .

Raj took in a sharp breath.

No more stalling, he told himself.

He looked down at Stacey. His gaze moved from her nose to her head. Gray moved to the opposite side of the bed across from Raj. Her jaw dropped when Stacey's forehead opened. So he was being a bit of a showoff. He had to impress a girl who could turn invisible somehow.

White light nearly blinding to the eye radiated out of Stacey's head. Gray squinted and turned away. This was nothing like Mrs. Court. This was nothing like Raj had ever seen before.

He stared straight into the brightness, transfixed. It consumed him and threatened to suck him in.

Raj pushed away from the bed and staggered back as though he'd been shoved.

Gray's eyes were wide as saucers. "That was incredible! What happened? Did you reach her? What did she say?"

Raj ran his hands over his face, holding his cheeks in his hands. Abruptly, he dropped them. "I'm sorry. There's nothing there."

Gray's face dropped. "There has to be. As long as she's still alive she has to be in there somewhere."

Raj shook his head. "She's gone, Gray."

Gray looked like she was about to argue then thought better of it. "We should go," she said. She walked out before Raj.

He glanced back one last time, half expecting to see Stacey's face twisted in an angry plea, but she remained serene.

Raj had lied. Stacey Morehouse was in there, all right, but she had nothing to say about her accident. There was no reason to burden Gray with what she had really said. A sentence she'd repeated over and over like a scratchy, broken record and then when Raj made no answer, screamed it one last time: "Let me go!"

Chapter 22

Gray waited by the elevator for Raj. They rode down in silence. Gray stole a sideways glance at him. Raj looked like he'd seen a ghost even though Gray was the one who should have been blown away.

She would never forget the way the layers of Stacey's forehead had peeled back and light poured out of her head. She had no idea Raj was such a powerful warlock. Even if he hadn't gotten any information, she was amazed.

They walked side by side out the front door and into the parking lot.

"Can you come over?" Gray asked. "I want to teach you the invisibility spell."

Raj sighed. "It's been a long day."

Was Gray hearing correctly? "A promise is a promise. Follow me home."

Raj nodded. Like he was going to say no to that.

Gray kept glancing at him in her rearview mirror. By now it was getting darker and Raj looked like a silhouette behind his wheel.

Poor Stacey Morehouse, Gray thought, followed by, *I'm a terrible person*, a moment later. Terrible because she wasn't really thinking about Stacey at all. Her mind was on Raj. Raj's hand in hers—the electricity she had felt when their fingers had intertwined.

"Mom, Raj is going to hang out a little bit with me," Gray called out once she'd led him inside.

Mom appeared in the hallway before Gray had a chance to make it to the stairs. Her mom's eyes went straight to Raj. "Hello, Raj," she said.

"Hi, Mrs. Perez."

"Would you guys like something to eat?"

Raj's lips lifted.

"Maybe later," Gray said quickly. "We have stuff to do."

Mom's forehead creased. "What kind of stuff?"

"Don't worry, it's kosher. Come on, Raj." Gray charged up the stairs. She didn't look back until she'd reached the upstairs hallway. She was happy to see Raj right behind her. "I'll teach you in my room." She led him inside and shut the door behind them.

"Tidy," Raj observed.

"Yeah, let's get to work," Gray said, standing in the middle of her room. Raj was still having a look about, and she'd rather he focused on her than her personal effects. "This spell is ridiculously easy. Have you heard of the graphic artist M.C. Escher?"

Raj shook his head then shrugged. "Maybe."

Gray pressed the shift key on her computer to wake it up and bent over the keyboard, typing. She brought up a picture and stepped back so Raj could see. "I'm sure you'll recognize his Drawing Hands."

"Oh yeah, he's done a lot of cool stuff," Raj said when he got a look at the black and white picture of two hands, each drawing the other.

"I like to think of the invisibility spell in opposite terms— as you, the artist, erasing yourself from a 3D canvas." Gray held up her hands. "I have this eraser in my mind and I'm moving it back and forth, picturing my hands disappearing and, as you see, my skin vanishes from sight." Gray held up two seemingly decapitated hands. "Pretty cool. Now you try."

Raj held his hands out and stared at them.

Gray watched his expression turn into one of steady concentration. She half expected him to peel back the layers of his skin right down to his bones. Yeah, a walking skeleton wouldn't go over so well.

"Stop concentrating so hard," Gray said. "Staring at your hands isn't going to make them disappear. I don't even look at myself when I'm going invisible."

Raj closed his eyes as though that would work. When he opened them he looked surprised to see himself fully in the flesh.

"Let's try a different analogy. This is by far my favorite. Imagine yourself as a drawing on an Etch A Sketch, and then shake it back and forth. I find that's the fastest way to make my entire body go invisible all at once. When I fill myself back in, it's more like a wax mold or glass of juice I pour color back into, but we'll get to that part after you accomplish invisibility."

Raj shook his body side to side.

"No, you have to do that in your mind!"

"I'm having trouble concentrating." Raj attempted a laugh. "I feel like my brains have been sucked out."

Gray filled in her hands. If she couldn't teach him to erase himself she wasn't going to get a chance for Lesson 2: Making yourself re-visible. "I'm not surprised. That looked pretty intense back at the hospital."

"This isn't normal. Usually I'm fine." Raj moved to the foot of the bed, the place he'd been standing in Gray's dream. A shiver ran through her and it wasn't half bad.

Gray cleared her throat. "What do you think Stacey's chances are of coming out of that coma?"

Raj pierced her with his gaze. "She's not coming out."

* * *

"He didn't stick around long," Mom said once Raj McKenna was out the front door.

"See? No funny business."

"You could've invited him for dinner."

Gray rolled her eyes. "Yeah, right, like he'd want to have dinner with me and my mom."

"You never know."

Mom ended up ordering Chinese takeout. It was nice, just the two of them sans Charlene's usual dramatics. Gray felt guilty thinking it, but it was the truth.

"What have you and Raj been up to?"

Gray dipped her spring roll in sweet sauce and gave her mom a look.

"Not being nosy," Mom said quickly. "Just making conversation."

"Raj helped me with something today so I'm teaching him one of my spells . . . or trying to teach him, rather. He couldn't grasp it. Not so great on the male ego."

"We all have our areas of strength. Raj may never learn it. There are certainly spells I was never able to master."

Gray chewed and swallowed. "Well, we're going to try it again Saturday morning. Whatever Raj did at the hospital sucked out all his energy."

Mom's chair creaked when she sat up. "What were you doing at the hospital?"

Oops.

Gray looked at her plate. "I went to visit Stacey Morehouse. I thought Raj might be able to help her, or at least get through to her." Even though her head was down she could feel her mother's eyes boring into her.

"Did he get through to her?"

"No, but the most amazing thing happened. Her head opened up and this white light started shining out. I thought for sure they were communicating, but Raj said she wasn't in there." Gray stuffed another spring roll in her mouth.

"That poor girl," Mom said.

"What happened to her?"

"I remember briefly hearing about her car accident. I can't recall much about it. You had just died. I was walking around in a fog at the time that happened."

Gray pushed her bean curds around with her fork. Did she dare say the words? "Do you think Charlene had anything to do with it?"

Silence followed. Gray was afraid she'd angered her mom, but when she glanced up, Mom was studying the wall behind her thoughtfully. "She couldn't have. Her powers are useless against Stacey. I made sure of that months ago."

"What about Ryan?"

"I can hardly imagine Ryan Phillips capable of attempted murder."

Was that Mom's way of saying she could imagine Charlene was? Gray jammed her fork into her bean curd and stuck it in her mouth.

"No, I really don't think she could have," Mom repeated. "Charlene was distraught after she found you—tearing at her hair, screaming. I thought she was going to hurt herself."

That was sorta touching. Crazy, but touching.

"I don't see how she could have managed to do something to Stacey Morehouse's car two days later. Charlene wouldn't leave her room for a week after you died. Now that I think of it, she even refused to see Ryan when he came by to check on her every day that she missed school."

"Well, that's a relief," Gray said, though she wasn't entirely convinced. Weird coincidences were entirely possible, but where there was a witch, there was suspicion. "I'm stuffed," she said after polishing off the last of the noodles from her plate.

"Save it for lunch tomorrow . . ." Mom started to say, then fell silent.

Gray looked down at her leftover bits of mushrooms and bamboo shoots. "This sucks."

"I know, honey. I'm going to fix it as soon as possible and then I'll have both my girls at the same time, all the time."

Right, until Charlene found out about Gray's incident with Blake. Once she did, she might very well kill her. Then again, Gray might have cause to blackmail her sister for life.

Did you do something to the brakes on Stacey Morehouse's car?

Gray wondered if Charlene would really answer that question. She tapped her pen against the open notebook. Gray was seated at the countertop, jotting notes before bed while her mom washed their scanty pile of dishes and moved leftovers to glass containers.

Gray followed her mom's progress then looked down at the notebook once more.

P.S. There was a slight incident involving Blake at school today . . .

Chapter 23

"Excuse me. Um, do you mind moving?"

Raj didn't realize the words were being addressed to him as he leaned against a locker across the hall from Charlene Perez and watched her arms fly around as she spoke to Blake Foster. Blake's jaw appeared wired shut, as though he planned to give Charlene the silent treatment.

"Can you please move over just a little so I can get inside my locker?"

Raj blinked and noticed the petite brunette speaking softly through a mouthful of braces. He moved to the side.

"Thanks," she said and opened her locker.

When the girl left Raj moved back. No sense going through the same conversation with the occupant of neighboring locker 324. Shay was hugging her text and notebook to her chest when she rounded the corner. She stopped beside Raj and followed his gaze across the hall.

"I wonder what she's thinking," Raj said by way of greeting.

Shay's eyes rolled up in her head. "I'm not breaking any vows for you."

"I didn't ask."

"Please, I know what you were hinting at." Shay planted a hand on her hip and looked at Charlene. "I don't need to read minds to guess what's going on. Her sister is no doubt messing things up with Blake. Blake is getting tired of the rollercoaster ride they're taking him on and is pulling away. Now Charlene is afraid she's going to lose him—thus the transparent black top and lace bra underneath. I wouldn't be surprised if she's sent home to change before the morning's out."

"Hmm," Raj said, rubbing his chin. "And you got all that from body language?"

"Like I said, people are so predictable."

"Nice skill."

"I call it the power of observation. Speaking of which, you've been going around wearing your heart on your sleeve. I hope Graylee Perez isn't taking advantage."

Raj grinned. "If Gray wants to take advantage of me, I don't mind."

"You're impossible, you know. Don't say I didn't warn you."

Blake's jaw had relaxed into a lopsided grin. Whatever Charlene had said had convinced him to follow her toward the set of double doors down the hall.

"What's going on?" Max Curry asked as he walked up. His eyes followed Shay's playful punch to Raj's shoulder.

Shay's smile brightened when she looked at Max. "Raj is on stakeout."

"Stakeout?"

Raj turned his head at the same time as Shay to the spot Charlene had occupied a moment earlier. She was gone now.

"Charlene Perez," Shay clarified.

"Excuse me," Raj said.

Just a quick peek, he told himself. He wasn't going to be late to first period.

Raj paused in the alcove outside the double doors and looked into the student parking lot. Charlene and Blake were getting inside her car. There you had it—they were taking off. Blowing off school. Not that Raj blamed them. He might as well turn around and head to first period.

But the car never rumbled to life. A minute later it was still parked.

Didn't matter. There was nothing to learn from Charlene in a parked car with Blake. It wasn't like she'd do any nefarious plotting with Blake the Mortal Jock. Raj looked sideways at the double doors. If he hurried, he could get to class just as the last bell was chiming.

He stepped toward the parking lot instead.

"Time for a little Etch-A-Sketch-erasing action," Raj said under his breath. He was a good visualizer. A bloody brilliant visualizer according to the personal coach his mom had hired once she realized he knew more magic than all the peer leaders at Gathering combined.

Just do it. Real quick.

Particles of Raj briefly floated in the air like specks of dust before disappearing altogether.

Awesome!

So he hadn't gone all at once, but he'd get there.

Raj took his first step forward, the familiar feeling of unsteadiness returning when he looked down and saw no foot. He couldn't wait to show Gray on Saturday morning. Maybe he'd knock at her door `a la invisible mode. Then again, Mrs. Perez might answer, and on the other hand, if Raj already knew the spell there'd be no reason for him to stick around as Gray gave him his tutorial before she dashed off on whatever mission she had planned.

The corner of Raj's lips turned down. He continued walking toward the Beetle. The driver and passenger seats were empty. As Raj stepped closer, he saw Charlene and Blake sucking face in the back seat.

Raj grabbed his left wrist—the fist that wanted to slam right through the window. *It's not Gray*, he reminded himself. *Not Gray. Not Gray.*

Charlene could make out with the entire basketball team for all he cared. Still, the sight was disturbing. Raj moved away.

Now he really was going to be late.

Gray was right. The first opportunity he had, he used the spell to play Peeping Tom. But he had done it for her. Lately he felt like everything he did was for her.

* * *

Raj was deciding between a frozen pita pocket, canned spaghetti, or starvation when there was a knock at the door. Both he and his father stared at one another.

"Go on and answer it," his dad said.

No one, besides religious crusaders and solicitors, ever knocked on their door, but when Raj opened up he was dumbfounded to find Gray's mother, Mrs. Perez, standing outside.

"Good evening, Raj," Mrs. Perez said. After greeting him she stared into the house.

His father's footsteps filled the narrow hallway as he advanced toward the open door. The smell of smoke moved with him. Raj was used to it, but with the fresh air hitting his face it suddenly felt overpowering in his nostrils.

Mrs. Perez shifted her gaze to his dad. "Hello, Richard," she said in an easy voice.

"Marney." He nodded. "How have you been?"

"Taking one day at a time."

Raj was grateful that his father was in the security uniform and not his usual white stained cotton T-shirt and worn jeans. Still, he shifted and longed to block himself, his home, and his father from Mrs. Perez's sight.

"I'm actually here to see Raj," Mrs. Perez said.

"Oh? And what do you need from Raj?" His dad took a step closer. Raj inched away.

"I need his help with a rather bothersome migraine I can't seem to shake. I'm afraid it's beyond my abilities and I remember Raj had something of a talent for the healing arts."

It was silent a moment and then from the corner of his eye Raj saw his father's shoulders sag and his face lift into half a grin. "Lord knows he didn't get it from me. Please, come in."

"No!" Raj said. "I find the best warm-up to a migraine disposal spell is breathing in fresh air. Let's take a walk around the block."

Raj's dad frowned. "At this time of night? In this neighborhood?" He glanced at Mrs. Perez.

His dad clearly wasn't using his head. If anyone had the bad idea to attack a witch and a warlock they were in for a world of trouble.

"We'll be fine," Mrs. Perez said before Raj could speak. "But thank you for your concern. Raj?"

Raj came out of his fog. "Right, be back momentarily." He stepped out of the house into the company of Gray's mother.

Their nearest neighbor had toys littering their yard—and not the bright, cheery kind. A wheel was missing from a rusty tricycle turned over on its side. Dolls missing various body parts stuck out of the muddy patches dotting the overgrown yard like quicksand. The next yard wasn't much better, with paint peeling from old lawn furniture and chipped potted plants that had toppled over. It looked more like an abandoned neighborhood in Chernobyl.

Raj walked briskly. Mrs. Perez matched his pace down the street, not that the scenery improved further down. Even if he hadn't read her aura already, Raj would have known the woman didn't have a migraine. It wasn't as though she'd come to his part of town if she did. Mrs. Perez had to have access to her own treasure trove of potions.

So what was this? Come to warn him away from her daughter? Of course Gray's mom would see Raj as riffraff not even fit for friendship with a member of her picture-perfect family. Okay, to be fair, the Perez family had problems, too. Nothing like what Raj had to deal with, though. At least Mrs. Perez cared about her girls. Hell, she'd gone to untold lengths to bring one back from the dead. Would Raj's own mother even visit his grave if he died?

"Gray told me she confided in you."

Raj waited for the shoe to drop even though he hadn't picked up on any hostile energy radiating off Mrs. Perez. For all he knew she had placed herself under a masking spell. It wasn't as though Mrs. Perez would drive over in the dark to wish Raj good luck in his pursuit of her daughter.

"I appreciate the support you've shown her during this difficult time."

"How'd you do it?" Raj didn't mean to be so abrupt, but he couldn't stop himself.

"I contacted the right entity."

"I can't imagine that came cheap."

The headlights from an approaching car lit Mrs. Perez's face momentarily. Raj saw peace in her expression. There wasn't an ounce of shame or guilt in those eyes. And he couldn't blame her.

The vehicle slowed as it approached them. Raj's jaw tightened then slowly relaxed after it passed.

"I gave up all my powers to get her back."

Raj instantly knew he hadn't misheard Mrs. Perez. What struck him wasn't what she'd confessed, but, like her expression a moment earlier, the complete lack of regret in her voice.

"You gave up your powers for life?" he asked. It was unheard of. A witch without power was like a whale without a tail.

"For life," Mrs. Perez confirmed in a serene voice.

Raj stared sideways at her. "Why are you telling me this?"

"I can't protect her, but you can."

"Why would you think that?"

Mrs. Perez smiled. "Because you like her."

Raj shrugged.

Mrs. Perez's grin widened as though she could see right through him, even though she was now as powerless as any non-gifted person. "I want to ask a favor of you, Raj. I want you to look out for Gray—protect her. As soon as I get word from my contact I must go. I might not get the opportunity to tell Gray. Do you understand what I'm saying?" Mrs. Perez stopped suddenly and looked at him as though possessed. "I might not be around to watch out for her."

"I understand," Raj said. He turned away, afraid Mrs. Perez would once more use her powers as an observant mother to see he not only understood, he cared more than he wanted to admit. His feelings were a personal matter, not something to be discussed with Gray's mother. Still, he wanted to reassure her. She'd gone to the trouble to come to him for help. Crazier still, she trusted him.

Raj led Mrs. Perez around the block and walked her to her car. Without her powers she suddenly seemed more vulnerable.

As Mrs. Perez fished inside her purse for her key, Raj lifted the locks on her car. She shot him a look that made him feel at once abashed. "Sorry, habit," he mumbled.

As she reached for the handle, Raj called out, "Mrs. Perez."
She waited.
"I'll do everything I can for Gray."

Chapter 24

Gray got up at seven on Saturday. When you knew you wouldn't be around the next day, it was highly motivating to get a crack on the day you did have.

As soon as Gray's feet touched the floor, she snapped her fingers for her worn jeans and favorite T-shirt, but nothing happened. She looked down. Still wearing the negligee. Okay. Gray snapped again for a pair of ripped jeans with fun fabric patches sewn in, but again she stood in the slip.

"Now what the heck?" she said, storming to her room.

Gray threw open her closet door and gasped. Empty.

She ran to her dresser and began opening drawers. Empty. Empty. Empty!

Gray raced back into Charlene's room and practically tore the cover off their communication notebook when she ripped it open.

Charlene had left her a simple message: *Maybe it's time you remembered you're supposed to be me and that means dressing and acting appropriately.*

Gray chucked the notebook across the room. It smacked the wall and dropped to the ground. "You are so dead, Charlene!" Gray didn't realize she was shrieking.

Footsteps came racing down the hall. "What's going on?" Mom's eyes widened when she saw Gray yanking clothes out of Charlene's closet. She held up Charlene's favorite pink cashmere sweater and began ripping it down the middle. Halfway down it would no longer tear and Gray screamed in frustration.

"Gray!" her mother shouted. "What are you doing?"

Gray threw the sweater down and sunk to the floor. She put her head into her knees and sobbed. "She took all my clothes. They're all gone."

"What?"

"My closet, my dresser—Charlene emptied everything."

Mom straightened up. "Well, then she can replace it all."

Gray sniffed.

"Come on."

"What?"

"Get up. We're going to breakfast."

"I can't go to breakfast. Raj is coming over this morning."

Mom didn't even blink. "Then I think you better get dressed."

"In what?" Gray cried out. "It's bad enough wearing Barbie prep wear to school. Now I have to spend my Saturday in the Clueless skirt. I refuse!"

Mom was trying not to smile.

"What?"

"As much as you hate the skirts, I think it would be more appropriate than the teddy."

Gray looked down and then back up at her mom. Maybe she was going crazy, because in the next instant she burst into hysterics. She fell back on the floor holding her stomach. Mom laughed above her. And just as suddenly Gray was crying again.

"Come on," Mom said. "Up with you." She extended a hand and pulled Gray to her feet. "We can go shopping later."

"Shopping," Gray said suddenly. "Good idea." *More like good excuse while she went out of town with Nolan soliciting help from Brock.* "Nolan and I were planning on hanging out at the mall today, anyway."

"Since when do you hang out at the mall?" Her mom looked her over.

Gray's anger momentarily subsided to be replaced by guilt and bashfulness, the bashfulness due to the slip better suited to a Frederick's of Hollywood catalogue model. A skirt wasn't sounding so bad anymore. Gray glanced at the garments dumped on the floor and snapped into the ruffled skirt. It was the closest to her sense of style. Did Charlene own leggings? Gray would have to be able to picture them to get them to snap on. She couldn't just go making stuff up.

The appearance of Gray in clothes only distracted her mom for a moment. "That's better. So today you're spending time with Raj and then Nolan?"

"Yeah."

Mom tilted her head to one side and looked at Gray sideways. "Honey, I think you're going to have to make up your mind and choose one of these guys."

Gray's hands dropped to either side. "What? It's not like I'm going out with either of them."

"Yes, but that's what they're hoping for and isn't that what you want: to go out with one of them?"

Gray studied the carpet. "I don't know."

"Well, I think they're both nice boys. You should go with your gut."

"Don't you mean with my heart?"

"No," her mom said, smiling wistfully. "Go with the gut."

That made sense in a way. Gut instincts were supposed to be the most trustworthy and it was in her gut where she felt the butterflies. The heart had its purpose as a blood-pumping muscle, but love . . . love blossomed and sparked through the body—originating from the gut.

How romantic. *I love you with all my gut.* Gray stifled a giggle.

"When's Raj coming over?"

Gray glanced at Charlene's alarm clock. "I told him to come at eight."

"On a Saturday?"

"Well, Nolan's coming around ten."

Mom clucked. "Cutting it close, aren't you?"

"It's not like I want to be juggling two boys. I have enough problems, thank you very much. But Nolan already made these plans with me. And Raj . . ." Gray lifted her shoulders. "I owe him a spell."

Mom headed to the door. "How about I get muffins and mochas from the Muffin Man? I'm sure Raj would appreciate a little pick-me-up this early on the weekend."

Gray wrinkled her nose. "He'll be here any moment. You're okay leaving me alone with a boy?"

"I trust Raj."

"If you say so."

Okay, weird. So obviously Charlene wasn't a virgin any longer (and who knew how many guys she'd slept with) and Gray was the same age as her—exactly the same age, in fact—but sometimes she felt like a younger sister: innocent and inexperienced when it came to the world of boys.

Gray's mom hadn't been gone five minutes when Raj knocked. She was happy to let him inside—the house felt eerily quiet, like that first morning she woke up from death.

Raj wore a snug burgundy ribbed sweater over black jeans. Gray felt like a guy copping a peek at a chick's chest. She looked away quickly and invited him inside.

Raj looked around. "Where's your mother?"

Gray rolled her eyes. "She thought we might like muffins and mochas. She'll be back soon."

Raj's eyes practically lit up upon hearing the words "muffins and mochas."

"Come on," Gray said. "We don't have much time." She started up the stairs, expecting he'd follow.

"Are you undercover today?"

Gray squinted at Raj. "What? Oh, right," she said, following the direction of his eyes. "The skirt. Not really. Charlene destroyed all my clothes. It was this or a silk chemise."

"She did what?"

The moment they entered her room, Gray began pulling open dresser drawers. She lifted her finger and the closet door sprung open, revealing empty hangers and a shoe rack without a single pair of shoes.

Raj looked around with a sort of stunned expression on his face, though nothing compared to the way her own eyes had bugged out earlier when she tried to snap herself into a pair of jeans and T-shirt and nothing had happened.

Gray wasn't angry anymore. She was beyond angry. Just wait till Charlene woke up the next day with a nose ring or "Blake's a dick" tattooed across her arm. Gray could make threats, too. She could threaten to break up with Blake and start going out with pimple-faced Bobby Phelps. If Charlene wanted to take away her clothes, Gray could show up to school naked. It wasn't like anyone would know it was her, except Raj, Nolan, Ryan, Shay, and Max.

Gray's cheeks heated, but luckily Raj's attention was diverted by the clothing raid that had taken place inside her room.

"What's in the drawer?" Raj nodded toward the one drawer Gray had kept closed.

She rolled her eyes. "Charlene left me my socks and underwear. Apparently she'd rather not share those items even though this is technically her body."

Raj stared at the drawer a moment longer. "Why would she do this?"

"Probably 'cause I slapped her boyfriend upside the head." Gray's lips quivered when she caught Raj's blossoming smile. Finally she couldn't hold it in any longer and burst into peals of laughter.

Raj laughed beside her. "I'm sure he deserved it."

"Oh, he did."

Raj's lingering smile sent shivers straight down to Gray's toes. She moved away and looked at her digital alarm clock. "Right," she said. "So are you feeling all rested, refreshed, and ready to go invisible?"

Raj frowned. "I can't concentrate in here. There's too much bad energy lingering."

"Oh, right, Charlene," Gray said, rolling her eyes skyward. "We'll go outside. Obviously her room would be a thousand times worse."

* * *

"We should probably stand behind the tree so we don't freak my neighbors out," Gray said once they stepped into the front yard. "Unless you know how to do a mind erase?"

"Nope," Raj said. "Not one of the tricks I have up my sleeve."

"Dang, I haven't met anyone who can do one of those."

"Or maybe you just don't remember."

Gray tilted her head to look at Raj and then laughed.

Raj clapped his hands together and rubbed them. "All right, so operation Etch A Sketch." He jerked his head side to side. "Did I do it? Am I invisible?"

Clearly, from his smile, he knew he wasn't.

"Maybe we should start with an object. Hand me your lighter."

Raj just looked at Gray's outstretched hand.

"Give it."

He sighed and slowly pulled the Zippo out of his pocket. Gray nabbed it from him then held the lighter in front of her face. "Now you see it . . . now you don't. Now you see it again. You try."

Raj held his hand out for the return of his lighter. Gray glanced at the Zippo between her fingers and smiled. "Let's give you a little incentive. I'll keep your lighter until you can make it go invisible."

"Hand it over," Raj said.

"Giving up already?" Gray tossed the lighter in the air and reached out her hand to catch it. When it landed in her palm, a dull ache traveled up her arm and burned at her shoulder. The Zippo felt as though it was about to scorch the skin around her palm even though the cap was snapped shut. She handed it back to Raj. "Take it."

"What's the matter?" Raj asked, studying her face.

Gray was frowning. "You shouldn't be carrying that object around."

Raj flicked it open and closed. "Why not?"

Gray kept frowning, trying to read the expression on his face. A dull throb still lingered in her arm as though it had been used to cushion a blow to the pavement.

Raj took a step closer. His face was contorted, angry. "Afraid I'll burn down another house?"

"I'm afraid that thing is hurting you!" Gray hadn't meant to yell.

Raj's eyes widened briefly and then his entire face dropped. Even his cheeks seemed to sink into his face.

Gray didn't like where this was going. "Keep the damn thing for all I care." She avoided eye contact as she bit out the words. "Let's just get back to the spell before my mom returns and I have to go. I thought you wanted to be invisible."

"I do," Raj replied calmly.

"Then concentrate! You have to want it."

Raj squeezed his eyes shut. Gray's breath caught. An image sprang into her mind of Raj holding her, kissing her like mad. She took a step back, but the image followed her. His hands caressed her shoulders, moving down her back. She tilted her head, exposing her neck to a trail of kisses, and then opened her lips to allow Raj's tongue inside her mouth.

Gray sucked in a quick breath, hoping the projection hadn't reached Raj. Her heart was hammering wildly inside her chest. It felt like a thousand drumbeats pulsing in front of a blazing bonfire.

Raj opened his eyes and stared directly at her.

Gray felt the blush high in her cheekbones. She pressed her lips together and shrugged. Raj's face darkened and he took a step toward her.

"What are you doing?" she asked in alarm. "Are you inside my head?"

"No," he said. "You're inside mine."

Gray felt her cheeks turn to flames. "Stop thinking those thoughts."

"Maybe you should get out of my head."

"I can't." Gray choked. She began to flail around and gasp for air. If she died suddenly would Charlene die, too? It wasn't entirely out of the question to drop dead in her front yard. It had happened to Gray in her own bedroom.

This time there was someone around to resuscitate her. Was that why Raj's lips were over hers?

Gray grabbed Raj by the shirt and kissed him roughly back. Where did that come from? Maybe Charlene's body instinctively knew what to do because it certainly couldn't be Gray wrapping her hands around the back of Raj's neck and pulling him closer.

It wasn't helping matters that Raj returned her kisses and caresses as though without them he'd perish.

He backed her up against a tree and kissed her roughly. Gray closed her eyes, seeing sparks light up all around them. She could feel them erupting all through her body. It was the most alive she'd felt since returning from the dead.

It was the most alive she'd felt ever.

Angry tires screeched and then sped up. Gray's eyes flew open, but all she saw was an empty road.

Gray opened her eyes and came back to earth. She took her arms off Raj and moved aside. "You have to go!"

Raj's face fell. "Why?"

"You just do."

"But what about the muffins?"

"You can't be here!" Gray cried. "Please."

The skin around Raj's eyes wrinkled. "Gray, I didn't mean to . . ."

"Just go," Gray said. "I'll call you later."

* * *

Gray paced the driveway. She'd eaten two muffins without really tasting them and become edgier the later it got. It was now ten forty-five. She and Nolan needed to get on the road right away if they were to have any chance of seeing this warlock and getting back by dinner.

On one hand, she'd rather be with Raj; on the other, she needed her body and twenty-four-hour access to it. How was she supposed to even entertain the idea of dating a guy when she went off to la-la land every other day?

Gray walked through the grass to what she now thought of as The Kissing Tree and leaned against it. She closed her eyes. Focus, Gray. Not the time to daydream about mind-blowing kisses.

Why was Nolan taking so long?

Finally, Gray couldn't take it any longer and went inside to call him. "Hi, Mrs. Knapp? This is . . . Charlene Perez. Is Nolan there?"

"Oh, Charlene." Mrs. Knapp's voice rose. "How are you, my dear? We miss seeing you at Gathering."

"Um, thanks."

"Let me see. Nolan left early this morning. I know he had a lot of homework to do at the library. Those teachers are always making everything due at the same time. I'm sure you know how it is?"

"Yeah," Gray answered feebly. *Where the hell was Nolan?* "Well, thanks for checking, Mrs. Knapp. Can you let him know I called?"

"Certainly, dear."

* * *

Once Gray accepted the fact that Nolan had stood her up, she drove to the hospital to visit Stacey.

Why Gray felt this sudden empathy for Stacey Morehouse was beyond her. Perhaps their balancing act on the tightrope between life and death was their shared bond. What had Stacey's last moments of consciousness been like? What could she tell Gray if she were to suddenly awaken?

When Gray walked into her room, a physical therapist was in the middle of massaging Stacey's arm. "That a girl," the therapist said. "We want you to be nice and strong when you wake up." She moved to her other side. "Your father tells me you play softball every spring, and honey, spring's coming."

Gray shut her eyes gently. The therapist's soothing voice continued. She could picture everything the woman did just by her descriptions.

"Now we're going to move these long, lovely legs of yours. Think how wonderful it'll be to walk again."

Gray tried to imagine that in addition to being invisible, she was weightless. She tried to imaging floating away from the room, away from the voice, the pain. Was that what a coma was like? Or was it like the days she didn't exist—when even the comforting voices of loved ones couldn't reach her?

She no longer had a body to return to. This replica of herself might appear similar, but it wasn't hers. It didn't bear the scar below her left knee when she'd fallen out of a tree at age ten just before her father died. He'd fussed over the wound and said he'd fix it. Gray had known he had the power to make it disappear forever. "No, Daddy, leave it," she'd said.

"Why, baby?"

"Because it is a part of me now."

He'd kissed her head gently and said, "You are wise beyond your years, Gray girl."

Gray opened her eyes and tears spilled out. They appeared on the floor in wet splashes—transparent yet totally visible.

Gray looked at Stacey lying unconscious on the bed. She was breathing. She still had a chance.

How long had Gray been lying in her bed—a lifeless corpse? Nearly four hours before her sister found her.

Gray choked back a sob.

The therapist stilled and leaned over Stacey. The room had gone too silent for Gray to risk walking out, but she couldn't help it. She rushed out of the room and down the hallway as though spirits were after her. She would have left altogether if she hadn't heard the receptionist speak as she passed.

"Good afternoon, Mr. Morehouse. I'll page Dr. Conway and let him know you're in Stacey's room."

Gray pivoted and followed on the heels of Stacey's father.

"Hello, Mr. Morehouse, we just finished Stacey's exercises," the therapist said when he walked in.

So far all Gray had seen of Stacey's father was his back. He wore no overcoat, only a dark suit jacket that matched his pants. "How is she today?" Mr. Morehouse's tone was businesslike—lawyerly.

"Her body is healthy and strong," the therapist answered. "It won't take her long to regain her full strength once she wakes up."

Gray wondered how much Mr. Morehouse paid the therapist to say that. Like the patchwork quilt and curtains, the therapist didn't look hospital issued.

He nodded. "Thank you, Shannon. You may go now."

"Sir . . . I thought I heard your daughter sob earlier."

"When?"

"Not more than five minutes ago. Right before you came in."

Mr. Morehouse took two large steps to the side of the hospital bed. "Stacey? Baby girl?"

Oh, god, Gray was going to hell. Except there was no heaven, which meant there wasn't a hell, either, so maybe she was okay.

When there was no answer or movement, the therapist grimaced. "I'm so sorry, Mr. Morehouse. I shouldn't have mentioned anything."

"No, you were right to. Stacey's a fighter. I know she's trying to come back to me, and probably frustrated as hell. But she'll make it. All in good time. We won't rush her."

The therapist nodded. "I'll leave you two alone." Gray didn't get a chance to intrude further on Mr. Morehouse's private moment when the doctor walked in.

"Hello, Mr. Morehouse," the doctor said, sounding as brisk and businesslike as the attorney.

"Dr. Conway."

Gray quickly moved to the side before Mr. Morehouse had a chance to run into her.

"Level with me, Doctor. How is Stacey doing?"

The doctor took a stance several feet from the bed. "If I may say so, Mr. Morehouse, at this point we aren't prolonging life. We're prolonging death."

Mr. Morehouse was bent over the side of his daughter's bed. After the doctor spoke, his spine straightened. He looked like a tree that had been momentarily blown over in the wind, only to stretch to its original grandeur. It was easy to see where Stacey's height came from. And when Mr. Morehouse spoke, Gray understood how the man had won every court case to come before him. "As long as my daughter has a breath in her body you will keep her alive. Do you understand, Doctor?"

* * *

Gray ought to use the Mr. Morehouse voice with Nolan when she finally tracked down the jerk. No show. No call. No nothing. What kind of guy did that?

"Hello, Mrs. Knapp. This is Charlene Perez again—just wondering if Nolan returned home."

"Oh, dear, yes, he did, but then he left again."

Gray waited for more, but apparently that was all his mother was going to say.

It was too late anyway, nearly three o'clock. Gray had already wasted one of her precious days waiting around for

Nolan. What had happened to that boy and why was there an uneasy feeling in the pit of her stomach? That usually didn't bode well.

Gray stomped into Charlene's room. The pink cashmere sweater still lay in a heap on the floor. Hmm, what would enrage Charlene the most: leaving it on the floor for her to find or putting it away and having it appear on her body ripped when she snapped her fingers?

Gray snatched it off the ground and tossed it into Charlene's closet. Then she opened The Book of Charlene, prepared to write something nasty. Nah, she had a better idea.

Gray grasped as much hair as she could get inside her hand, pulled it over her shoulder, took the scissors, and cut through the chunk in one long snip.

She swore she could hear her sister's scream the next morning.

Chapter 25

N*o calling Gray*, Raj told himself for the tenth time since the soul-searing kiss she'd pressed into his lips earlier that morning.

Fine, but he had to do something.

Raj drove to the edge of town and parked on the street outside of Adrian's business. He pulled out his lighter and snapped it open and shut, staring at the building for what felt like an eternity before getting out. Raj hadn't been by in two months. Finally, he pushed open his car door and stepped to the pavement.

Adrian's place didn't have an awning like the surrounding shops, but an Old English– style sign hanging from a hook against the building.

Hedrick the Healer

The bell over the door jingled when Raj entered. "Adrian, you here?"

"In back."

"Are you with someone?"

"Not for another hour."

Raj followed Adrian's voice into the back room. Adrian closed a text as Raj walked in and shoved it into an open space on his bookshelf. "I knew you'd be back. Great timing, too. I just let your replacement go."

"Not up to par?"

"He made a man grow hair out of his nose rather than on his head."

Raj did a quick scan of the packed bookshelves before resting his eyes on Adrian. "Adding cosmetic enhancements to the menu?"

"Baldness is an unfortunate condition." Adrian's lips curled back as he ran a hand through his own thick locks. "I hope you're not rusty, McKenna, because I'm backlogged."

"Actually, I'm here for a favor."

"Favor," Adrian repeated with a sneer, as though the word was worse than baldness.

"Do you still have your primordial texts?"

"I keep everything. What are you looking for?"

"Body transfers."

Adrian smirked. "Getting a little too big for your britches, are you? Why would you want to look up a thing like that?"

"For a friend."

"Raj, buddy, you have talent, but stay away from the body transfers. That sort of thing generally doesn't go well."

Raj rubbed his hand over the lump the Zippo made in his jeans pocket. "I'll give your bald man hair . . . on his head."

"I have three more screw-ups that need fixing."

"Done."

"And a long wait-list."

Raj sighed. "Book them after school."

Adrian clapped his hands together. "We're back in business!" He smacked Raj on the shoulder. "Don't worry about your friend. Under my direction you'll get them their thinner body or younger exterior or whatever enhancement their heart desires."

Again Raj sighed.

The bell on the front door clanked abruptly. "Adrian!"

Adrian's grin widened as he pushed through the curtain to the main chamber. "Coming."

Raj followed behind Adrian. A hunched older woman walked forward. With her babushka tied under her chin she looked like one of the matchmakers from *Fiddler on the Roof*. She set an old Superman lunch pail and soup thermos in the center of the round table. "Lunch."

If this was Adrian's mom, just how old was Adrian?

"Thanks, Nan."

Ah.

After Raj had finished staring at the beat-up lunch box he noticed Adrian's grandmother staring at him. "Hi," he said.

She pursed her lips. "You need to stop making mistakes— very bad for business."

Adrian laughed. "That was Marcus, Nan. This is Raj. Raj never screws up."

Her face relaxed . . . slightly. "I have boils."

"Boils, please!" Adrian said. "Boils make Raj yawn." Adrian escorted his grandmother to the front door. "Thank you for the lunch, Nan. I'll put you at the top of the client list."

His grandmother placed a hand on Adrian's cheek. "Don't overwork yourself."

"I won't."

"And eat your food."

"Eat your food," Adrian repeated with a snort after the old woman had left. "As if I could resist Nan's cooking."

Raj stared at the thermos. Even Adrian had family who cared whether or not he was fed. "Are you and your grandmother close?"

"Hey, we're not here to talk about my Nan." Adrian stepped behind the curtain. "I'll be right back. Don't touch my lunch."

When Adrian returned he dropped a tome that had to weigh at least ten pounds into Raj's hands. "Take a look at this one—body transfers: the hardcore stuff. Basics bore me."

Raj cracked the book open and looked directly back up. "This isn't in English." Adrian already had his lunch pail open and had arranged smaller containers around him with the tops off: a pickled beet salad, long bun, and some kind of gelatin substance with apricots and cream.

Adrian spun the lid off his thermos. Steam rose from the enclosed stew and tickled Raj's nostrils. His thoughts darted from Gray to the muffins he never got to eat back to the book in his hands.

Adrian lifted his nose. "You don't know Latin?"

"Should I?"

"All witches and warlocks ought to know Latin."

"I don't."

Adrian sighed. "Warlocks today." He bit into the roll and began chewing.

Raj tucked the text under his arm and headed for the door. "Enjoy your lunch. I'll catch up with you later."

"You don't really believe I'm going to let you leave with that, do you?"

"Yeah, it's going to take me hours to translate."

"Leave it," Adrian said. "I'll do the translating. Just make sure you're here at three sharp Monday. At the end of the week we'll discuss your friend."

Raj gripped the volume. "We may not have a week."

Adrian stopped chewing. "Not my problem."

Raj dumped the book on the table and walked out. He'd just find someone else then. He didn't have time for Adrian's shenanigans. Despite what the man thought, there were other warlocks who could perform body transfers—and with far less fanfare.

* * *

That night, after his dad left for work, Raj slipped into his mother's house. Mom and Aahana were now living on the south side of town in a wide ranch home. The floors and countertops were clean. He noticed a few familiar furnishings and décor. Raj tiptoed into the kitchen and opened the fridge. Light spilled onto the linoleum floor, but not on him. He was invisible.

Raj carefully pulled out the glass Tupperware containers and set them down gently on the countertop. He found a fork and stuck it into the creamed spinach. Warming the food was too risky. Raj had never cared for cold food in the past, but tonight it tasted wonderful. He opened a second Tupperware and began eating couscous straight from the container.

The first door he walked past was his mother's. She'd left it wide open. Further down the hall, Raj came to a closed door with a monkey sign reading, Keep Out. Raj smiled and turned the doorknob gently.

Seeing in the dark was a nice complement to invisibility. Raj stopped several feet from Aahana's bed. His sister looked like a sleeping angel. He didn't linger long—didn't want to be creepy, but the thought of returning to the dump across town stopped him from crossing the threshold.

Raj lowered himself to the plush floor and rested his back against the wall. He sighed.

There was a movement from the bed. A second later, Aahana's head popped up. Her face wrinkled. "Raj?"

"Don't freak, okay? I'm invisible."

Aahana stood on her knees and began looking around the room. "Don't freak? That's awesome. You have to teach me. Where are you?"

"Here," Raj said, appearing a few feet away from Aahana's bed.

"No way!"

"Shhh."

"Aahana!" their mother yelled from down the hall.

Raj went invisible right before his mother walked through the door. Aahana, who had been staring at him, quickly moved her eyes to her mother. Raj saw that Mom's own eyes were narrowed. "Who are you talking to?"

Aahana screwed up her face. "I thought I told you to knock before coming in here."

"Answer the question, Aahana."

Aahana rolled her eyes. "I'm practicing for theater tryouts. I've decided I want to be an actress."

Raj had to bite his lip to keep from laughing, especially at the look of horror that crossed his mother's face. Still, the woman wasn't entirely gullible. She sniffed the air. "What's that smell?"

Raj took a step back.

"You don't think I could make it in Bollywood? Why not?"

At least that captured Mom's attention once more. She straightened. "You come from a long line of healers, Aahana. Theater and sports are activities better left to the ungifted– it would be a waste of your talents."

Aahana's lip turned over and Raj couldn't be sure if her pout was more than an act. "I would have thought being a witch meant having fun."

Their mother's entire upper body stiffened. "You know I do not like this word."

"Fun or witch? Fine, healer, whatever," Aahana said when Mom didn't answer. "Can you please go now?"

"Aahana . . ."

"I said please!"

After their mother's footsteps receded, Raj appeared again. He glanced at the crack in the bedroom door and shut it all the way. It wasn't as though it'd do any good to lock it.

Aahana huffed. "As you can see, nothing's changed."

Raj's lips turned down. "Did you really want to try out for the school play?"

"No, but what if I did? She's as bad as my friend Chung-Hee's mother, who says she has to be a doctor when she grows up. I wish I could live with you and Dad."

"Trust me, you're better off with Mom."

Aahana sat back on the heels of her feet. "Raj? Does Dad ever talk about what happened?"

"He doesn't talk about much of anything. Like you said, some things don't change." Raj ran a hand through his hair. "Speaking of which, I better head home. I didn't mean to startle you—just wanted to see you, you know?" Raj started for the door.

"Wait!" Aahana's eyes widened. "Don't go," she said softly.

"I can't stay."

"I know! I have a sleeping bag you can borrow." Aahana got out of bed and went to her closet.

Raj watched as Aahana rolled the sleeping bag open beside her bed. "You know Mom would have a fit if she found out."

Aahana grinned. "Easy. I'll perform a sleeping spell on her."

"You know she can always tell when a spell's been cast over her. Anyway, you shouldn't do that to Mom."

"Fine then, I can keep my voice down."

"Can you now?" Raj asked, grinning.

Aahana answered by drawing a finger across her lips.

* * *

All was quiet on Gray's street Sunday morning. No one had ventured from their cozy homes yet. It was too early. Raj had snuck out of Aahana's room at six, rolling the sleeping bag into a ball before tiptoeing out. It was seven fifteen now. He'd gotten a black coffee to go at the shack up the road as soon as they opened.

The Perez house was several houses up. Raj didn't expect any activity for at least another couple hours, but just in case . . .

He flipped through his mother's copy of *The Art of Healing the Misplaced Soul*. He'd nabbed it off her bookshelf on his way out. It was a long shot, but worth a try. At seven thirty a woman jogged past, the wires of her earbuds hanging past her neck.

By nine forty, Raj had read halfway through his mother's book and, as he'd suspected, it contained nothing of use in regards to body transfers. He drank down the last of the coffee, cold now, and looked up in time to see Charlene walking out to her car. Raj tossed the book on the passenger seat.

He had to be careful to follow Charlene at a safe distance, especially as there wasn't much traffic at this time. It would have been a lot easier if he made the car invisible, but that was asking for bad karma. Wouldn't it be swell if someone rear-ended him?

Raj expected Charlene to make for Ryan Phillips's house. What he didn't expect was for Charlene to drive up to the blue brick building where Gatherings were held. Gray had told him Charlene was no longer an active member of the coven.

Raj parked in the farthest corner then proceeded to pace in front of his car.

Shay, if you're in there, please meet me outside in the parking lot.

Raj watched as more cars arrived and parked in front of the building. As soon as Shay came out the front doors, Raj started toward her.

"Raj? What are you doing here?" They stopped a foot apart. Shay's lips turned down. "Oh, no."

"What?"

"You have a favor to ask me."

"Please, just take a quick peek inside her head."

"Raj . . ."

Raj stepped closer. "She's already responsible for one girl's death."

"Stacey isn't dead."

"She's worse than dead."

Shay glanced over her shoulder. "I need to get back inside."

Raj put a hand on her shoulder as Shay turned to go. "You don't have to tell me anything—just make sure she doesn't plan on hurting Gray."

Shay's face was unreadable. "If Charlene truly wishes another witch harm then it is my duty to report her." Before Raj could thank her, Shay's face tightened. "Then again, Gray is supposed to be dead. No one on the council knows she's alive. On the other hand, Gray didn't do anything wrong—her mother did." Shay looked into the distance then glanced at Raj. "I'm not making any promises."

Raj thanked her even though there might not be reason to. He waited two hours in the parking lot for her reemergence. In that time he finished the rest of *The Art of Healing the Misplaced Soul*. While the text offered nothing in the way of instruction on body transfers, the information could come in handy should someone ever require his assistance banishing unwanted spirits or performing a full-on exorcism.

When the first members of the coven began exiting the building, Raj made himself invisible. He moved to the walkway just outside the building. There was no reason to hang back when no one could see him. Shay, no doubt, would be one of the last to leave. She always held back to help with chair-stacking spells and other clean-up.

Raj flicked his lighter open and closed. A man passing by glanced his way, an expression of perplexity appearing over his features when he saw nothing. Raj quickly replaced the lighter in his jeans pocket.

Why wait? It wasn't like anyone would see him if he went inside, though it was easy to imagine Shay's ire if he were to try consulting with her in the Gathering's sacred space. It wasn't as though Raj had been banned or anything. He'd just elected not to attend. He didn't exactly feel welcome any longer.

And speaking of those who chose not to attend, Charlene stepped out of the building . . . arm around Nolan Knapp. Finally, activity of the interesting variety. Raj followed the pair around the building.

"You are so sweet wanting to help me and my sister out," Charlene cooed. "Mom always said you were one of Kent's most gifted warlocks . . . not to mention one of the cutest."

Nolan's chest lifted. The dolt was grinning like a fool. Couldn't he tell Charlene was playing him? Of course not; Nolan Knapp was an idiot. Raj wondered what Gray could possibly see in him.

He's not the one she kissed, he reminded himself.

"So you want to go now?" Nolan asked.

Charlene batted her lashes. "Are you game?"

Nolan's voice lifted an octave. "I'll tell my parents I'm spending the afternoon at the library."

Charlene giggled. "You're so bad. I'll be waiting for you in my car."

Road trip it was then.

* * *

Raj's initial guess, that Charlene was on her way to the city, hadn't panned out. She hadn't taken any of the Seattle exits and now she'd even passed Everett. Cityscapes had turned to open fields and farmland. They were roughly fifty miles into the I-5 headed north.

Canada.

Charlene was making a run for the border.

Raj squeezed his steering wheel. At least the witch was making good time. That hadn't been as helpful when Raj had to pull off for gas and scream back up the highway to catch up to the speeding vehicle.

It looked as though they were going to buzz through Bellingham until Charlene suddenly cranked over and barreled down an exit—no blinker. Raj was following far enough behind to have time to trail after her down the off-ramp.

They ended up in a residential neighborhood, parking on the street outside a small ranch home with hedges and rose bushes lining the walkway up to the front door. Roses shouldn't be in bloom yet, nor lilies, freesias, or dahlias. If Charlene and Nolan were soliciting aid, Raj shouldn't be surprised that they'd gone to a witch.

Nolan was the one who knocked. A large, burly man filled the doorframe. Words were exchanged and then the pair was invited in. Raj didn't have time to hear the exchange. He'd been parking several houses down as Charlene and Nolan made their way up to the house.

Raj was once more invisible. He peeked through the windows. The figures inside looked ghostlike through the sheer, gauzy, lace curtains. Great, probably another warlock with granny issues.

Raj put his ear up to the front door. No sound. He couldn't risk coming in with the entrance leading directly into the living space.

"Thank you for seeing us, Brock," Nolan said after the door opened and he stepped outside with Charlene. Her smile was tight. Maybe that was a good sign?

"Crap!" Charlene said the moment the door closed on them.

Nolan's lips turned down. "Don't worry. We'll figure something out."

"Figure something out—she's trapped inside my body! God, it's like having a Siamese twin stuck to my brain."

Stop walking, Raj silently commanded them. Once they got inside Charlene's car he'd be cut off from their communication. Oh, to have Shay's mind-reading abilities.

"Something needs to be done," Nolan said. "It is your body, after all."

Charlene suddenly stopped and turned slowly toward Nolan. "You're right. It is my body, and if she can be put inside it, she can be taken out."

* * *

Raj pounded on the door of the warlock's home. He nearly fell inside when it flew open.

"Yes?" A burly figure straight out of a fairy tale stood in the doorframe. With his facial hair and long mane, he bore a striking resemblance to Gimli the dwarf warrior in *Lord of the Rings*.

Raj cleared his throat. "I need to know what you just told that couple."

The warlock scratched his beard and looked down at Raj.

"And why should I tell you?"

Raj straightened. "Because a girl's life depends on it."

The warlock glanced over Raj's shoulder. He jutted his chin toward the door. "Hers?"

"No, her sister's."

"The sister anything like that one?"

"Nothing alike . . . except in appearance."

The warlock rolled his head from one shoulder to the next then turned. "Follow me to my living room. Have a seat there."

Raj looked at the antique rocking chair in front of the window. "I'd rather stand."

"Have a seat."

Fine, what choice did he have?

"Name?" the warlock asked.

"Raj."

"Last?"

"McKenna."

"Coven and status?"

What was this? An interview?

"Kent. Inactive." Raj rocked forward. "What is your name?"

The warlock settled onto the middle cushion of the couch in front of him. "Brock."

"Mind telling me what Charlene and Nolan were doing here, Brock?"

Brock folded his hands over his lap and studied Raj a moment. "You're a healer."

Raj suppressed a sigh. "That's right."

"I was never good at the healing arts. I hope you appreciate having the skill."

Brock continued to stare at him so Raj answered, "I do."

"It's a lonely calling—always helping others. One's in danger of neglecting themselves." Brock leaned forward. "Like I told your friends, it's too late for the sister to get her body back. Can't transfer a soul into a decomposed body." He thought a moment. "Well, could in theory, but I doubt she'd want to go around looking like a flesh-eating zombie."

Raj's feet hit the floor. "Now what?"

"You can't stuff two souls inside a body. One of them has to go."

Chapter 26

On Monday morning Gray went straight to the bathroom mirror. Her hair had been trimmed and now landed just above the shoulders. It looked pretty cute—not that she'd get to sport the new look to school.

For once, the communications notebook was blank, but Mom had firm instructions in regards to lengthening her hair before stepping foot in McKinley. Add hair growth, right alongside tanning, to the daily spell regiment.

"I told Charlene the two of you are going to have to learn to get along," Mom said as she walked Gray through the spell.

They'd blessed a bowl of water, snipped a small lock of Gray's hair, and placed it inside the bowl.

Gray had never messed with her hair length so the whole thing was taking a while. Okay, maybe she was taking long on purpose. She was in no rush to get to school any earlier than she had to. Extra time meant possible encounters with Nolan, Blake, Ryan, or all three. The only person she wanted to see was Raj, but as Charlene she had no business being seen with him.

Mom had one of her spell books open to the page on hair growth. "Repeat after me: Long and flowing like a river. Make my hair grow quicker and quicker."

Gray turned her head side to side in front of the mirror. "I like my hair the way it is."

"I like it, too, and you can cut it any way you want once you get your body back, but for now you need to keep it the way Charlene likes."

Ah, yes, the daily reminder that Gray had no rights over the body she was borrowing.

By the time Gray got her hair flowing down her back, she was running seriously late for school. Again, teleportation would have come in handy that morning. The school parking lot was full of cars, vacant of students. Except for Raj McKenna.

He sat waiting on the hood of his car. Raj slipped off as soon as he saw her. "Gray, we need to talk."

Sooner or later Gray was going to have to own up to her part in their kiss, but right now she had graver concerns to contend with, not to mention more immediate ones—like getting to class on time. "Can we talk about this later?" she said as she rushed past Raj. He fell into step beside her. "I'm running late for biology."

"We have bigger problems than biology."

Gray craned her head to look at Raj.

"It's important," he said.

Fifteen minutes later they were seated at their usual table at The Daily Grind. The barista raised her eyebrows when they ordered, but Gray hardly noticed.

"Charlene went to Gathering yesterday."

"Charlene? Gathering?"

Raj pushed his finger into the table. "I followed her there and waited. She came out with Nolan Knapp." Gray was just reaching for her mocha when her hand stilled. Raj looked at the surface of the table as he spoke. "He got into her car and I followed them."

"Where did they go?"

"They visited a warlock named Brock in Bellingham."

Gray forgot to breathe. She nearly gasped for breath a moment later. "That jackass!"

A man glanced up from his newspaper one table over and frowned.

"Nolan was supposed to pick me up Saturday to see that same warlock. The weasel stood me up."

Before Gray could grumble further, Raj cut in. "Is that why you sent me packing Saturday morning? You were meeting up with Nolan later?"

Oops.

He didn't have to give her the face. Gray had real problems on her hands. She straightened in her chair. "Well, he offered to actually introduce me to a warlock who does body transfers, which is more than I can say for you."

Raj's jaw tightened. "I'm trying to protect you."

"I don't need your protection. I need help!" Gray rose from her seat.

"Sit down!"

Did Raj really just issue a command? To her? Gray's nostrils flared. "If you think you can boss me around, McKenna, think again."

"Charlene plans to purge you."

Gray's mouth opened. Her butt hit the chair with a thump. "What?" She blinked several times.

"Shay confirmed it. During Gathering all she could think about was how to extract you from her body for good."

"I thought I told you I didn't want Shay Baxter messing in my affairs."

"What do you have against Shay? She broke a personal oath to take a look inside your sister's head . . . to help *you*."

Now not only was Gray frustrated, but she felt like a jerk on top of everything else. "I'm sorry," she said. "I'm just stressed. I don't know how much time I have left. Do you have any idea how Charlene plans to purge me?"

Raj frowned. "No, but that's because Charlene doesn't have any idea how to do it at this point, which is a good thing."

Gray tapped a finger against the table. She pushed her mocha aside.

"Gray . . . can I ask you a question?" Raj studied her face. "What happened? How did you die?"

"I don't know." Gray shrugged. "Something called SUDS."

"I find that hard to believe. I remember driving myself mad thinking if somehow I could speak to you, you'd be able to tell me what really happened."

"I don't know. One day I went to sleep and the next I woke up and found out I had been dead."

"Think, Gray."

"My mom already had the coven look into it. There were no mystical circumstances surrounding my death."

"They're certain?"

"Yeah."

"So think harder."

Why was he being so hard on her? She'd died, for crying out loud, and now her own sister was trying to purge her from existence. A little compassion please.

"I don't even remember dying!"

"What events do you remember leading up to your death?"

Fine, that wasn't too difficult. In her head that'd only been a week ago.

"Nothing out of the ordinary. I went to school. Came home. Did some homework. Snacked. Hung out in my room. Had dinner . . . God, what a lame last day of my life. It's sad."

Raj rolled his hand in the air impatiently. "Had dinner?" he prompted.

"Then went to bed." Gray shrugged.

"Did you feel okay before you went to bed?"

Gray wrinkled her nose. "No, actually, I felt sick to my stomach."

"What did you have for dinner?"

"Salad, but that's a moot point. I started feeling ill before dinner."

"What else did you eat?"

"I was fine after lunch. Then I came home and ate some chocolates." Gray's eyes widened. *Chocolates that Charlene made.*

"What?" Raj asked.

"I need to go."

Raj stood up after Gray. "What is it? What do you remember?"

"It was Charlene," Gray gasped. "Charlene killed me. She didn't mean to, but she did."

* * *

"Are you sure you don't want me to come with you?" Raj asked after he pulled up next to Gray's car in McKinley's parking lot.

Gray stared forward. School was still in session. It seemed so insignificant compared to everything she'd been through. Charlene had tried to kill Stacey—twice. She'd succeeded in killing Gray instead and now she was trying deliberately to purge her from existence forever.

"I want to talk to my mom alone."

Raj nodded.

Gray felt a sudden urge to reach for his hand, to squeeze it, a human connection. How long would she have that? "Can we meet up later?"

Raj swallowed. "Yeah, of course, but first I'm going to see Adrian."

"Adrian," Gray repeated blankly, as though she'd never heard the name before. Then she snapped out of it. "I'll go with you."

Raj's shoulders lifted and dropped. "You should talk to your mom. Let me deal with Adrian. If I do some work for him he'll play ball."

"Fine." Gray made like she was going to exit the car then leaned over the seat and kissed Raj on the lips. Then, in a flash, she got out of his car and headed home.

"Mom!" she cried as soon as she entered her house. "Mom!" Gray rushed into the kitchen, the scene of the crime. No sooner had she stepped in, she froze. There was a note on the countertop. Her heart began that wild beat that made her feel halfway between a stroke and fainting episode. She leaned over the counter, her hair falling over her shoulders as she did so.

Girls:
Got the call.
Hope to be back soon.
Love you both.
Mom

That was good news, wasn't it?

If so, then why was there a lump the size of Texas in Gray's stomach?

To think she'd worried that Charlene would want to kill her for slapping Blake. She already had killed her! And that weasel Nolan was helping her now.

That's it. If Charlene was going to play dirty then so would Gray. She snatched the keys to the Beetle and stormed out of the house. It was time she met Adrian the Avenger face-to-face. Gray had some serious avenging to do.

Chapter 27

G ray pulled up in front of the sign announcing Hedrick the Healer. Locating Adrian had been ridiculously easy. He was listed in the Yellow Pages.

A bell jingled when she walked through the front door. She stepped into a cramped room. There was a small round table covered with a cloth in the center. All that was missing was a crystal ball.

Raj was pacing, a large text in his arms. He looked up abruptly. "Gray? What are you doing here?"

"My mom's gone."

"Gone?"

"She heard from her contact."

Raj was about to speak when a young man pushed through a curtain and entered the chamber. Adrian Hedrick Montez might not have his powers, but his presence reeked of supremacy. He was built like a fireman—one who started rather than put flames out.

A smile spread over Gray's face even as Adrian looked at her as though she were trivial. "Who's the skirt?"

"No one," Raj said at the same time Gray said, "Graylee Perez."

"Well, Graylee Perez, your boyfriend and I have work to do so if you don't mind . . ."

"I'm not here to see Raj. I came to see you."

"Oh, really?" Adrian studied her with renewed interest. Mostly he stared at her chest and legs. His eyes ping-ponged between the two.

"I'm in need of your services."

This earned a look in the eye. Adrian swept his hand over to the small round table in the center of the room. "Take a seat. What ails you, my dear?"

"This body," Gray said as she settled onto the hard wood chair.

Adrian's eyes roved her once more. "I see nothing objectionable about the one you have now. Don't tell me Raj has told you otherwise—a breast enhancement, perhaps?"

Raj snapped his book shut and stepped forward. "That's enough."

Gray didn't break eye contact with Adrian. She folded her hands and set them flat on the tabletop. "Flattering, Mr. Montez. This isn't my body. I'm borrowing my twin sister Charlene's body at the moment and I wish to extract her. Permanently."

"Gray . . ." Raj's mouth dropped at the same time a smile spread over Adrian's face.

Gray ignored Raj. "Can you help me?"

Adrian leaned forward. "So you're the one who needs a body transfer, are you? The question is, where is your own body, Miss Perez?"

"My body's not an option."

"And why is that?"

"It's decomposing at the cemetery."

Adrian's eyes nearly popped out of his head. Now Gray had his full attention. Adrian placed his hand on his chest.

"You mean you died and were brought back?"

"That's correct."

Adrian looked at Raj. "How could you keep this from me?"

Raj crossed his arms. "It's on a need-to-know basis."

Adrian looked back at Gray. "I'll do it, but I don't want money. I want to know how the spell was performed."

Gray snorted. "It didn't even come out right."

"Is that all you can think about? You were brought back from the dead. Death is final." Adrian leaned in closer. "I wonder, why you?"

Right, because Gray was nothing extraordinary. That's what Adrian was implying, wasn't it? She narrowed her eyes. "Sorry, can't help. Don't know a thing about it."

Adrian leaned back and folded his arms over his chest. "What's in it for me?"

Gray stretched out of her chair and ran the tips of her fingers along the table as she circled to Adrian's side. "Poor Adrian. Can't perform magic anymore." She came to a stop beside him.

Adrian shot her a menacing look. "What do you know about it?"

Gray squatted so that she was eye level with Adrian. "I know what it's like to have your powers blocked. All we need to do is find the responsible party and then . . ." Gray paused for emphasis. "We put a fissure in their spell."

Behind her, Raj sucked in a breath.

Adrian's eyes glittered.

* * *

Raj wasn't just flicking his Zippo open and closed, he was slamming the palm of his hand over the lid to snap it shut. They stood on the walkway just outside Adrian's shop. "Why did you promise to unblock his powers?"

"He's not much good to me if he can't perform the purge or whatever it is I need to do to keep on existing."

"There are other options. We can still do a transfer, just not to your body. Adrian could have instructed me. I could have performed the transfer!"

Gray didn't like the way Raj raised his voice with her. He wasn't her boyfriend. She didn't need to listen to this. "I'm running out of options, Raj! And I'm running out of time."

"So your only plan is to stoop to your sister's level? You might want to think about the consequences before you rush in."

Gray's mouth flew open. "I wouldn't be in this mess if it weren't for my sister!"

"I don't like where this is leading, Gray." Raj shook his head.

First her mom deserted her, and now Raj. It was too much. Did they expect her to just lie back and let her sister take the life force out of her? No thanks, she'd already done that once. "Then walk away," Gray bit out. "And let me deal with the dirty work."

Raj stopped flicking his lighter. He grabbed Gray's hand so suddenly she gasped. "What are you doing?"

"You want to play dirty . . ." Raj said. He grabbed the handle on Adrian's storefront roughly. "Let's settle this once and for all."

Adrian grinned as they walked inside. "Back so soon?"

"First we try a transfer," Raj said. "And if that doesn't work we move on to the purge." When he looked at Gray she nodded. "It's most likely someone in the coven blocking Adrian's powers. Probably Holloway. What do you suggest, Gray?"

Both men looked at her. She felt like shrinking under the weight of what she had to do; instead, she straightened her spine. "Truth spell. Does anyone know how to do one?"

Adrian grinned. "My Nan practically invented the truth spell."

Gray rolled her eyes. "Why am I not surprised?" She looked from Adrian to Raj. This time Raj was the one to nod. "I'll give it to Marc Phillips, he's Holloway's second in command. And then—I'll get the truth."

"I'll have Nan make you up a potion. She doesn't give out her spell."

"Fine," Gray said. "Just get it to me soon. Time's running out."

"Give it to me and I'll get it to Gray," Raj said.

"Or I could bring it to Gray directly."

Raj's jaw tightened. "No."

Adrian smiled. "Very well, McKenna." He turned to Gray. "You do realize that if we transfer you into an ungifted body you'll keep your powers, but you can't pass them on to your children?"

Gray lifted her chin. "Sign me up."

Adrian bowed slightly. "Miss Perez, a pleasure. I look forward to exchanging services."

"Just get Raj the potion, stud."

* * *

"Charlene?" Marc Phillips raised a brow when he saw Gray standing on his doorstep.

It was dark out by this time, but at least Adrian had gotten the potion to Raj that same day. Actually, it turned out to be a powder, not a potion, sealed inside a tiny plastic bag. The white powder looked like crack.

Mr. Phillips was looking over Gray's shoulder. "Ryan's at Paul's house playing video games."

"Do you mind if I come in for a moment, Mr. Phillips?"

"Please do," Mr. Phillips pulled open the door. "Is everything all right, Charlene?"

Gray squeezed several tears out of her eyes. "I miss my sister."

Mr. Phillips put a hand on her. "Does your mom know you're here?"

Gray's lip folded over. It wasn't part of the act. "She left town this morning."

Mr. Phillips stopped and ran a hand through his hair. "Can I get you something? A soda?"

Gray lifted her face slowly with the wounded doe-eye look. "Could I have a cup of warm tea?"

"Tea! Good idea."

Brilliant idea, especially as Gray planned to request Mr. Phillips's favorite—Earl Grey—which would easily lead to two cups of tea, one in which she could sprinkle the truth powder. She settled into a chair on the dining table adjacent to the open kitchen. Mr. Phillips set a kettle on top of the stove. He cleared his throat. "I was pleased to see you at Gathering yesterday. In times like these it is even more important to have the support of people who understand you." He looked at Gray and she nodded to show she understood. "I wish your mother had come with you."

Gray shrugged. "I'll mention it to her."

"She needs the support of her coven."

Gray pursed her lips. She didn't like Mr. Phillips telling her what her mother needed. She was a grown woman. She could make her own decisions.

The kettle whistled.

Mr. Phillips further irked Gray by setting out one teacup, filling it with hot water and a teabag and setting it in front of her. He took a seat across from her. Gray stared at the empty space directly in front of him as she blew on her tea.

"At times like these guidance is particularly important," Mr. Phillips continued. "You and your mom could have benefited from Holloway's lecture two weeks ago. Accidents and illness are especially hard on the gifted. We tend to believe ourselves beyond the reach of misfortune and when it does strike it not only feels unfair, but unacceptable. We believe we ought to be able to reverse it somehow. I did everything I could to reach out to your mother after your sister died, but she turned her back on me and on the coven."

Gray's lips tightened. She was beginning to understand why her mom was done dating warlocks. She tipped her teacup back, swallowed, and winced. Not only was she unable to sprinkle the truth powder inside Mr. Phillips's absent cup, but she now had a burnt tongue. "Ouch."

"Too hot?"

Gray nodded.

"Want a glass of water?"

Water—great idea. "I'm fine, thanks," Gray said quickly. She looked at Mr. Phillips over the rim of her teacup as she blew over the steaming liquid.

"I'm happy you and Ryan have remained close, but I worry about your mom. She hasn't kept in contact with anyone in the coven. She has no friends to get her through the grief. What she needs"—Mr. Phillips next words were temporarily caught off by a deep cough—"is to turn to those (cough, cough) who understand . . . Sorry, I seem to have something in my throat." Mr. Phillips's torso shook with the force of his hacks.

Gray set her teacup down. "Let me get you a glass of water, Mr. Phillips."

"That's all right, Charlene, I'm fi . . ." A full bout of hacking swallowed the last of Mr. Phillips's words and he nodded through tears.

Gray smiled the moment her back was turned to Ryan's dad. She grabbed a glass from the cupboard and filled it with cool tap water. While Mr. Phillips coughed she reached into her bra, pulled out the packet, and sprinkled the powder into the water. It fizzed and then dissolved.

Mr. Phillips took the glass from Gray's outstretched hand and began to drink. When he was finished he set the glass down. "Thank you, Charlene, much better. Sorry about that. What were we talking about again?"

Gray took her place across from Mr. Phillips. The good news was the effects of the powder were instant, according to Adrian, anyway. The bad news was it only lasted five minutes. Gray had to tread carefully—this was a truth, not a memory, spell, meaning Mr. Phillips would remember their conversation after it took place and she didn't wish to say anything to make him suspicious after she left.

Mr. Phillips's eyes lit up. "Oh, right, the importance of regular attendance at Gathering."

"Mr. Phillips!" Gray hadn't meant to sound so desperate. The man startled in his seat. "I ran into Adrian Hedrick Montez in town this afternoon. Actually, I was passing his shop when I saw him. He tried to get me to come inside. He said he could dull my feelings of sorrow."

Mr. Phillips's eyes narrowed. "You want to stay far away from Adrian Montez."

Gray made a show of shrinking into her chair. "Is he dangerous? I thought he had no powers, but people say he uses magic on his clients."

"Adrian is no longer able to perform magic."

"How can you be sure?"

"Because I, along with Mr. Holloway and Mr. Curry, are blocking his abilities."

Gray's eyes widened. Three of the coven's most powerful warlocks were blocking Adrian. This was going to be more difficult than she thought.

Gray let out a breath. "Oh, thank goodness, I feel much more secure knowing that, but how can you be sure the block will stay in effect?"

Mr. Phillips stared at Gray so intensely she thought for a moment the spell had worn off early. Then, slowly, he drew a pendant out of his shirt and held a small vial between his fingers. "Blood," he said. "We each have a drop of Adrian's blood in a vial. We have to wear it around our necks at all times." The blood was encased in a silver tube. There were etchings— words—wrapped around the narrow enclosure.

"All the time," Gray repeated.

Mr. Phillips tucked the vial back under his shirt. "It's a small sacrifice to keep the world safe from Adrian's mischief."

"I thought blocking spells didn't require . . . props." The one Charlene and Ryan had performed on her certainly hadn't. Those two hadn't gone around with a drop of Gray's blood below their throats. Ick.

"Blocking spells are weak at best. You usually have to be in close proximity of the person to impair their powers. We needed a guaranteed way to control Adrian at all times no matter where he was."

"What a relief. And there's no loophole for him to break through the block?"

Mr. Phillips smiled. "Not so long as we have the pendants. Don't worry, Charlene."

Oh, she wouldn't. Not anymore. Gray tipped back her teacup and drank the last dregs of black tea.

* * *

"He's going to need a memory wipe, otherwise, he'll know it was me." Gray paced in front of the table in Adrian's shop.

Adrian leaned against a bookcase, a smile stretched over his face. Raj had his arms crossed, standing a foot away from the wall. Daylight had never broken through the clouds and now it was pitch-black. The surrounding storefronts were dark and deserted.

Gray stopped pacing and looked at Adrian. "Am I correct in assuming your grandmother has some kind of powder for that, too?"

It didn't seem possible for Adrian's grin to widen, but it did. "She already has a batch made up. Nan gets banned from certain establishments from time to time and likes to give a little dose to the proprietor or, in the last instance, her dentist."

"Heaven help us," Raj said, rolling his eyes skyward.

"I can have it here in twenty minutes. Are we doing this tonight?"

Gray nodded. "I have three and a half hours left."

"I suggest we split up," Adrian said. "Three of them, three of us. I'll take Holloway."

"No," Gray said. "It'll be easier for me to get all three pendants. I can turn invisible."

"So can I." Raj stepped forward.

Gray's mouth hung open. "For how long?"

He shrugged. "Four days."

"So Saturday you were just pretending you didn't know the spell?"

"Oh, Raj," Adrian said, voice lifting. "Well done. He's sneaky, that one."

Raj frowned. "I'm not sneaky. I just didn't get a chance to tell you."

"Maybe because your lips were otherwise engaged," Gray snapped.

Adrian pushed away from the bookshelf and chuckled. "I'll get the memory potion. Do me a favor and refrain from killing each other until after we get the pendants."

Gray and Raj glared at Adrian's back as he left. Raj's expression softened as soon as Adrian was gone. "Gray . . ." he said, taking another step forward.

Gray sighed. "Don't worry about it. You've done nothing but help me, which is more than I can say for anyone else."

Raj shoved his hands inside his pockets. "What's the plan?"

"We go together."

Raj nodded.

Gray wrapped her arms around herself. "We'll wait till they're asleep. If anyone gives us trouble you'll hold them down with your freezing spell."

Chapter 28

They started with Marc Phillips. It turned out that performing a memory wipe on a warlock was a lot more complicated than, say, a doctor or a waiter. There wasn't actually a powder or a potion. What Adrian brought back was magic smelling salts with the reverse effect of knocking a person out cold, which was what they needed in order to perform the memory wipe along with candles that required time to burn out completely. They only had to clear a small chunk of memory, the one involving Gray's visit earlier.

Adrian's instructions to Raj had been hasty and she hoped it worked. At least the magic salts had. Once Gray unscrewed the lid and held it under Mr. Phillips's nose his head rolled to one side. Apart from the rise and fall of his chest, he practically looked dead.

Gray exchanged a look with Raj. She reached around Mr. Phillips's neck and unfastened the pendant. She fastened it around her own neck for safekeeping.

Raj was already pulling candles out of his backpack and setting them on Mr. Phillips's dresser: three white and three red. The Zippo flicked open and he lit each wick. Then he pulled out the scraps of paper, reading over the first before burning it as he spoke: "Bit by bit Charlene shall fade, shall disappear."

Raj held the next scrap into the flame of the next candle. "Day by day this is as I say."

The third: "Memories from this afternoon shall disappear."

The fourth: "Sunk into a forgotten bay. As this paper is consumed in flame, memories of her shall burn away."

And the final candle: "All encounters and words gone from today."

There was no point making themselves invisible as they tiptoed down the stairs. If they made a noise, Ryan would hear them whether or not they were see-through, and it was a lot easier to take the stairs quietly when they could see where they were placing their feet.

Max Curry's father was next. Raj sat outside the Currys' driveway, drumming his fingers on his steering wheel. Gray was determined not to rush him even as her last minutes ticked away. "Sorry," she said.

Raj continued drumming his fingertips on the steering wheel. "About what?" He stared absently out the windshield.

"For dragging you into this whole mess."

Raj stopped drumming and looked sideways at her. "I wanted to be dragged into it."

Gray stared at him a moment before climbing over the armrest and landing in his lap. She pressed her lips to his. At first Raj was so taken aback he didn't respond, but then he was kissing her, holding Gray cocooned in his embrace. Warmth spread from his hand where it was pressed in the hollow between Gray's shoulder blades. Raj's arm wrapped around Gray's lower back. He caressed her with a delicacy that put Gray into a trance. The movement sent shivers of pleasure through her body. All her muscles relaxed. Raj's body felt warm against hers.

Gray pulled back slightly to look at Raj, but only briefly. Looking at him made her want to kiss him anew. Their lips fell into a delicate rhythm. It seemed like it should feel awkward, kissing Raj McKenna, but it wasn't. Gray could kiss him till the end of time.

How could she have died and missed out on this?

Of all the reasons to be brought back, this was the best. Everyone should experience a kiss like this before parting.

Gray pulled away, but only so she could nestle her head against his shoulder. Snuggling felt good, too.

"Um, Gray."

Gray closed her eyes. "Can't we stay like this a little longer?"

Raj ran a hand down the side of her face. It made her want to weep.

"Not if we want to get the last two pendants tonight."

Gray sighed. "Do you think Adrian will help me once he gets his powers back?"

"I'll make sure of it."

Gray glanced up. She took a deep breath then sat up in Raj's lap. "We better get to it then."

* * *

The smelling salts had to be used on both Mr. and Mrs. Curry. They slept on opposite sides of the bed, backs turned to one another. Gray held the salts under Mrs. Curry's nose, screwed the lid on, then tossed it over the bed to Raj. He caught it easily, held it under Mr. Curry's nostrils, then removed the pendant.

Mr. Holloway was single, like Marc Phillips. The coven's leader didn't even have children. Raj cursed when they stopped across the street from his house. Lights blazed from a room downstairs.

Gray glanced at the clock on the dash. One forty-eight.

She had a little over an hour left.

"Once he goes to bed it'll be easy," Gray said to reassure herself.

"If he goes to bed," Raj said. He pulled his lighter out and began flicking it open and closed. "We have to get that last pendant. Once Phillips and Curry wake up and find those pendants missing it'll be impossible to lift Holloway's."

Gray glanced down then slowly unlatched the first pendant around her neck followed by the second. She handed them to Raj. "Save them for me, will you?"

Raj took the pendants and nodded.

They watched Mr. Holloway's house in silence.

At two twenty Gray cleared her throat. "I guess we're going to have to do this the hard way."

Raj stuffed his lighter in his pocket and turned the keys in the ignition.

"What are you doing?" Gray asked.

"Taking you home. I'll see to Holloway."

"The hell you will." Gray reached for the key and turned it toward her.

"You're almost out of time. I'll come back and wait for him to turn in."

As Raj reached for the key again, Gray covered his hand with hers. He looked at her. "We do this together," she said.

Raj stared at her a moment then relaxed his hand and nodded. They stepped out of the car simultaneously, pushing their doors gently shut. "We'll go invisible," Raj whispered as they crossed the street. "I freeze him and you hold the salts under his nose." Raj handed Gray the vial as he spoke.

It felt like it would slip from her sweaty palm. "How do we get in?" Gray asked.

"Like this." Raj lifted a terracotta stepping stone from the front yard and hurled it through the front window.

For a moment Gray was so startled she couldn't remember how to turn herself invisible. Thankfully, she managed to disappear from sight before Mr. Holloway burst through the front door. He leapt over the three steps leading from his porch to the front lawn and charged into the yard.

Gray and Raj took that opportunity to fly up the stairs and through the open door into the house. At least that was what Gray hoped Raj was doing. She didn't want to be inside Holloway's house alone. The living room was just off to the left of the entryway. The room was well lit from floor to ceiling. A book had tumbled to the floor in front of an armchair.

Gray didn't dare breathe, let alone say, Raj's name. There was hardly time to regroup with Mr. Holloway storming back inside the house. He lifted a finger and the lid on a heavy old trunk sprang open against the wall.

Holloway's footsteps shook the house like a giant's. He leaned over the trunk then stopped suddenly and whipped around. Gray's heart leapt inside her throat. Holloway scanned the room and stood quietly. Gray held her breath and froze in place beside the couch.

When the front door slammed she jumped in place. The bolt clicked shut. When Mr. Holloway moved across the room it looked like he was coming straight for her. Gray's jaw dropped. She tried to move, but she couldn't and then, thank god, Mr. Holloway froze in place.

"Now!" Raj cried.

Gray's fingers shook as she untwisted the cap off the salts. She held it under Mr. Holloway's nose. It wrinkled. Even his lips curled back.

Gray stepped back.

Mr. Holloway's eyes hadn't closed. If anything, they seemed wider. Then he started laughing. "You think your salts will work on me?" The laughing ceased. Mr. Holloway attempted to speak. His eyes narrowed when no sound emerged. He stopped trying and then he smiled, a heinous grin that sent chills through Gray.

She didn't think she could approach him again. She was once more frozen in place—her own terror holding her hostage. Gray saw the pendant lift out of Holloway's shirt and float briefly in the air before disappearing.

"Time to go," Raj hissed.

She followed his footsteps to the door. The bolt made a weak clicking sound like a dying battery on a car remote. It didn't budge. The sound of shattering glass made her nearly leap out of her shoes—again!

The jagged edges surrounding the broken window were kicked away.

"Come on!"

Gray hurried toward the window and Raj's voice. He grabbed her hand as she lifted her leg through the window. When she glanced inside one last time she saw the same horrid smile frozen on Mr. Holloway's face.

There was no breath left in Gray's lungs. Her legs wouldn't move. She couldn't even gasp for air. Raj's grip tightened around her hand. He dragged her forward, across the lawn, across the street, and to his car. He opened the passenger door. "Get in!"

He didn't make himself visible until they were out of Holloway's neighborhood. It took tremendous effort for Gray to fill herself back in. She glanced at the clock on the dashboard. Two fifty-one. "We're never going to make it."

The wheels on Raj's car squealed in response. "Gray!"

Gray leaned back into the seat.

"Gray!"

"What?"

"Concentrate! Can you turn the lights green?"

"Doesn't matter," Gray said. Her voice sounded a million miles away. "Still won't make it."

"Gray!"

"No problem." She stared through the windshield. They could have run red lights for all the traffic that was out at almost three in the morning. But Gray made them green and when Raj screeched into her driveway he screamed, "Go!"

His shout was like an adrenaline boost. Gray threw the car door open, then the house door, and flew up the stairs. The numbers on the digital clock glowed like green eyes in the dark as Gray leapt for her bed. Two fifty-nine.

* * *

Gray sat up, gasping. Her heart was lodged inside her throat as though no time had passed. So intent was she on getting air into her lungs that it took her a moment to notice that not only was she not in her own bed, she wasn't in Charlene's, either.

The room was dark, but she could still make out the movie posters tacked to the walls and action figures on the dresser across from her. There was a smell both familiar and unfamiliar. A soft chuckle invaded her eardrums from directly beside her.

"Fascinating. I wish you could see the transition for yourself."

Gray clutched the sheet to her chest and turned to face Nolan. He was under the covers with her, topless, elbow propping up his head.

Gray didn't know what was worse: the fact that she was naked in Nolan's bed or that she was about to cry in front of him. *Fury! Focus on fury.* She wasn't about to let the little twerp watch as she wept.

Even fury was out of the question. Gray stared forward, her eyes adjusting. She pulled the sheet higher. She couldn't look at him. "Why are you with my sister?"

Any illusions Gray had that he'd express guilt were quickly shattered. "You screwed me over, Gray, so I switched sides."

"What are you talking about?"

"I saw you kissing Raj McKenna. I came by early to pick you up Saturday . . . to help you . . . and that's when I saw you sucking face with that dirty, rotten warlock." The sheet tugged under Gray's folded arms as Nolan sat up. "You were just using me, Gray. Jerking me around while you were screwing McKenna. Your sister told me about how you ruined things with her boyfriend. This entire time you've only cared about yourself. Now we've turned the tables on you."

"I hate you." She barely caught the shrug of Nolan's shoulders.

"Hate me all you want, just remember you were loving me a minute ago." Nolan turned to look at her with a smug smile. Luckily, he had no place to aim it.

Gray was gone. Or so it appeared.

She had vanished the moment she stepped out of bed.

Nolan swallowed his smile.

"Gray?" Nolan threw the covers back and stepped out.

He had on underwear. Gray did not. She didn't have a stitch of clothing. Even the slip was preferable to this. She had to keep her body from shivering in the room's draft, but mostly she had to keep from shaking with rage.

Nolan looked around the room. "Crap."

He picked Charlene's clothes off the floor and shoved them inside a dresser drawer. At first Gray thought he was holding her garments hostage, but the longer she lingered the more it became clear he thought she'd teleported . . . otherwise, he wouldn't have settled back into bed.

He leaned over and inhaled the pillow Gray had been on. Sick freak. She ought to suffocate him with it the moment he fell asleep. But Nolan lay there with his eyes open, staring at the ceiling.

Murder's not the answer, Gray chanted as she waited for her moment to escape.

That was Charlene's department.

Goosebumps rose over Gray's flesh. She crept toward the door, then looked at Nolan. He'd closed his eyes, but she doubted he was sleeping. Gray glanced at his dresser. Wouldn't it be great if she could dress herself without snapping?

If Nolan heard her, he could tackle her before she had a chance to get out of his room.

She placed her hand on the doorknob and turned it gently. Once her arm was twisted she pulled back slowly. Every movement she made was deliberate until she was out the front door and running, barefoot, on the wet pavement outside. The Beetle was parked two houses down.

The car growled to life as though feeding off the energy of her anger. She floored the gas pedal and tore down the street toward home. Gray nearly hit the garage door when she roared into her driveway.

Once inside she turned visible. Her teeth were now chattering, body shaking. She ran up the stairs and turned on the shower. Once the water was warm enough, she stepped in. The washcloth scraped at her skin. Gray increased the temperature until it scalded her. She scrubbed herself raw and remained in the shower so long the water began cooling until it stopped altogether. She sank into the tub, head resting against her knees. Cold seeped into her bones.

Not her bones, Charlene's.

How could she have been so wrong about Nolan?

She had really believed he meant to help her. Not only had he aligned himself with Charlene, he'd gone about it in the worst possible way.

Gray ground her teeth together. She wouldn't cry. She refused to shed a single tear over a vengeful jerk who couldn't handle rejection.

Chapter 29

Raj slept in late on Tuesday. He and Gray had managed the impossible. If they could break into the homes of three coven leaders and make off with the pendants, the rest should be a piece of cake. Thank goodness Gray hadn't made the switch inside his car. Explaining Charlene's sudden three a.m. appearance in his passenger's seat probably wouldn't have gone over well. Worse still, Charlene would have been suspicious and they couldn't have her snooping around messing things up before they had a chance to transfer Gray safely to another body.

Attending school today was out of the question. Raj drove straight to Adrian's. The first thing off was the bell. It didn't ring, being that it was no longer attached above the door. Raj stepped inside Adrian's chamber and cursed under his breath.

Everything was gone except the table, now cleared of its cloth.

There was a chuckle and the curtain above the back room flew to one side. Adrian entered as though upon a stage. "Don't worry, I haven't skipped town . . . yet."

Raj only relaxed slightly.

Adrian began clapping. "Bravo, Raj. Bravo. You and the little missus cleaned up good. And I feel fantastic!" Adrian waved his hand over the table and a bottle of champagne and two flutes appeared. "Drink?"

"No, thanks," Raj said.

"And the missus?"

Raj ground his teeth together. "Is out for the day."

Adrian poured himself a glass and lifted the flute in the air. "Ah, well, then a toast to her and you, as well." Adrian took a sip then set the flute down. "I tell you, Raj, don't ever take your powers for granted. They're a terrible thing to be without."

Raj folded his arms over his chest. "We kept our end of the deal. Let's talk about yours."

"Already on it." Adrian waved his hand and the champagne and flutes were replaced by a set of syringes filled with bright liquids. Every color of the rainbow was present.

Raj frowned. "What are those?"

"These?" Adrian smiled. "I call it Plan C." He grabbed a syringe and jabbed it inside a vein in his arm. "Always have a Plan C, D, E, and F. If you learn one thing from me, Raj, remember that." Adrian emptied the syringe with the red liquid into his vein and shuddered.

Raj tried without success to get a reading on what kind of potion Adrian was injecting himself with. When that didn't work he studied Adrian's aura. It turned white briefly.

"If this is Plan C, then what's Plan A and B?"

"Plan A: I have excellent news! I found a fresh one—terminally ill girl, same age, looker, going to croak any day."

"Don't talk about people that way," Raj said.

Adrian's brows arched when he smiled. "Or there's always Plan B: The Purge."

Raj nodded at the syringes. "And Plan C is poison yourself?"

"Possibly. This is a very delicate spell—never been done before, but then, there's never been a known case like this. Don't worry," Adrian continued. "I never go back on a bargain. Do you have the pendants, by the way?"

"I'm holding them for Gray."

The second syringe hovered above Adrian's opposite arm. "Thinks she can put a leash back on me if I misbehave, does she?"

Raj straightened. "I removed the blood from them. They no longer pose a threat."

"I want them destroyed."

"That's not your call," Raj answered.

The request didn't surprise Raj in the least, but Adrian would have to live with the disappointment. They were saving the pendants to use on Charlene. The coven had no idea how dangerous she was. It was up to Gray and Raj to prevent her from hurting anyone ever again.

Adrian studied Raj a moment. "I see."

"See what?"

"I'll simply need to take it up with the missus." The second syringe still hovered over Adrian's arm, yellow liquid inside. "I need to know what day she died."

"Why?"

"For this spell is why. We don't have time for twenty questions, McKenna."

This was a bad idea, a very bad idea—Adrian attempting a spell that had never been done before. Sure, that would turn out well. Raj had to make sure the transfer worked. For now he'd answer Adrian's questions. It wasn't like it was secret information or anything. "February ninth."

"Well, isn't that tragic." Adrian stuck the needle through his skin. "So what did she die of?"

"She was poisoned."

"Poisoned! How?"

"By her sister—unintentionally. Death by chocolate." Raj's lips curved up at the absurdity of it.

"If the sister killed her we should definitely purge her."

"Let's focus on the transfer. You say this girl is about to pass on. How can you be sure?"

"The doc was practically reading her last rights . . ." Adrian looked at Raj and grinned. "But then, you're the expert. By tomorrow she could be in the morgue, which still works for us so long as the body's preserved, though good luck explaining that one to the coroner when she rises from the dead." The remainder of Adrian's chemistry set vanished following the wave of his hand. "The rest will have to wait or I won't be of any use."

"You do realize that if you double-cross Gray she'll bury you," Raj said. "I once did a spell on her and she nearly strangled me for it."

The warning, unfortunately, had the opposite effect on Adrian. His smile widened. "Got something of the sinister in her, does she? Sure you can handle a witch like that?"

Instead of taking the bait Raj sighed and said, "Just get the job done."

* * *

Raj waited for Gray in the parking lot at McKinley on Wednesday morning, but she never showed. Once the warning bell rang, he got inside his car and drove to her house.

"Gray." Raj pounded on the front door. "Gray!"

They'd cut it close the last time he'd seen her. Hopefully she hadn't run into any trouble with Charlene; not that Charlene could really do anything—like keep her hostage. Could she?

Raj beat on the door. Suddenly it flew open and he fell forward as he put his weight into his fist.

Gray stood at the top of the stairs in a black turtleneck and jeans. She'd cut her hair; it hit just above her shoulders. Her eyes were heavily outlined in dark liner. It wasn't just the top or eyeliner that surrounded Gray in black. Clouds of it hovered around her, turning the edges of her aura black like charred kabob.

Raj gently closed the door. "What happened?"

Gray descended the stairs and stopped at the edge of the banister. "What do you mean?"

"Something's wrong."

"I'm trapped inside my sister's body. No kidding something's wrong."

Raj reached inside his pack and pulled out the three pendants. They dangled from his fingers. Gray's eyes lit up and she smiled, but her aura didn't change. "It got pretty hairy in the end, but we did it." Raj held Gray's gaze and willed away whatever malice troubled her. She appeared as focused on him as he was on her.

Gray reached out and wrapped her fingers around the chains dangling from Raj's fingers. "Thank you. You did good work the other night, which is more than I can say for myself. I choked."

"Did not."

"Raj, I choked." Tears glossed over her eyes and were quickly blinked away. "If you hadn't been there . . ."

Raj cleared his throat. "Mr. Holloway was a bit intense."

When Gray looked at him he grinned and suddenly she was chuckling softly. "God, he freaked me out. He always seemed so unassuming at the podium during lecture—not like something from a children's horror story."

"I'll never forget the way he rushed out of the house," Raj said.

"Or the evil grin." Gray shuddered. "You know he's gotta be demonic."

Raj laughed. "I'm sure he's thinking the same thing about his attackers—probably wanted to leave an impression."

"He did that." Gray turned with the pendants and Raj followed her into the kitchen. Gray pulled the stoppers and caps off the pendants. "They're empty."

"I emptied them."

Gray turned toward Raj. "Adrian has his powers back?"

"I wanted him to be ready to perform the transfer."

Gray nodded and turned away.

"Have you heard from your mom?"

Gray couldn't stop her shoulders from sagging. "No, and I've left her a dozen messages. She may have gotten the call, but it's still going to be too late."

The kitchen countertops were polished and empty. There wasn't even a fruit bowl set out. When Raj's eyes found Gray again she had a kitchen knife poised over her wrist. Before he could speak she sliced herself open and held the first vial to her wrist. Raj hurried over and took it from her, replacing the stopper and lid as she filled the next vial. They worked in silence. When each vial was filled and sealed, Gray rinsed them once more in the sink then dried them off on a kitchen towel.

Gray handed Raj a pendant. "You'll take one?"

He nodded and clasped it around his neck then tucked it beneath his shirt.

"Thank you. Is Adrian ready?"

"He's located a lost soul in Seattle."

Gray let out a breath. "Good." Her aura morphed into a dull, heavy gray.

"Are you okay?" Raj tried asking again.

Gray looked around the kitchen. "It's weird being inside Charlene's body, you know?" She looked at Raj.

He didn't answer. He had the feeling she didn't expect one.

"I know it looks similar to my own, but it's not and I feel it's not. As strange as that's been I can't imagine being inside someone entirely unfamiliar to me."

Raj took Gray's hands in his. "It will still be you."

Her hands trembled briefly and then she pulled away. "I know. Anyway, I'm done with this body. Onward and upward, right?"

Raj tapped a finger against the outline of his Zippo inside his pocket. "Yeah. Shall we?"

"Can we stop by the hospital first?"

Gray wanted Stacey to have one of the pendants. It was only fitting that she should be one of the individuals blocking the powers of the person who'd stolen her consciousness. After slipping the pendant around Stacey's neck, Gray made it invisible.

Chapter 30

Adrian clapped his hands together and rubbed them when Gray entered his barren workshop. "All right. Who's in the mood for a body transfer?"

Gray gave him a stony stare. She reached around her neck and unclasped the third pendant. Adrian's eyes followed the chain as Gray pulled it out from under her turtleneck. She held it out. "A souvenir."

Adrian snatched it. "And the other two?"

Gray inclined her head toward Raj. "Raj has one. Mine is in safe keeping. That's Charlene's blood in there. You can wear the pendant after the transfer or return it to Raj. Once you put it on, Charlene's powers will be blocked. That means mine will be blocked as well."

Adrian's brow rose. "Not a good feeling."

Gray took a deep breath. "No."

"Let's go then."

Being powerless was a wretched feeling. Gray had already felt her abilities weaken after she clasped the first pendant around Raj's neck. He naturally was against entrusting one to Adrian, but Gray found it fitting that the three people involved in the transfer should be the three to block Charlene's powers. Once the transfer was complete, Gray would get her pendant back from Stacey. Every day that she had to look in the mirror and see a stranger's face, she'd at least take comfort from the vial of Charlene's blood hanging from her neck and know that her sister would never practice magic again.

If Gray's transfer was unsuccessful and Stacey should die, the pendant would go with her. The chances of Charlene regaining all three pendants would be next to nil with one hanging invisible around a corpse under the ground.

"I'll drive," Raj said.

They were the last words Gray heard. As she stepped toward the door a fluttering feeling rushed over her right before she disappeared.

* * *

So this was what teleportation was like? It was quick. No whooshing portal or ethereal passageway leading from one place to the other. Or maybe that was because Gray wasn't the one teleporting herself. She simply reappeared in her living room.

A shiver coursed through her body. All the windows were open. The draft prickled her skin as it had that morning. Terror gripped her by the throat. Nolan. Holloway. Her mind tripped over the two names, chanting them like a death mantra, but it was only Ryan.

"Hello, Gray."

The voice sounded different, smooth, but Ryan's pear-shaped face was as familiar as ever. He stood in the living room

Oh, for goodness' sake.

Gray's hands landed on her hips. "What are you doing here, Ryan?"

"I'm here on Charlene's behalf."

"Are you now? And did you help put Stacey Morehouse in a coma on Charlene's behalf?"

Ryan grinned. "Charlene didn't need my help with Stacey. She's a very powerful witch, you know."

"You mean psychotic."

Ryan squinted. "That's not a nice thing to say."

"Speaking of psychotic . . ." Gray said, walking toward the door. "Get out of my house." She reached for the door handle, but the door didn't budge when she pulled on it.

When she looked at Ryan he was grinning. The boy might be pear-faced and short, but at the moment he'd taken on an entirely morbid look. "I'm not going anywhere, Gray, and neither are you."

Ryan was juiced up on something, and had props. He'd pulled out a glowing orb that kept her rooted in place, back flat against the living room floor. The front door, which Gray couldn't open moments earlier, was now wide open, in addition to the windows.

Thin trails of smoke rose to the ceiling like pieces of white string. Ryan was burning white sage in porcelain bowls. After lighting incense in every room downstairs he'd gone upstairs, Gray could only guess, to do the same in all the rooms above her.

"You little sh . . ." The words had died on her tongue when she tried to speak.

Fight, Gray told herself. *Break through the magic.*

Gray didn't know whether she wanted to laugh or wail. Of all the people to take her down, she couldn't believe it would be Ryan Phillips.

An image of Gray's mom entered her head—her mom lost in the mountains, searching for a contact who'd beckoned her to get her out of the way. It all came down to the final battle of the twins, didn't it?

Gray saw her mother coming home: Gray gone again, this time without a trace—not so much as a cold corpse for proof. Even with a second chance at life, she hadn't gotten to tell her good-bye; to give her one last hug. Tears leaked out the sides of Gray's eyes.

Gray managed to thrash slightly. Ryan's eyes widened. He stood above her, reading aloud from an old text. He set it down and grabbed a porcelain bowl that wasn't smoking. His fingers slipped inside then flicked above her, sending droplets over her face. They mingled with her tears. "With this holy water, spirit be gone."

Gray would have laughed if she had the use of her vocal cords. Nice try, Pear Head.

Then something began pulling at her insides. She gasped aloud. It should have alarmed her that Ryan found that encouraging, but she was a little too distracted by the sensation of floating away from the floor like one of the smoke trails streaming from white porcelain.

Gray was floating. Except she wasn't floating. Her sister's body was still on the floor.

"Go to the light, Graylee Perez."

Screw you, Ryan Phillips.

There was a second gasp, only Gray hadn't made it—the body on the floor had. The girl sat up suddenly, choking, then stopped. She looked at Ryan with teeth that gleamed like the Cheshire Cat. "You did it. You freaking did it!"

Oh, crap.

Chapter 31

Raj wasn't good at locator spells, but Adrian was. Any misgivings he'd had about returning Adrian's powers were put to rest when the warlock went immediately to work arranging four candles around his spot on the floor. He set one North, South, East, and West.

"Was Gray just purged?" came Raj's first terrified question the moment Gray disappeared from sight. He'd considered she might have turned herself invisible, but only for a second. Her absence was tangible.

Adrian had studied the last place she'd stood. "That wasn't a purge. That was an abduction, and a cowardly one at that." Adrian lit the candles and jasmine incense.

Raj set a goblet of water in front of Adrian.

"Let the water show the location of Graylee Perez," Adrian said. "Let the water show the location of Graylee Perez." He repeated this two more times.

The water rippled then smoothed. A house appeared faintly then cleared.

"That's Gray's house," Raj said, heading for the front door.

Adrian was right behind him. They jumped in Raj's car and once more he screeched through the streets. From the corner of his eyes he saw Adrian's set of syringes appear. One by one he injected himself with the remaining colors. "Once we take care of Gray you'll need to get me to my Nan for detox."

Raj flew into Gray's driveway, coming to a skidding halt beside her car. From the street he'd seen the front door open and went racing inside.

Ryan Phillips stood over Gray. She was seated on the floor, trying to get to her feet. Raj started toward Ryan, to deck him, before helping Gray up. When he took his next step, however, she turned and smiled—a grin that stopped him in his tracks.

"You're too late, McKenna. You're too freaking late." Charlene began laughing.

Raj fell to his knees and put his head in his hands.

The laughter abruptly died, as did the self-satisfied smile on Ryan's face, when Adrian walked in. "Oh, it's never too late," he said smoothly. He stared directly at Ryan. "Ryan Phillips." Adrian's lips curled around the last name. "Your father has been a very bad warlock. Like father, like son. Sit down."

It was a toss-up as to whether it was a spell or pure terror that made Ryan take a seat on the couch.

Raj rose slowly. The grief and hatred were equally intense and just about to rip him apart.

Adrian turned to Charlene, who now stood. "And you, my dear, are a wicked witch."

"Screw you!" Charlene yelled.

"I don't think so." Adrian snatched Charlene's wrist and pulled out a dagger.

She screamed as he carved something into her palm and did the same on her second hand. Adrian sliced into his palms and then grasped Charlene's, joining their open wounds.

He began chanting in Latin.

"Stop him!" Charlene shrieked.

Ryan leapt off the couch and jumped onto Adrian's back. Raj sprang to action and tackled Ryan. He had no idea what Adrian was doing, but anything at this point was worth a shot.

Adrian finished his incantation then dropped to the floor with a loud thud.

Charlene's mouth opened and closed. She held her arms open and examined her body from her chest down then held her palms open in front of her.

"Charlene?" Ryan asked shakily from the floor.

Raj held his breath.

"He cut my freaking hands!"

Ryan followed Charlene to the kitchen. Water filled Raj's eardrums—a gushing onslaught of liquid.

It looked like Adrian was dead. "Adrian." Raj touched him with the tip of his shoe. "Adrian!"

Raj crouched beside Adrian and turned him over. The smile on the warlock's face sent an unsettling shiver over him. Adrian tried to laugh, but it came out in raspy huffs. "Get me to my Nan," he said.

Raj pulled Adrian up by the arm then half carried, half floated him to his car. Adrian crumpled onto the backseat, slumping across all three seats. When Raj drove over a pothole, Adrian moaned.

"She existed before and so too shall she exist again," he mumbled. "February ninth. Death. Life. Purged. Returned."

Raj's knuckles tightened around the steering wheel. He wished Adrian would stop with the rantings. Gray was gone. This wasn't the three a.m. switch. This was Charlene reclaiming her body all to herself. Why couldn't she and Ryan have given them more time? They had come so close to doing the body transfer.

Raj punched the dashboard. Pain splintered through his fingers. Laughter rose from the backseats.

"You think she's gone, ye of little faith," Adrian said. "My spell is infallible, but it takes time and patience. You'll see. You'll all see. They thought they could stop me. Me! Adrian Montez!" His voice rose.

Raj glanced in his rearview mirror, half expecting to see Adrian pop up, but he remained down for the count and didn't speak the remainder of the way, except to groan occasionally and mutter, "February ninth."

Adrian's grandmother made a big fuss when Raj dropped him off, lamenting in some language he didn't recognize. Raj didn't have time for dramatics. He dumped Adrian and headed for the south side of town.

Once arriving at his destination, he pounded on his mother's door.

"Raj?"

He was staring at the ground. His lower lip quivered.

"Come in."

They sat in silence in his mother's living room until Raj began sobbing. He hid his face in his hands. His entire body shook. At some point his mother moved from the chair across from him and took a seat beside him. When her hand touched his back, Raj inhaled sharply.

"What happened?" his mother asked in a soothing voice. "The night of the fire?"

Raj stared straight ahead and blinked several times. "Dad attacked me. He was drunk. He threw me against the wall." Raj took a deep breath. "Then he pulled out a cigarette and flicked open his Zippo."

The hand that had been stroking Raj's back stopped. Raj swallowed. "I snatched the lighter from him. He said to give it back. I said if he wanted it, go fetch it. Then I threw it in the living room. While Dad was hammering me with his fists the curtains caught fire. I didn't realize Aahana was sleeping on the couch."

The silence that followed was unbearable. As soon as Raj's mother wrapped her arm around him the tears rushed down his cheeks, and this time she didn't try to stop them.

His mom could be very abrupt. She also had one of the most soothing voices he'd ever heard—when she chose to use it. She used it now. "Raj, give me the lighter. It's time to let go and come home."

Chapter 32

This time, when Gray went invisible, it was different. She floated like a spirit. She was incapable of speech or physical contact.

What she could do was travel at warp speed and go through walls.

She passed through the walls of Valley Medical Hospital and came to a stop at the foot of Stacey Morehouse's bed. There was only a moment's hesitation before she dove inside. It was rumored that if a soul still lingered, a battle for the body would ensue, but Stacey Morehouse had long given up.

But not entirely.

Graylee Perez.

Gray heard Stacey's voice crystal clear, but she couldn't see her through the white haze.

Suddenly the voice was closer—in her face.

Glad you could stop by.

Before Stacey exited the body she played Gray her last horrifying moments before hitting the light post. Gray nearly threw herself out of the body as the vehicle lost control and accelerated toward the steel post.

At the moment of impact, Gray sat up in the hospital bed, gasping. The movement triggered the alarms on her monitor. At first she thought the beeping was inside her head. A nurse ran in then nearly fainted when she saw Gray sitting up in bed. A second nurse followed and made the sign of the cross. "Sweet Jesus," she said. "It's a miracle."

Mr. Morehouse was there within ten minutes, hugging Gray against his starched shirt. "I knew it. I knew you'd come back to me." He stood up. "Out! Everyone out! Give my daughter room to breathe, except you, Dr. Conway. I'm holding you personally responsible for making sure Stacey stays in her current state."

No one had addressed Gray directly, as though she were mute or might have lost all motor functions, but now that the initial shock had died down, Mr. Morehouse bent beside her. "Stacey, do you know who I am?"

So she had amnesia now, did she?

"Very funny, Dad. What's going on?"

* * *

Gray turned her head side to side in front of the mirror: Stacey Morehouse's mirror. After chasing the local news reporters away, Mr. Morehouse had insisted on taking her home, despite Dr. Conway's entreaty to keep her in the hospital for observation. One just didn't argue with a lawyer.

Gray's hair was now golden blond. This was weirder than being inside Charlene's body. She was also nearly a foot taller.

Gray opened Stacey's dresser drawers. Nice clothes. Not really her style, but she could learn to adapt. Gray found a pair of faded jeans she liked and snapped her fingers. Surprise mixed with relief washed over her when the jeans appeared on her legs. She hadn't been entirely convinced her powers would transfer with her into the body of a biologically ungifted human.

Gray touched the pendant at her throat before filling it in and unclasping the vial. She set it on top of the dresser.

Gray rushed down the stairs and was stopped by Mr. Morehouse's voice as she started toward the front door.

"Where do you think you're going?"

Gray turned slowly. Last she'd seen, Mr. Morehouse had set up shop in his study. Now his papers were stacked in piles around his laptop on the dining room table.

Gray pasted a smile over her face. "I've been cooped up for two months, Daddy." *Daddy* sounded like a word Stacey would use.

Mr. Morehouse's facial features relaxed. "You're right." Gray thought that'd be the end of it until he stood up. "I'll take you wherever you want to go."

"Um, okay, let me just run up to my room and grab my sweater." Gray dashed back up to Stacey's room and closed the door. She picked up the phone and dialed home. "Pick up. Pick up. Pick up."

"Hello?"

"Mom?"

"Who is this?" The voice was much clearer now.

"Meet me in front of the bookstore. Five minutes." Gray hung up the phone. She grabbed a sweater out of the closet and raced down the stairs. "Ready, Daddy."

"Where to?"

"The bookshop."

Mr. Morehouse looked her over carefully. Maybe Stacey was disinclined to read.

"I'm going to need a pile of magazines," Gray said. "Got to catch up on all my celebrity gossip . . . and world events, naturally."

"Naturally," Mr. Morehouse said with a chuckle.

* * *

Gray's mom was already pacing in front of the bookstore when Mr. Morehouse pulled into a front row spot. As they approached the front door, Gray yelled suddenly, "Ms. Perez!"

Her mom turned and looked at her blankly.

Gray kept walking toward her and only stopped when she was a couple feet away. "I go to school with Charlene. My name's Stacey Morehouse."

Mom's mouth opened.

Gray turned to Mr. Morehouse, who'd caught up. "Dad, this is Ms. Perez. She lost her daughter, Gray, two days before my accident."

Mr. Morehouse, who had stretched his hand out toward Mom, pulled her to him when their fingers touched and embraced her. "Please accept my condolences, Ms. Perez." Mr. Morehouse stepped back. There were tears in his eyes. "I know something of your pain. I nearly lost my little girl."

Mom's eyes began to glisten. Both adults were on the verge of waterworks. Gray cleared her throat. "Couldn't leave my pop alone. He's single. I don't know why. He's such a great guy." Gray twirled a strand of hair around her finger. "Ms. Perez is single, too."

"Gray!" Mom cried out.

Mr. Morehouse squinted at her mom.

"What I meant to say . . ." Mom swallowed down what sounded like a sob. "Gray was the light of my life." She looked straight at Gray. "She still is."

* * *

Convincing Mr. Morehouse to let her out for an afternoon hadn't been too hard; talking him into starting school back up was more difficult. He'd gotten it into his head to hire a private tutor to homeschool her for the remaining seven weeks of the semester.

"Dad, you have to be kidding," Gray whined. Mr. Morehouse might be a lawyer, but she'd discovered the quickest way to get him to bend. "I was trapped inside a coma with no family, friends—no one to talk to. Don't trap me inside this house with some stodgy old tutor for company."

What Mr. Morehouse wouldn't budge on was driving. This was absolutely forbidden. "I'll hire a driver," he said.

"Or I could take the bus."

"You? Take the bus?"

"As opposed to being chauffeured every day—uh, yeah. Doesn't sound very economical, Dad."

Mr. Morehouse stared at her a moment before breaking out into a grin. "Always the good head on your shoulders. You know money doesn't matter when it comes to your happiness, but if you would prefer to take the school bus I won't stop you."

"That's what I want."

* * *

Twilight Zone revisited would best describe Gray's first day back at school in a new body, only this time Gray was treated like a returning celebrity rather than a mental case. Students formed circles around her. The braver ones hugged her. If Gray happened to forget certain details of her life before, it was waved off as post-traumatic stress, selective amnesia—totally understandable.

With all the Stacey Morehouse admirers following her around, it was difficult to get a moment alone.

"You're like Miracle Girl," Trish Roberts said, stroking Gray's hair as though touching the divine.

"Give her space!" Pete Sutherland cried when Gray walked up to Stacey's locker. It didn't matter that she had no clue what the combo was. It was amazing the amount of leeway people allowed a girl waking from a two-month coma. The office staff had provided a paper copy of Stacey Morehouse's class schedule and locker combination.

"I'll hold your books for you while you put away your coat," Pete said.

Gray glanced at him. As Stacey Morehouse, she could probably get any guy at McKinley High, but there was only one boy she wanted holding her books. She listened for the sound of the Zippo. She turned to look down the hall. Gray felt someone staring at her, but it turned out to be the daggers from Charlene's eyes prickling the back of her head.

Charlene had her locker door open, but she faced into the hallway, glaring at Gray.

Gray unzipped a small pouch on her bag and pulled out the pendant. Hopefully, Raj and Adrian were wearing theirs. She clasped it around her neck and tucked the vial under her shirt.

"Excuse me a sec," Gray said to her groupies. "Mind guarding my locker a moment?"

"My pleasure," Pete answered.

Charlene's eyes narrowed as Gray approached. "Hi, Charlene," Gray sang out in Stacey's peppy voice.

Charlene looked her up and down. "Welcome back."

"The doctor said it was a miracle."

Charlene's lower lip stuck out.

"I'm just ready to move on with my life and pick up where I left off."

Charlene grasped her hands. "If you know what's good for you, you'll stay away from Blake."

"Or what? You'll try to kill me again?"

Charlene started.

Gray moved within inches of her face. "I know what you did to me."

Charlene's jaw dropped. She cowered, and it made Gray stand up even taller. These long legs of Stacey's were nice. There was fear in Charlene's eyes. There ought to be.

This was for Stacey Morehouse.

This was for Gray.

"Who told you that?" Charlene asked. "They're lying!" she said when Gray stared her down. "If it was Raj McKenna, you should know he has a weird fixation on me."

Gray threw her head back and laughed. "Stop lying, Charlene."

Charlene eyed her suspiciously. Her lower lip quivered in the next instant when she looked into Gray's eyes. Gray made them flash the way only a witch could, sending an electrical current like lightning crackling around her irises. It sent pinpricks of pain back to her eye sockets, but the effect was dramatic.

"I know what you are, Charlene. I know what you did, and now I've taken your powers."

Gray looked at Charlene's legs. Her sister followed her stare. A wave of pale white skin rolled over her legs like stockings being stripped off. At the same time Charlene was losing her perfect tan, Stacey's skin filled with color.

"You can't do that!" Charlene cried. "It's not possible."

Gray leaned in. "If I were you, I'd keep my voice down—wouldn't want to end up in an insane asylum." Gray spun on her heel and left Charlene opening and closing her mouth like a guppy.

There was only one thing left to do.

* * *

Gray was waiting on the hood of Raj's car when he walked out at lunch. The luck amulet he'd given her dangled from her fingers. She watched Raj's eyes alight upon it. Gray swung it into her palm and closed her fingers around it.

Raj approached her cautiously. "Pretty amazing recovery," he said.

She pushed herself off the hood. "No doubt."

"Is this permanent?" Raj asked, waving a hand to indicate the towering figure that was Stacey Morehouse.

"Twenty-four-seven." Gray smiled. "I suppose I can learn to live with being a size zero."

"I don't care what size you are so long as it's you."

"Aw, say stuff like that and I might have to kiss you, McKenna."

Raj's lips, however, were pressed together in a non-kissy kind of way. "So Adrian's spell worked?"

"What spell?"

"When we arrived at your house you'd turned into Charlene and Adrian performed some kind of Latin spell—nearly killed himself in the process. His grandmother left town with him."

Gray poked her tongue against her cheek and stared at Raj. "I didn't see either of you after the extraction."

"Extraction?"

"Ryan succeeded in extracting my soul from Charlene's body, but he didn't destroy it." Gray snorted. "He told me to go to the light. I went to Stacey's body, instead."

Raj's entire body sagged. "I thought I lost you again." His voice cracked, making Gray's heart ache for the pain he'd gone through a second time.

She smiled with reassurance. "Nope. This witch ain't going nowhere." She uncurled her fingers around the amulet. "I am going to need new initials put on this, however. Think you can get used to calling me Stacey?"

Raj's eyebrows drew together.

"What about Lee?" Gray asked. "It's Stacey's middle name—sorta fitting really."

Raj looked Gray in the eye. "It's not just the name. Your life is going to be different from now on. Are you sure you don't want to exchange me for the senior class president or captain of the basketball team?"

Gray pocketed the amulet before putting her arms around Raj. She brushed her cheek against his then whispered in his ear, "Not for all the magic in the world."

When they kissed, it didn't matter whose lips Gray used. Her soul had survived and found companionship with an incredible guy who just happened to be a warlock. It had taken a trip to the bone yard for Gray to recognize what was right in front of her.

Most people didn't get a second chance. Gray didn't plan on wasting hers.

She wrapped her arms around Raj and breathed in his scent.

"I wonder what it is Adrian thinks he did," she mumbled against Raj's sweatshirt.

Raj chewed on his lower lip before answering. "He kept muttering something about February ninth."

Gray glanced up at Raj.

"The day I died. I wonder why."

"He seemed to think you were coming back that day."

"Well, I'm already here. Thank god I don't have to wait until next year. I'm done being dead."

Raj squeezed Gray against him, enfolding her in his warmth.

"Good," he said. "I've never cared for graveyards. Promise you won't disappear on me again, *Lee*."

Gray nudged him with her shoulder. "Invisibility is sorta my thing, remember?"

"You know what I mean."

Gray's throat grew thick with emotion.

"Don't worry, Raj. I'm not going anywhere."

Her place was among the living, with Raj. She'd defied death twice and lived to tell. Graylee Perez was here to stay.

Want to know what happens next? The magical mayhem continues in the second Spellbound novel: Duplicity!

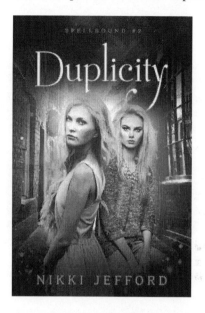

If Graylee Perez thought sharing a body with her twin sister was bad, dealing with a duplicate of herself is two times worse. Gray the second doesn't seem to get that Lee's boyfriend is off-limits. Then there's the problem of Adrian Montez. He expects one of the Grays to be his.

Nearly a year later, the council is on to them for past misdeeds; Lee, along with the rest of the coven, has lost control of her powers; and, Gray is being stalked by what looks like the Grim Reaper.

If the two Grays work together, they may stand a chance of setting things right and making it out alive.

About the Author

Nikki Jefford is a third generation Alaskan now living in the Pacific Northwest. Author of the Aurora Sky: Vampire Hunter series and Spellbound Trilogy, she loves fictional bad boys and heroines who kick butt. Books, travel, hiking, writing, and motorcycle riding are her favorite escapes. Visit her online at www.nikkijefford.com

79435512R00144

Made in the USA
Middletown, DE
10 July 2018